RACE
FOR THE
SUN

MINETTE LAUREN

The Soul Watcher Series

RACE
for the
SUN

Published Internationally by Minette Lauren
Magnolia, TX USA
Minettelauren.com

Copyright © 2020 Minette Lauren

Exclusive cover © 2020 Fiona Jayde Media
Interior Design by Tamara Cribley, The Deliberate Page

PRINT ISBN: 978-1-7340968-6-6
EBOOK ISBN: 978-1-7340968-7-3

This is a work of fiction. Names, characters, places and incidents are either the prod-
uct of the author's imagination or are used fictitiously, and any resemblance to
any person or persons, living or dead, events or locales is entirely coincidental.

ACKNOWLEDGMENTS

A sincere thank you to Faith, Laurie Wellington, Joanna D'Angelo, and Amy Sharp for their editing, help and guidance in bringing this story to life.

A special thanks to Cristina Donoso for your continued help and assistance. Your friendship means the world to me.

To my dear husband, Georgios, you are my knight in shining armor, who has always championed my endeavors. You are my favorite cheerleader and the best man I know. You are my Onegan.

To my mother, who raised us to believe we could be anything, you are everything to me.

In memory of my sister, Rebecca, who battled type-one diabetes. I wish I were even half as brave.

To Ginny, you make me a better person, and I love you dearly.

To Faye, I hope to see you on the other side.

PROLOGUE

The stately man in the impeccable white linen suit looked at her with a bland expression. "Soledad, you are here of your own accord. Do you remember the actions that brought you to this place?"

Soledad. The name seemed familiar. Was it her name? Why did she not remember? The answer danced on the tip of her tongue, and like a feather caught in a summer breeze, her thoughts chased it further away. She struggled to sit up, but nothing presented itself to push against. Her weightless body floated, and her eyes darted left and right, taking in the absence of surroundings. There was nothing. She was captured in a sea of fog for as far as the eye could see.

A growing surge of panic tingled through her. "What place? What's happened to me?" Her eyes widened in sudden realization as she stared at the translucence of her hand jutting out from a plain ivory robe.

"Soledad, do you know why you have returned?" The man in the suit was not unkind but seemed to be waiting for her to catch up. "Take your time. The manner of all important things will reveal themselves." With his words, a beam of light flashed from his form, and Soledad remembered his name, Alekeen.

He stood motionless as she floated to an upright position. A flash of light blinded her, and Soledad's last moment of consciousness unfolded like an old-time movie projector rewinding a vintage celluloid film. First, she experienced a backward walk through the clouds, seeing people she recognized who were long gone but well-loved; some she had not loved or even liked; and others who were strangers to her, beings she never knew.

As she was thrust into a dark, icy tunnel, fear crowded the space in her brain reserved for rational thought. Soledad felt the most alone she could ever remember. Discomfort coursed through her body, and she couldn't breathe. Searing pain assailed her as the salty liquid pushed from her lungs.

She saw black, for what seemed like an eternity, then light. In an abrupt moment, there was air and the gasping for it. Pelting rain cascaded over her, trying to force her below the ominous depths of the open sea. Soledad watched in horror as her body flailed, fighting the heaviness of the water.

She reflected on the vision and remembered her intention to let the waves capsize the small craft and devour her fiberglass casket into the watery depths. Her human form flailed and thrashed instinctively as great swells of saltwater had swirled through her mouth, stinging her nose and eyes, but the truth was, her short life ended before she had time to regret the course of her hasty actions.

The rewind of her life as Katia Grey filled her with great sadness. She was a suicide. In the darkness of night with too much champagne, she took a small sailboat off the coast of Key West into a great storm. Her grief was born of her desire to join her son, but she knew now in her disembodied state the unlikeliness of her wish. While still possible, finding what you wanted in the afterlife was like looking for water in the desert.

Her husband of twenty years had left her for his twenty-three-year-old legal secretary. The year after the divorce, their son drowned while scuba diving off the coast of Australia. It wasn't long after that her ex celebrated the birth of a daughter to replace his loss. She was too old to know such comfort. Her years of childbearing were in the past. Both of her parents died early from heart disease and smoking-complicated ailments. Her siblings had their own families. Soledad decided she could no longer bear the pain.

At forty-two, it was too late to start over. Her doctor diagnosed her with severe rheumatoid arthritis after her son's death. The early creaking in her joints foreshadowed decades of pain and deformity. Once her hands gnarled and twisted, she would no longer be able to paint, and without her talent, she felt empty. Belief in God, at least in the way religion portrayed him, deserted her. She expected no existence after death, except to be free from the pain of living. Her body would become part of the earth again, feeding the ocean and becoming one with the great body of water she had loved her whole life.

"I failed again," she announced. Sadness tinged her voice. Heard only by Alekeen in this empty place, she weighed out her existence. "The life I spent as Katia Grey was—" She paused as her tongue untethered itself in her mind. Her energy piqued as she spoke in a positive tone. "It wasn't all bad. I was quite happy until the past few years. A successful artist and mother, a mostly perfect wife, making more good choices than bad." She counted off her past credits on her fingers, drifting across the never-ending, fog-covered expanse. She moaned with longing for her embodied form as regret soaked her luminous existence. *How did I go so wrong?*

Soledad looked at the man before her with shame. She remembered him as her spirit guide. His soul name was Alekeen, just as hers was forever Soledad. Her presence had visited the in-between world many times before. It was pointless to ask who he was, why she was here, if there was a God, or what would happen next. He had responded to all her questions more than once, but never with answers that would satisfy her curiosity. She lived and soul-watched many times, and knew death provided her with as much confusion as life. Still unsure if there was a heaven or a hell, or if an ultimate God existed, she thought of the bureaucracy of the afterlife as a slow-moving chess game, leaving her longing for an end to it all.

She had never met with any other spirit guide. Suspecting Alekeen had spent a long time away from the living, Soledad noted that he never shared any knowledge beyond *her* current existence. If he was privy to any details about God, he was elusive. She knew so little about so many things, but she was painfully aware of what would happen next. Call it punishment or a chance to progress—it depended on the angle in which one viewed the task. It was time to choose.

First, she should identify a goal for her next life. The obvious thought, not to commit suicide, flashed through her mind. She was guilty of the act in several past lives for many different reasons, but avoiding this sin wasn't her true goal. All souls walking the Earth chose to give up at least one life, often their first. Lives came and went, and souls took human form in a revolving eternity. Each life lesson achieved was a skill to assist in the next spirit rotation.

The only information Soledad gleaned from her conversations with Alekeen in the in-between world was that one day, she would be like him. Contemplating the promotion, she didn't think she wanted his job. His existence didn't seem all that fulfilling—spending an eternity counseling others, asking what they understood and how they felt, in order to move their chess pieces farther across the board. In her opinion, it wasn't a great way to spend the ever-after. Heaven's social worker, a continual public servant for soul servitude—ick!

In between each life, a soul spent time watching other embodied souls. The disembodied were known as soul watchers. The living claimed these watchers were guardian angels, but it was a definite mistaken identity. All spirits were at varied levels of advancement with different agendas. Soledad was sure of her good heart and tried to believe the rotation held a noble purpose—love, advancement, finding peace in her existence. All were significant goals she meant to achieve, but some souls had an entirely different outlook on their expansive development. Maybe their spiritual guide was an alcoholic or on holiday. Who knew? Information was limited to the counseling of past lives, current existence, and which life you would watch in between.

No one ever mentioned the others, but she saw them. They watched over small stray dogs or lingered without a living being in sight. Their roles were different than hers, and she didn't understand their purpose. She imagined these entities were damaged souls or ghosts as the embodied called them— disturbed spirits that lacked the will to live or to watch over the living. It scared her to think she might end up like them one day, especially if she kept ditching her embodied lives. Soledad shivered as memories of her past mistakes pricked her conscience.

Interactions with the living were forbidden if you were not the assigned watcher. The embodied path was a journey between the living and their guardian—if they possessed one. The mistake she made long ago involved a young woman sitting on the bank of a swollen river, waiting to drown her newborn babe in the light of the morning sun. The baby's wail called to Soledad in her soul-watching state. Channeling energy with fervor for the woman to stop, Soledad became desperate and took shape, begging the woman to reflect on the future result of her actions. The woman pulled the child from the water, brought it to her breast, and convulsed in tears. Soledad's only reward for saving the small life two centuries ago was the knowledge she'd acted out of love. For her violation, she was sentenced to absence of partnership, penalized separation from her soulmate for many lives. Though she knew this sacrifice would be the result when she interfered, the heart of her energy could not turn a blind eye to the innocent child's fate.

It terrified Soledad now to think she would never again share a life with her soulmate. How long was the penance for influencing another embodied soul, that was not yours to guide—even if it was for a good cause?

Not every existence had a soul watcher. She had felt like she was without one most of her last life as Katia Grey. The loneliness in the end was more than she could bear. Losing her only son proved too great a pain. Soledad could let go of that ache now, in her present disembodied state.

The task at hand required her to choose from a list of needy souls that she would follow in the next stage of her existence. The one she chose would help or hinder her own advancement to the next embodied life. Whomever she did not choose might never have a soul watcher and could spend a miserable existence alone, struggling. She hated this part of the process because every soul needed a watcher to guide them. If there was an all-powerful-good God, why did he permit such sadness and pain for them to bear?

"Are you ready?" Alekeen's voice was calm but authoritative, drawing Soledad's attention back to him.

"No time like the present." Soledad smiled at the irony. Time was not linear as most living beings believed. Her humor transformed to despondence as she contemplated how many lives she must live before advancing. It was unfortunate that choosing to not exist was not an option. She had asked many times.

"Soledad, you may choose from six souls this time. Each is at a different life stage. Pick the oldest one, and you can make short work of it, but as you have learned, those can be the most difficult." He raised his eyebrows and peered knowingly at her, reading her thoughts without her voicing them.

Soledad remembered the soul watcher's life she had chosen many life-cycles ago. She picked an eighty-eight-year-old woman, who lived to one hundred and five, and never listened to any of her energy channeling or projections. Soledad spent many years after the stubborn woman's death watching her silently as the woman soul-watched for a great-grandchild. Luck was on Soledad's side. The old woman had not failed as a soul watcher, and when she incarnated, Soledad walked with her through another portion of life until the old woman's goal was complete. It was a rare occurrence to sit idle through a soul-watching life, and you could neither channel to the embodied or disembodied. The learning experience was a form of mandatory reflection for not fulfilling your previous duty as a soul watcher.

Some spirits fulfilled their purpose early in their embodied lives and left young corpses behind. This occurrence was good since the soul would advance, but the embodied found it difficult to withstand. The living didn't understand the death of an innocent child. Other spirits lived long lives without ever coming close to their original intentions. All souls faced multiple lessons, and a soul watcher was only with their charge until the most important task was complete. The embodied soul was left to experience additional lessons alone or in the company of a different watcher.

Soledad held her hand over her mouth like a horn and tilted her head back, impersonating a boxing announcer, as she made a trumpet sound. She gifted Alekeen with a brilliant smile that she did not truly feel. "Okay, Obi-Wan Kenobi, spin the wheel of fortune and let the games begin."

He returned her smile, widening his arms as he rolled his eyes. At least her spirit guide had a sense of humor. She knew he could simply put the images in her mind, and all options would be known at once, but he understood her spirit well. She enjoyed grand theatrics and the excitement of a show. Above his head was a hologram showing an old man in his garden, mourning the loss of his wife. He wore black slacks and a nondescript, button-down shirt. The old house behind him dated back to any year from 1900 forward. She absorbed the old man's feelings. His soulmate died, leaving him alone in his older years. His children were alive, but they had their own families. A steady decline in his health was imminent. If he continued down this path, the remainder of his existence would be cut short.

As a soul watcher, one's duty was to choose a soul to help, but to what end was never revealed. Most embodied goals were transparent. It was easy to see that the old man's lesson was embracing independence and finding worthiness in a life alone. The benefit would be great if she could turn this soul around, since she too had abandoned a life of loneliness. But he might also die before she had time to help him, indenturing her to him throughout his next soul-watching life. If that happened, Soledad would be sentenced to watching him again through another embodied life, and that could be a lengthy task.

A little girl playing with dolls in her room appeared next. It looked like 1970-something. Soledad was familiar with the era, recognizing the Barbie Dreamhouse that graced one corner of the room. Time was not linear. It continued all at once, as a collective. No one could jump much farther into the future than a few decades past the life they had farthest lived, but anyone could trek through history. Most souls moved forward through time for the modern conveniences and easier lifestyle, but some returned to a warmer past with heavy toil and the simple love of family.

The little girl was happily playing, but Soledad absorbed the feeling that things were about to change. Her family was doomed to fall apart and send her innocence spiraling in a different direction. Soledad could not change the course of events scheduled to disrupt the little girl's world, but perhaps she could influence the choices of the young one, to help cope with the despair.

Next, a young boy with brown skin and short-cropped hair was crying in a stone tomb. He stood with several others, trapped and panicking. It was Egypt, 486 BC, and he was one of many servants chosen to spend eternity with his pharaoh. Soledad absorbed that there were only hours left until this life ended. The chances of turning his fear to tranquility and light, to help another soul before he departed, would be too great. His life of abuse would lead him to spend many lives soul-watching before he could successfully help others. She sighed with regret. It was too long to wait. Her soulmate was out there somewhere, and she craved a better existence for herself. It might be detrimental to her ultimate advancement to choose speed, but it was a feeling she could not conceal. She didn't care to advance as much as she longed for a happy existence.

In Soledad's experience, it was rare to find one's perfect match. Approximately every twentieth embodied life and every tenth soul-watching life, one was blessed with a short reprieve from the struggle of their own presence. She supposed that every spirit, like her, longed for those breaks. Existence with her soulmate imprinted deep, cherished memories in her subconscious, never failing to lure her into the game of the Gods—or God—whoever was responsible for her never-ending struggle.

The only comfort Soledad found in existing without her soulmate was through soul-complements. This cosmic gift included family members, friends, and spouses who surrounded her throughout her many lives, giving comfortable joy. Soledad found these soothing spirits in almost every embodied life, but they didn't give her the same sense of fulfillment she felt when paired with her one true partner. In these lives, a union of golden light propelled her to her destiny, and a world of knowledge, understanding, and empathy urged her to advance. She didn't know if this was every soul's reality, but she knew it was hers. Soledad almost envied spirits like Alekeen and Mother Teresa, who obviously needed other factors in existing. The love of one soul had little or nothing to do with their crowning achievements.

Soledad's addiction was finding her soulmate. It was like a drug addict looking for their next fix. In a past life, she was an addict who found relief in opium. Because of the abuse of an alcoholic father and an uncle that used her in ways no little girl should ever know, daily toil was impossible. She was tortured by demons and burdened with a flood of daily life-fears. In that short, perilous existence, she wasn't able to function in normal society, because she remembered all the atrocities of her past. Subconscious memories set her brain's synapses on fire. The opium was her only reprieve.

The next hologram shown above Alekeen was a woman in her thirties, divorced, no kids, a dreamer. This soul was lost in life and struggling with an abundance of family issues. Soledad knew the woman's energy and had helped her through previous lives. The candidate for soul-watching was one of Soledad's soul-complements and was her sister's child in her last life as Katia. The funny and creative child that Soledad remembered was grown now. Soul-watching would be entertaining at least, and as a guardian, she would get to see the siblings she had left behind. It would be frowned upon to whisper to her niece that Katia was okay, but Soledad still might have a chance to bring peace to the family. However, she knew what seemed to be the easiest path was often the hardest. She might be taking a path that would bring her both joy and sorrow. The love she felt for this soul could be too close to her past failure.

The vision of the last two spirits lay in tandem above Alekeen. They presented themselves as newborn twins. Instinctively, she knew they were future relatives of her spiritual line. They might be her children or great-grandchildren of a future life. The hospital was sleek and new. She could tell by the uniform dress code of citizens that it was a few decades after her last life. It was best to guide when you weren't so sure of the possible outcomes or the actual relationship. Sometimes you helped a member of your family in the future and then went back to live the life that linked you. Who knew what sort of task would await her by choosing one baby? She would see both lives unfold but could only assist one. It would bring her great pain if the other failed, and she stood by watching. The task was too daunting.

The show ended as quickly as it had begun. Alekeen waited for Soledad's answer, and though she had decided, she did not want to say the name just yet. It was probable that Alekeen already knew, but the in-between world had its own process. Each embodied soul presented needed a soul watcher in the trials of life. The Egyptian boy needed her most in his hour of darkness, but choosing him would fail to advance her. Part of her growth was knowing who to help and who was lost. Knowing she could not play God and understanding where to put the most effort was something she had learned over time.

The old man grieving in his garden would bring constant gloom. The prospect of trudging through his loneliness and misery did not draw her to his existence. The girl playing dolls was her most assured path to advancement, but the affection she felt from her previous life dragged her to aid her sister's child, Ally.

Ally Cat was the name she had lovingly called her niece. The image Alekeen shared was of Ally paddle-boarding on a lake. The serenity the image portrayed fell apart when Soledad searched deeper, recognizing the pain beneath the glaze of her eyes. Ally emitted low energy, signaling to Soledad a despondence in living. The aura surrounding her lean, athletic form was a hazy gray. The energetic spirit that most of Ally's friends and family believed her to be was burdened by life's disappointments, and her will to fight was waning. It was obvious to Soledad that the woman's heavy heart weighed her down.

Soledad floated aimlessly through the mist, contemplating her next steps. She stopped and turned to Alekeen. "I'm sure you already know my choice."

"Indeed I do, and best wishes to you in all your endeavors."

His smile was dazzling as he exploded with light. One moment she was staring into shimmering gold sparks, and the next, she was racing into the sun. Wind cascaded through her hair as air currents warmed her luminous face. She took in the brilliant blue sky with its white puffy clouds then scanned the landscape whirring past. A blooming cactus jutted from the desert-dry earth, but the abundance of squat, spiraling, green trees made her think she was not in the Sahara. Soledad could feel the engine rumble beneath her. Holding tight, she wrapped herself closer to the rider. Never having ridden on a motorcycle in any of her previous lives, the experience was invigorating. It was nice to be a spirit and free of the fear of mutilation. She didn't know what it might have felt like as an embodied rider. Maybe the risk or the challenge to push the limits would make it more exhilarating.

The road before her unwound like a floating ribbon through an endless sky. A series of curves and hills sent the throttle forward then back, accelerating and slowing the motorcycle as the rider whooped with pleasure. Soledad could feel the rays of positive energy exploding from the body she clung to, making her smile. It wasn't that soul watchers could read the living's thoughts so much as they could *feel* them. Certain knowledge was granted at the time of the review. When a soul watcher chose a soul, they knew every part of that soul's past up until the time of attachment. She knew the embodied rider was Katia's niece, Ally, and though bursts of pleasure radiated from Ally now, Soledad understood she was there for a reason.

Ally was not a tortured soul of loss like Soledad was in her previous life, but she'd met tragedy in her thirty-six years of living. Soledad felt Ally's mind return to the stressful events from that morning. It started with a phone call from Ally's sister, Jessica. It was a rare occasion to hear from Jess, who was a type-one diabetic approaching forty. Her kidneys were failing. Ever since Ally went to New York and told her sister she wasn't sure she could volunteer to be a donor, Jessica had been very cold.

Soledad could feel that Ally wanted to help her sister, but she was afraid. Ally contended that, as the one able-bodied person who remained in their small family, she felt reluctant to risk her own health. Her youngest sister, Alyssa, was born with special needs and required twenty-four-hour assistance. Their mother's partial disability from a weak heart prevented her from many activities, and Aunt Rose was too flighty to be there when they really needed her. It wasn't like their grandmother from their father's side could step in to watch Alyssa if anything should go wrong. Gran was eighty-seven. The bottom line was that their mother couldn't do it anymore. If Ally died giving her kidney to Jessica, who would look after their younger sister? Ally had paid for Alyssa's care for years. The attendants were great, but they still needed supervision. Alyssa was dependent on Ally's love, money, and visits.

Jess was angry about her sister's hesitancy to donate her kidney, but Soledad knew it was a decision that Ally would never get to make. Like a corrugated timeline, she knew certain aspects of the future, while other events were hidden in the nooks and crannies of the upcoming days, months, and years.

At nine this morning, Jessica went into a rage, yelling at Ally during their phone call for ignoring the urgency of the situation. It was a repetition of their fight six months earlier. Soledad felt memories of the last trip to New York sift through Ally's thoughts as she turned the throttle of the bike. She leaned into the curve, gripping the tank with her thighs, remembering the abominable visit, and how Jessica had raged on about the injustice of her declining health.

In New York, Jess had shot angry looks at Ally on their drive home from the hospital. "If you knew you weren't going to be a donor, why did you come?"

"I didn't say I wouldn't, Jessica. I came here to listen to the doctors and find out what becoming a donor would entail. It's not like you have done anything to help your own health—I mean, here you are mad at me when you are eating junk daily. The smoking and drinking won't help you get on a transplant list. You were told five years ago you would end up on dialysis if you didn't change your lifestyle, and here you are!" Ally was angry. Why should she be known as the evil sister when she hadn't done the damage to bring Jess to this dire health crisis?

"You want to blame me for being born diabetic? My therapist said I need to cut people like you out of my life. She said I would be in this situation no matter what I had or hadn't eaten. I ate the bacon, egg and cheese biscuit this morning because I was having an insulin reaction, and I quit smoking three years ago!"

Jessica turned to look out the window, and Ally spent the rest of the drive angry at Jess. She had bent over backward for Jess her whole life. She was always there for both her siblings. When it came down to it, Jess only wanted Ally there if she was willing to donate her organ. The truth hurt.

Presently, Ally gripped the bike hard, feeling regret for not telling Jessica she was sorry. She knew Jess was scared. Ally was, too. They weren't a religious family, and not knowing what came next was difficult when facing one's mortality.

Soledad's role of protector would begin sooner than she thought. She could see the dog in the middle of the road up ahead, but Ally's mind was still intertwined in her struggles. Soledad channeled her energy to warn Ally.

'Ally, look ahead. See the dog. It needs your help. Ally, wake up and see the road. Ally, you can make a difference right now. Help the dog. Slow the bike. Slow down—Ally!'

Soledad exhausted herself with pulses of energy that she directed at her ward. She began to wonder if there was any connection between her and the embodied soul of her niece. The living couldn't hear or see their watchers, but they could feel the channeling of energy if they were open to assistance. They absorbed the thought, and the embodied soul's subconscious would decide to listen or not. *"Come on, Ally!"*

CHAPTER 1

Hair raised up on the back of Ally's neck in awareness as her daydream skidded to an abrupt halt. The back tire swayed dangerously as she squeezed the brake of the motorcycle too hard. She felt her pulse spike in alarm before her feet landed firmly in the rocky, dust-covered turnout. Ally lingered in a daze before looking at the road where the stray pup sat thumping its tail.

She lifted the tinted visor of her full-face helmet and pulled her leg over the bike. "Well, look at you, little buddy."

The pup ran to within a foot of Ally. She eyed the poor thing's ribs. It was just a few months old, by the look of the young eyes on the scruffy mutt. It was the middle of nowhere, so where had the dog come from? Ally scanned the open land to see if she could spot a small cottage or even a tent. She could tell the pup was in bad shape. Who knew how long he had been looking for food and water? It was sad that people just dropped animals off when they didn't want them or couldn't afford them anymore. Humanity could be cruel.

Chunks of fur were missing, and the dog's skin was pink and irritated along the bare patches. Ally had seen the malady before. The little guy probably had mange. Ally had nowhere to put the dog on her bike, and touching it might make her own skin itch. She stood in the sunbaked dust, wondering what she could wrap it in when a state trooper drove around the bend. She waved frantically, hoping he would stop. The trooper obliged, pulling into the turnout and rolling down his window.

"Ya broke down?" he asked with a big Texas drawl.

His hat shielded his face, and his eyes were hidden by sunglasses that reminded her of an old episode of *CHiPs*. She lifted off her helmet and shook out her long dark hair. She might look a mess, but she smiled and tried to appeal to his sense of helping a damsel in distress.

She stared at the mange-riddled mutt sitting at the road's edge. It scratched and whined but was too nervous to approach. "No, but this poor pup could use a hand."

He smiled appreciatively, looking her up and down with surprise. "What can I do for ya, ma'am?"

He probably thought she was a guy when he stopped. The tight leather clung to her from head to toe. It was her protection against the asphalt, but it also drew a lot of attention when she got off the bike.

"Poor thing. Looks like it hasn't had water or food for a while. Probably homeless. Could you help to get it back to my place?" She paused, watching him process her request, knowing he probably had something more important to do. "Please. I'd do it myself, but as you can see…" She trailed off, pointing at the bike.

He blew out a long breath and eased out of the patrol car.

Taking off his hat, he revealed sun-streaked, sandy hair tinged with silver. She guessed him to be in his mid-forties. She loved the Nordic planes and angles of his chiseled features. A lot of people with Germanic heritage called Austin home. He was light compared to her dark complexion. Her entire family had moved to Austin when Ally was sixteen, and, at first, Ally wasn't impressed. She longed for the clear blue water and white, sandy beaches of Florida, but the people were so nice in the hill country that she quickly called Texas home with great pride. Texas gentlemen were part of the state's appeal. She had traveled all over the US, been to Europe a few times, Canada, Mexico, and a few of the islands, but there was no place like home.

Putting on her best smile, she moved toward the officer, "Hi, I'm Ally."

Soledad watched the trooper pull a cardboard box from his trunk along with a dusty old blanket. The puppy was skittish and wouldn't cooperate at first, but the officer pulled a sandwich out of his patrol car and kindly donated it to the box. It took the pup about two seconds to jump in after the sandwich. Soledad could feel Ally's heart breaking as she watched the poor thing gag after a few bites. Its stomach had gone too long without food. The trooper poured water into a coffee cup he had been drinking from, and the thirsty puppy lapped it up. The officer placed the box in the back seat and followed Ally home. She lived about twenty minutes away, but the officer assured her that he needed to check in at the station nearby, so it wasn't too much of an inconvenience.

Having a patrol car follow them the entire ride seemed to mute Ally's glee. The only energy Soledad could feel was anxious tension about the puppy and maybe too much attention to the speed limit. Ally carefully maneuvered the curves that led them home and parked her bike outside the large wrought-iron gate. The property was vast, but the little home that sat back behind the trees was quite modest. It was a small two-story with wood siding and a large, wraparound porch. There were two comfortable rocking chairs with a table between them and a white wooden swing off to the side.

Soledad lifted high above, to get an aerial view of the property. There were more than three acres of land, covered by live oaks and gnarled cypress trees. The house faced the morning sun, and sunset poured champagne-colored light across the cliffs on the opposite side of the lake. There were several small, detached buildings that were situated just behind the main house. Soledad floated down, peering into the closest one. It was an art studio. Paintbrushes littered a large worktable, and many canvases with beautiful portraits lined the walls. Further investigation turned up two storage sheds. One was used for garden supplies and vintage furniture. The other housed one mint green motorcycle and another painted pearl white, with thick tires. Both leaned on kickstands in opposite corners. Extra riding gear lay along a wooden shelf, and a battery tender was plugged into an outlet in the vacant space in the center.

Like a beacon in a storm, Ally's nervous energy drew Soledad back to her and the officer.

The patrol car parked behind her, and Ally removed her helmet, placing it on the bike. The officer moved around the car to lift the box containing the puppy, and Ally hit the remote on the gate. A big yellow lab came barreling down the drive, all legs and tail, jumping on Ally, then smelling the box the officer held.

"Ella, down!" Ally admonished, but the lab continued sniffing. "Sorry, she's a big baby. Company gets her excited."

"No worries. I have a black lab of my own, Jake. He often rides with me when I'm not on duty." He looked down at the box. "Where would you like this new addition?"

"Let me put Ella up, and you can place him on the porch. The whole property is fenced. I just don't want her to get infected or infested with whatever this poor guy has." Ally started up the drive, pushing the remote to close the gate behind them. She felt self-conscious as the officer followed her to the house, as she wasn't used to having strangers visit. Since her divorce, she didn't have many male friends. She spent a lot of time helping her family and throwing herself into her work. The officer looked a good ten years older than herself but very handsome in a rugged Marlboro Man way. His crisp blue eyes contrasted with his sandy-colored hair. Too many days in the Texas sun had drawn lines around his mouth and crinkles at the corners of his eyes, but it was a face of character and charm. He followed Ally to the porch, and she opened the door to push Ella inside.

She smiled. "Officer, can I get you a cup of coffee or tea? I don't think your cup can be used anymore."

"Name's Travis, Travis Stark, ma'am. And thanks for the offer, but I need to get back to duty. Another time perhaps." He tipped his hat and backed away, then stopped after a few steps. With one hand resting on his hip, his other stroked the short growth of after-five-shadow. "I have a bike of my own in the garage. Maybe we could ride out to the falls one day and have lunch. You can tell me how this little guy recovers." He pointed to the white ball of matted fur still lying in the box. Its nose was tucked into its body as if hiding from the world.

She was taken off guard and not sure what to say. "Oh, you have a bike."

"Yep, an old kick start, 1976 Harley. My grandpa left it to me. I have a couple other garage queens, but that's the one I like to ride most. I like the feel of it. Next Saturday is supposed to be sunny and seventy. Wanna join me on a ride?" His confident casualness made her feel a tingle of excitement, but she was unsure if he was interested in her, or maybe he just liked company to ride with?

"Uh, sure. Sounds great, but I get to buy you lunch. I'd like to thank you for all your help today." Ally held the porch column, trying not to give away her feeling of awkwardness. "I couldn't have slept tonight if I had left that little guy in the road. I would probably be out looking for him with a flashlight." She was only slightly joking. She would have been in her Jeep now, driving back to rescue the pup if the officer hadn't come to her aid.

He tipped his hat and smiled. "It's a date. I'll swing by here at eleven Saturday morning. Meet you outside the gate," he said over his shoulder as he walked down the drive.

Both excitement and anxiety ran through Ally as she pressed the remote to open the gate for him. It had been nearly two years since her divorce, and a year before that, she had separated. Not that she had been looking for a relationship, but she had wondered more than once if any man might ever notice her again. Now that one had, she was nervous at the prospect of an actual date. Ally had been off the market since she was seventeen and had married her high school sweetheart. She thought she'd never be single again. Her friend, Amy, had told her she emanated *don't even think about it* vibes. Ally had never thought of herself as unapproachable, but she admitted she hadn't really been looking. Until now, she thought that part of her might be dead.

Scratching came from the front door, and Ally remembered Ella inside. She looked at the sleeping pup in the box and thought she needed to get moving before the vet closed. She couldn't put Ella at risk, so she pointed the key fob at her Jeep and started the engine. The pup was startled by the noise. Ally soothed it with soft, rambling endearments, and it nudged itself under the old blanket. She picked up the box and laid it gently into the back cargo area. Dr. Ted would only be open another hour, and she didn't want to miss him. She backed the Jeep out of the drive then went back to the house to open the dog door for Ella.

"Sorry, big girl. No ride today, but I'll make up for it when I get back." Ella's tail thumped as she happily waited for directions. "Go on, girl, go play!"

Ally tossed the tennis ball beyond the house, and Ella made a mad dash for it. Ally's guilt at not taking Ella was a palpable thing as she slipped out the front gate and left her behind.

CHAPTER 2

Soledad watched Ally for one full day. Compiling everything she had learned from her ward's actions, she saw Ally as a free spirit who loved her bike, her family, and animals. She was close to nature and kept her surroundings natural rather than the manicured lawns that were so common in this part of the lake area. Ally's shyness left her lacking when it came to the opposite sex. Soledad didn't understand the confidence issue. While Ally wasn't a supermodel, most men would have noticed her when she walked by. She was striking in a unique way. Her sharp, aristocratic features and light eyes spoke of Swedish possibilities, but her long, dark hair hinted at Native American ancestry. She wasn't a cookie-cutter type, and her multifaceted personality could connect with most people on any level.

Soledad stood looking down at the sleeping figure with the large yellow lab at her feet and a freshly washed mongrel wrapped in a towel in her arms. It was a shame that her ward didn't have children. Soledad was sure Ally would have been a great mother. But motherhood wasn't meant for every soul. She knew the marriage ended because Ally's husband was mentally an eternal teenager, and she supposed Ally had her hands full with the one child she'd married. He broke them both with his drinking, expensive gambling habits, and lust for new toys. He quit working soon after she landed her first big show in New York and had been a wannabe playboy ever since. Ally wasn't averse to being the only breadwinner, but his treatment of her grew abusive over time, and she eventually quit trying to save him, opting instead to save herself.

Ally's sleeping form shifted with a sigh then looked up at Soledad as if she could see her standing there. Soledad knew Ally couldn't sense her presence, but there had been those who had said they could see the disembodied. Ghosts were much talked about amongst the living.

"Don't feel sorry for me. I've made my choices, and I can live with them. Nice of you to watch over me though—or maybe you are here for the little guy. He could use a guardian." Ally paused then snuggled closer to the pup. "I guess that's my role now." As quickly as she had awakened, she pulled the lamp chain and went back to sleep.

Soledad was aghast. Ally had seen her or felt her presence and wasn't afraid at all. She must have felt Soledad's contemplation. Making a mental note to put a cap on her channeling, Soledad tried to quiet her meandering thoughts. Ally needed guidance, not an opinion on her life to date. At a glance, Soledad would say her ward needed help trusting in relationships again and forgiving herself for not succeeding in her marriage. Her heart was obviously big and needed an outlet for her love other than the strays she picked up to take to Dr. Ted.

Luckily for the pup, it had a form of mange that came from the mother while nursing and would go away on its own. It wouldn't be a danger to others, so the dog could be comforted with lots of hugs from Ally and Ella.

The next morning Soledad sat watching Ally wake to her phone vibrating on her nightstand. Soledad thought of yesterday's incident on the bike and the memory of Ally's phone call with Jessica. Ally looked at it with loathing and let it continue to vibrate. Soledad felt Ally's thoughts. *I don't need the added stress on a day that already promises to be more than I can handle.* She understood that it wasn't that Ally had any pressing business to attend to, it was the lack thereof. It was the unexplained anxiety her ward woke with, making her ask herself why she got up and made her bed every morning. *Thirty-six years of living and I make up the bed, just to unmake it at night and redo the whole thing over the next day.* Ally enjoyed her trips to snow ski, to lay on the beach, to see castles in Europe. She enjoyed hot tea, walking her dog, and riding her bike, but Soledad understood there were mornings when Ally asked herself how long she would want to continue to get up and make her bed, to keep breathing air—to live.

Soledad sat in sadness beside Ally and could not bring herself to channel positive thoughts. She felt like a hypocrite. Wasn't that exactly how she had felt in her last life? There was a point where life lost its luster, and all days were the same. People continued because of family and duty, but her life as Katia, in the end, had none of those worries. Soledad reminded herself that Ally did have responsibilities. She had two sisters and a mother who depended on her. Even her ex-husband still needed her financial help. He was on a set allowance that they agreed upon during their separation. Ally was not obligated by law but knew he would end up homeless if she didn't continue to dole out cash.

Soledad was proud that Ally had reached the point in life where she realized that money and material objects were just that. Sure, life was much simpler if you didn't have the added stress of how you were going to pay for things, but in the end, all the things collected, coveted and stowed away for safekeeping—things that were fought over, stolen, greedily grabbed up, or sacrificed for—they were just things. Ally was one of the few embodied souls who understood that when life was over, the things that mattered most would be the relationships she'd had with her family and friends. The necklace her mother gave her would belong to someone else. The house she loved so much would be someone else's home. The saying "you can't take it with you" was pure, uncontestable truth.

Ally sat propped up on a stack of pillows against the headboard. Soledad could feel her thinking. *What's it all for?* Her life in California while attending college wasn't riveting. The summers in Alaska working a tourism job weren't life-defining, but it had inspired her to paint. She was now a successful landscape and portrait artist who loved painting pristine places untouched by man. Natural beauty inspired her, and she captured emotion in the creases of weathered faces or youthful smiles like no other Soledad had ever seen. Ally grew successful selling her work in a local gallery in Anchorage until a New York agent walked in one day, and Ally's life was never the same.

Ally's thoughts meandered as she contemplated what it would be like to photograph the officer she'd met. His slow swagger made her think of an old spaghetti western. She used her camera to capture images for most of her paintings but doubted he would be amused if she whipped out her cell phone and started zapping photos the next time she saw him. Maybe she could draw him from memory.

Her collective photography was extensive and sought after. Like taking in air to breathe, painting was in her blood. Soledad shuddered as Ally's mind moved to Katia Grey's life. Right now, she could hear Ally's thoughts as clear as if they were having a conversation. *It's not like I can take all the credit. It's a genetic gift. It's too bad she never lived to see my paintings. I wonder what she would have thought.* Like thunder rolling across a dark sky, Soledad felt the simmering disappointment Ally emitted over memories of her youth. She was sure that Katia's death had an effect on the family, but feeling Ally's hurt emotions struck a deep chord of regret.

The question boiled back to the surface of Ally's mind. *What is the point of it all?* Her family was small. Her friends were few, but those who called themselves friends were many. The California Crew, as she called them, and the New York Nesters were her two groups of *see and be seen* acquaintances. They liked to attach themselves to Ally at every big gallery showing or party, sucking the energy right out of her. Ally didn't covet fame. She had never flaunted her success and loathed parties celebrating her work. She was glad people liked her art and the possibility that a part of her might survive this life to be remembered. She supposed that was what it was all about. To give visual pleasure to others that might last more than one lifetime.

Ally had taken several trips to Paris and loved looking at the oils on canvas. Paintings that had lasted for centuries hung in golden frames, pleasing the tourists. She silently hoped that in the millennia to come, art would still exist in this way—that people could admire the world's beauty for one frozen moment in time, through the eyes and hands of a human artist.

Soledad felt Ally's mind ramble, churning up a memory of standing in the Sistine Chapel at Saint Peter's Basilica. As she had stared up at the work of Michelangelo, Ally had been amazed that so many people crowded in to see it. When she had seen posters of it or viewed it on television, it looked so large. She presumed it was the whole ceiling, but in the end, it was just another panel floating among a sea of other paintings. Why did the whole world attribute such success to that one piece? Soledad felt prodded when Ally's mind revolved back to the moment at hand. *How to get out of bed and go on.*

Soledad knew it was time to play her part. There were no rules about communicating with animals. Starting a gentle channel of energy to Ella, she sent the big yellow lab's tail thumping, which woke the little ball of fur in Ally's arms. Both engaged in a serious face-licking that finally caused Ally to giggle and throw the covers back.

Ally laughed. "Enough! Enough! I give."

Standing, she stretched like a cat then headed to the bath to do the usual morning grooming. When she emerged, her mood had lightened. Grabbing two leashes from the hook on the door, she breezed out of the house with the happy pooches trailing behind. She didn't always feel like a walk, but Ella did, and by the time she was finished, Ally always felt better for having done it.

She liked having a routine to start her day. It somehow grounded her anxious nature and put her in the present. The repetitive actions let her view life as a series of moments rather than a sentence of years. A walk, feeding the dogs, making tea, and setting up canvases in her workshop were all the rituals of her day before a frenzy of paint glided over the canvas. Her art fueled her consciousness until she exhausted her mind, and the worries faded. The mundane chores she had to do, to keep life functioning, were sometimes her savior. She clung to these comforting days, being home and feeling like a real human being. It would only be a few short weeks before she was back at the gallery in New York. Ally would rub elbows with the elite of the art world and long for home, Ella, the puppy, and her bike.

She would see Jessica this trip. They had agreed to meet for dinner before the opening. Probably not her best idea, but Ally needed to see her sister face to face and talk things out. The unsaid words were leaving a gap between them that was starting to feel like a chasm. She shouldn't delay since Jessica's health would only get worse over time.

Why was I born without any health issues, yet not equipped to help either of them? Both of her sisters suffered from congenital disabilities, and she had never even suffered so much as a sprain. Life was unfair, and she would have traded places with them both if she could. She loved her family and hated to see them struggle. Their misfortunes shaped her life and her personality. When she painted, she often drew from their energy and the life hurdles they overcame.

Ally had a secret stash of art that would never be seen by the gallery patrons. The paintings were for her creative and emotional therapy. She had painted a portrait of her sisters and herself together, without any flaws. Jessica at a healthier weight with good color and Alyssa standing without her wheelchair. Ally loved the one she had painted of Alyssa running through a field of bluebonnets. It was inspired after Ally bought Alyssa her first motorized chair, and she had giggled, racing the chair down the drive. It made Ally happy and sad all at once. She knew her younger sister had never known the experience of running and imagined this was the closest thing to it. When she returned home, Ally broke out a fresh canvas and painted a series of Alyssa in an alternate life where she could walk. She depicted her standing at a ballet bar, ice skating in an outdoor rink, swimming in the ocean, and running in the surf. Her sister's disability was buried in swatches of color that hid the darkness of reality.

Ally supposed there was a reason for everything, and maybe one day she would understand. It kept her angry at God for now, even though her rational mind told her no one was really to blame for her sisters' ailments. It was just life.

Soledad watched as the painting unfolded itself from a mash of colors into a beautiful golden angel. It was like something out of a very old Bible with illustrations for children. The iridescent wings and ivory flowing robe was so lifelike. Sprays of golden light illuminated the godly image. Soledad smiled. "I wonder where you got that idea from?"

Ally stopped in mid-stroke. She looked around but didn't find anything except the two sleeping dogs at her side.

Soledad was intrigued. "How intuitive you are. Well, since you seem to pick up more than the average living do, I'll clue you in on a few things." She knew her immortal voice wouldn't be heard literally, but she felt that Ally might absorb some energy that would sink in and maybe do some healing. "There are no such things as angels, at least as far as I know. I am here to help you, but how, I haven't a clue. The wings are a beautiful addition to what you think you saw last night, but I'm about as flawed as they come."

Soledad grimaced as Ally frowned. "Okay, I'm not all that bad, but I'm no angel either. Your sisters are the way they are because of their past lives. You have no physical impairments because of the lives you lived before. Alyssa has a sharp temper because she is still bitter from her last life. Her mistreatment of her son, who was born with deformed legs, is why she lives with cerebral palsy in this life. She has chosen this existence to improve her spiritual growth. Her completion of this goal cannot be fulfilled until her soul watcher time.

"Jessica is a new soul and hasn't lived as many lives as you. Like many others, she chose to come into this world to learn a hard lesson. She has taken a few wrong turns and will probably have to repeat this period of learning another time. I'm with you on the *life is cruel and unfair*, but we reap what we sow." Soledad paced back and forth behind Ally as her brush dotted the canvas with light accents. Her guardian spirit stopped to search her ward's face. *Has anything I've said penetrated your thick skull?* Channeling energy was an art of sorts. It had taken many soul-watching lives to hone her skills, and she felt quite proficient. The energy she was weaving now wasn't eloquent or refined, but it could eliminate some of Ally's internal guilt.

Ally dabbed at the blue sky with little white strokes of paint. No real identifying expression surfaced.

Soledad continued in a whir of energy, spinning round on her heel. "This anxiety you wake with most mornings is depression. I know you don't realize it, but you *too* have a lesson in this life before you can go on to soul-watch and then be born again. The only real reason to go through all this trouble is to meet your soulmate. At least, that's where I think you will find the most fulfillment. But, Ally, your soulmate could be standing right in front of you, and you wouldn't give him the time of day. You have to take down that wall and let others in."

Soledad started to work herself into a fervor. "You are burying yourself underneath a mountain of life's tasks, and have you ever heard the expression, 'Life happens, while you are planning other things'? Well, this is it, and you are going to miss out! So—what? Peter Pan wasn't the one, and you're upset things didn't work out. Join the rest of humanity. You are still young and have time to find the sweet existence we all pine for. Put yourself out there and take a chance. Disconnect from the past and live for a future without guilt and solitude. Do it before it's too late and you end up like me."

Soledad took a long pause, thinking over her own lost life. She had not found her soul-partner and had lost her son. Life had been empty, except for her art, and even that had been forgotten in the tragedies she experienced. She should have thrown herself into her creativity and toughed it out. It was the abandonment of her life that put her apart from her soulmate, Onegan. She knew his soul name like she knew her own. She wondered where he was now and if she might be successful enough to meet him in her next life. The lives in between were like winters of the soul.

Ally set her brush down in a glass and stood, stretching her back, moving to look out the window. The dogs in the corner bed stirred to see what had changed. Ella's big tail thumped in question. Ally smiled down at her and reached for the cup of tea by her brushes. She drank the last of the earl grey in her cup and studied the swirling leaves for a moment.

"Okay, big girl, time you and I do our fence walk and show the new kid what it's all about."

Ella did two circles and barked twice. Ally walked to the wall where another set of leashes hung. She opened the door and waved the dogs out, walking gingerly through the green grass beyond the small studio. She held the leashes in her hand in case she should need them but let the dogs roam free as usual. It was convenient to have a little cabin behind the house on a decent amount of fenced land. She had a few goats that kept the grass from overgrowing. Ella loved to herd them and check the fence for any openings they could get through. It was Ally's afternoon therapy and Ella's playtime.

The new pup galloped after Ella, yapping with joy. The size difference between the two was comical. The new little dust mop could fit in a medium-sized purse, and the yellow lab was a good ten pounds overweight. Since her other older lab passed, Ally had meant to find Ella another companion. She believed it was cruel to have one dog at a time. They were pack animals, and though Ally was the pack leader, she couldn't be home twenty-four hours a day. The new pup lucked out. It now had a home with a big yard, a furry friend that would protect it, and a human companion who would spoil it rotten. She supposed she should start thinking of a name.

CHAPTER 3

Harley bounced off the couch and ran through the dog door before Ella could even lift her head. Ally tied the leather strings of her chaps and grabbed her jacket from the hook. It was Saturday, and she only half expected the nice officer from earlier in the week to show up, but according to Harley, someone was here.

Ella looked at her with sleepy eyes. "Better watch out there, old girl. I think someone has sharper ears than you," Ally warned.

Ella's chocolate nose twitched as she slowly stretched, thumped her tail, and followed the white ball of fluff out the dog door. In hindsight, Ally should have named him Checkers. The poor pooch had come back from the groomer with his hair brushed out and trimmed, but still missing a few patches of fur.

Officer Stark was getting licked to death by the two swarming canines as Ally walked down the drive.

He smiled and stood when he saw her approach. "I see the little guy found a home."

Ally couldn't help but appreciate his casual stance and the way he so easily bonded with the dogs. His helmet was loosely tucked under one arm, and his other hand was casually scratching Ella in her favorite spot above her tail.

He smiled at Ally with casual confidence. "I see you're ready."

She smiled back at him. "I'm always ready when it comes to riding. It's my therapy."

"I have to admit, I don't know many females who like to ride. I was impressed by you the other day. Most women like to just sit on the back." His steel-blue eyes assessed her.

Ally knew he was trying to figure her out. *Let him try*. She smiled and headed for her bike. "Ella, take Harley home," she said firmly and pointed to the house. Ella bounced and barked her way back to the front porch with her tail moving around and around like a propeller. Harley immediately took chase to see what all the excitement was about. Ally took advantage of the distraction to move her bike down the drive, closing the gate behind them.

There wasn't much chatting after that. When she asked him where they were going, Travis said they could lunch at the falls after they rode Lime Creek Road. Ally knew the route well and took the lead. Slowing, she took a back seat after the first ten miles. She wanted to see how he handled the road and watch if he would make any hotshot moves to grab her attention—like stretching his arms as he took a curve or wheelies on the straight shots. She took safety seriously and wasn't falling for any guy doing circus tricks. In fact, they were marks against a rider in her book. Guys who rode dangerously lived dangerously, and she didn't care to share the road or her life with them.

Travis rode with skill and ease and wasn't a showoff. His vintage bike was beautiful and had Ally already planning her next purchase. She had what they called MBS, Multiple Bike Syndrome. She had owned several motorcycles throughout her life but hadn't ridden for many years until after her divorce. Her immature spouse had been the hotshot sort, so she sold her bike and bought him a new car. Four wheels were much safer than two when you liked to drink as much as he did. She had sacrificed a lot in her marriage, but she hadn't known just how much until she bought her first Harley after the divorce. Since then, she had bought two others, one for touring and another for off-road. The vintage bike that Travis rode was a beautiful sky-blue classic. She noticed the tightness of his thigh muscles when he hit the kick start and was impressed that his bike started on the first try. He might be a little older than she, but he was ruggedly handsome and fit.

Lunch at the falls was beautiful, as always. The lake lapped glittering gold waves on the shore as boats sped past. The sun danced over its mirrored surface, and Ally was glad she wore her sunglasses to protect her eyes from the shimmering light and Travis's assessing gaze. She had never met a man like him. He was confident and looked at her directly when speaking. He had a coolness about him that made everything seem breezy and uncomplicated. His warmth made her want to open up and share thoughts without being prompted.

The white tablecloth and the formal setting were at odds with their biker attire, but it was a sunny day at the lake, and the restaurant's outdoor seating invited a display of all fashions. They sipped iced tea and ate a light fare of sea bass with grilled asparagus. She was glad he didn't order a cocktail.

A lot of riders did enjoy a beer or two, but it was her own strict rule about riding not to imbibe. She never drank on road trips.

"Do you like wine?" he asked. It was as if he had read her thoughts.

"I do, just not when riding. I have enough problems trying to stay alert. I'm bad about daydreaming when I relax," she admitted.

He smiled. "I know what you mean. It's easy to get lost in the beauty of the surroundings and forget you have a thousand pounds of iron under you."

Ally wasn't sure if he was agreeing or making a joke. "I've had the problem since I was a little girl. I get caught up in something and poof, I'm off to never-never land." She waved her hand in a flutter, then shrugged her shoulders. "I don't have to speed or do anything crazy, but there is a certain freedom when I ride. The only other time I feel it is when I paint, walk with my dogs, or snow ski. Those things truly set me free. What about you? I'm sure you see excitement every day with your job. What frees your mind?"

For the first time, he looked away from her, staring out at the lake. A boat passed, pulling a skier who waved to some unknown person on the shore. Travis's form was relaxed. His legs sprawled out from the chair, and one leather boot turned out along the deck while the other rested comfortably on the chair rung beneath him. "I guess I could say the same. I do have a passion for riding and anything to do with the outdoors." Pausing, he looked at her. "My mind is free right now. It's not often that I get to ride with a pretty lady and just turn the world loose for a day."

"I would believe you if you hadn't looked away first." Smiling to buffer the observation, Ally made sure she looked directly at him. She didn't want him to take what she said too lightly.

"I mean what I say. I've never been flowery with words. My wife used to say I was the reason she had to read romance novels." He laughed. "I guess I'm not much of a Prince Charming."

Ally almost choked on the ice cube she had been crunching. "You're married?"

"Yes." The confirmation came with a hand shooting up to stop her rising conclusion. He straightened in his chair, giving her his full confession. "I mean, no. I was—I'm a widower. She died of cancer three years ago. We met in college and got married because she was pregnant. She lost the baby halfway through the pregnancy, and she was never able to have children, so it was just the two of us for twenty-something years. I was never any good at keeping count." A guilty expression crossed his strong features as he studied his plate.

"I'm sorry. I didn't mean to pry." Ally felt humbled and a bit embarrassed.

"No, I understand. What kind of man would I be if I were married and out with another lady riding around the countryside?" He smiled and threw her a lighthearted wink. "You know, the internet, dating, and all. It's amazing what you have to do to find someone decent these days. Women have to watch out for men. Some of us are unscrupulous."

"I have to admit, I've been divorced a few years now, but the internet seems too impersonal to me." Ally perused the dessert menu, knowing she had no intention of indulging in sugary treats.

"Dessert already?" he asked with a teasing smile.

She appreciated him not delving further into the question of her dating status. "No, I just like to see what the pastry chef is offering. It's too hard to ride on a full stomach."

They ate their food and exchanged casual conversation about the weather, upcoming events in the city, and bike mechanic talk throughout the rest of lunch. The sun started to wane, and they collected their gear to return home.

The Devil's Backbone was a favorite of Ally's and Soledad's, who had been quiet throughout lunch. She forfeited channeling in lieu of supervision. A strange bitterness hung around the beautiful man that Ally rode with, but it wasn't his own. The soul that shrouded him was like a fog that wouldn't let the whole of his sunny energy pour forth. Soledad wasn't sure if the fog was a soul watcher, or one of those spirits who lingered and never passed to the other side. Whatever it was, it kept Travis's heart in chains. He was obviously interested in Ally, and together they might be soulmates, but the fog was thick and causing waves of interference that translated to wariness and distrust. She could feel the radiant happiness floating off Ally, but the breaks in her energy were borne of the hurt she had endured from her previous bad romance. Ally doubted a man as nice as Travis could really exist.

Soledad clung to Ally as the bike sped down the crooked path, worrying about the way her ward's energy pulsated. Ally would build a mental shield against the physical attraction she felt toward Travis then tear it down with the throttle of the bike as she sped through another curve. His beautiful physique and the vibration of the bike beneath Ally worked over her most sensitive parts. Soledad felt like she was intruding on something private but was glad Ally was breaking down the negative energy inside. It had been too long since she could trust someone enough to get close, and Soledad was elated by the small possibility of Ally connecting with a man who could be a real partner. Travis was confident enough to support her on a level that she had only dreamed of before—*a real adult relationship*.

Soledad knew Ally was vulnerable. The lingering fog around Travis's aura didn't bode well. She'd seen it before, a good soul that wanted the right things, but a spiritual mist camouflaged the opportunities for happiness and success. If the fog lifted, Soledad was sure Travis's vision would clear. It was the only thing standing in the way of his happiness and success. If that happened, he would be perfect for Ally in this life. Soulmate or not, true happiness in the embodied state was a rare gift.

When they came to a light at a small intersection just before town, Ally lifted her visor and smiled at him. He lifted his own and returned her enthusiasm. He looked younger in this moment, and Soledad knew he had enjoyed their time together. She felt a physical push as Ally tried to let go of her prudish ways. Her thoughts punctuated her aura like bullet points. *Life is not an old-style Harlequin. It does not have to end after divorce. I don't have to remarry to have sex.*

Soledad started her channeling at once, telling Ally to let go and be free, to take her heart to a level she had never achieved before. Though she'd just opened her own pathway, Ally immediately dug her heels in and fought against Soledad's waves of energy. The hurt Ally had experienced was too intense, and she had paid tenfold with her heart and half of all her assets. Divorce was a dirty fiasco, and it was understandable that she didn't feel like setting herself up for future failures.

"Geez, Ally! It's not like he is ready to walk you down the aisle, I'm saying to let yourself enjoy a day of bliss without analyzing it. Just appreciate being admired and feel something besides regret, guilt, and pain for a change." Soledad said the words more out loud to the wind than for Ally to actually absorb.

When the riders stopped for gas, Soledad floated away a distance from the couple to contemplate different tactics to relax her ward. She leaned against a gas pump and observed both riders fueling their bikes. Each seemed to be contemplating life and reflecting on the day's conversation—both going down their lists of pros and cons. Travis returned the pump to its lever and smiled at no one in particular. Her ward needed a vacation from herself. Soledad hated to think that her niece was so uptight, but it must be the reason Soledad had been given the option to be Ally's soul watcher.

She noticed Ally looking around the gas station, searching for something. Her cascading hair blew in the wind, and the fine hair on her neck rose. Ally swiped at the static electricity ruffling over her arms and shivered. Soledad knew Ally had felt her presence before but didn't seem scared. It had inspired the angel painting. Ally thought she had dreamed of an angel watching over her, and it lifted her spirits not to feel so alone, but Soledad knew that the static electricity Ally felt now was not from her.

She saw the shadowy fog move from Travis to Ally. As it grabbed at Ally's hair, Soledad pulled all her energy together and pushed the air around the spirit in warning. She couldn't physically touch anything living or dead, but the channeling of energy could move air and objects. The shadow retreated but sent Ally tripping into the pump.

Pink flooded Ally's cheeks as she grappled with the hose connected to the tank. The fog's attack angered Soledad. How had she let the misty figure get so close? No telling what kind of nefarious deeds it had planned. She would have to be more aware of present dangers and do better at protecting her ward from any further incursions. Soledad might not be able to steer Ally away from her own demise, but she could keep the shadows at bay. Evil intentions had the ability to harm, but Soledad was not without her own powers.

The day sped away as quickly as it began, and the riders came full circle. As they turned into the gated drive, Ella and Harley sped out of the house and charged the gate. Ally and Travis turned off their engines and removed their helmets, laughing together at the excited greeting.

"Wow, what a great day. Great ride…" He trailed off, looking up at the sky.

"I know. I usually ride alone, but it was fun riding with you. Nice to have someone understand what I feel when I go through the curves." Ally shook her head, looking down at her bike. "So many of my female friends just don't get it." She laughed with a sudden thought. "Even my male friends like to shop."

He arched his brow in disbelief then gave her a slow grin. "We should do it again soon."

"I would love that, but I have a gallery show coming up, and the rest of the week will be packing up the paintings to be shipped to New York then flying there to host the whole affair. I could be gone most of the month."

"No problem. I'll still live in Texas when you get back." He winked at her, but then his gaze turned serious, and his smile flattened. "Unless you'd rather not." He waited for her to respond.

Did he suffer from past insecurities as well? He had been so confident until now. "A man who can wait." She smiled to reassure him. "I love it."

"A man who can't is a fool." He made light of his words by tipping his imaginary Stetson. "On that note, I'll let you go inside and make your nest for the evening. I should get back to feed Jake. It's steak night, and I'd hate to disappoint him. If you're hungry, you're welcome to join us. Jake makes a mean ribeye." His eyebrows waggled.

Ally chuckled, hugging her helmet to her chest. "I would love to, but I'll take a rain check tonight."

Travis smiled with understanding. She loved the crinkles that framed his beautiful blue eyes. He nodded as he kick-started the vintage bike, and it came to life with a roar. She called out a thanks, but her voice was lost in the engine throttle and explosive tailpipes as he sped away.

Ally attended to Ella and Harley, adding bits of grilled chicken and steamed broccoli to their kibble. The dogs usually ate better than she did, and more regularly. She was enchanted by her day and was left with a sense of hope and possibility. Her energy aroused passions she thought were long dead, and suddenly, she felt a need for release.

Ally walked out the backdoor of the main house to her studio and flipped the switch to the overhead fluorescent lights. She dug out the large canvas she had constructed but left buried in the back of the studio storage room. She had never attempted any painting this large.

Ally didn't know what she was about, but her emotions flooded over her and begged for release. She linked her phone to the speaker system, which then pumped a mixture of baroque and alternative rock through the studio. As the music sent her paintbrush in great swipes over the canvas, she swung her hips to the rhythm. The black paint flowed first, creating a backdrop for the center. Then the red burned from her brush, spreading flames of scarlet with wide, flicking strokes. The creation teased the viewer to wonder what lay just beyond the golden swipes of paint, inspiring other topics of the canvas to stay slightly out of focus.

As she worked through the night, time evaporated. Ally stopped when a ray of sun pierced her face through the small studio skylight. She set the brushes down and stepped back. It was a lifelike image of a man sleeping, woven in red silk sheets in a dark room. A window above peeked at a setting filled with urban blight, a police car visible through the glass. The man's identity was mostly shielded by the golden highlights of tawny-colored hair. His lower lip and chin hinted at his sleepy vulnerability. Taut muscles tapered down his back, disappearing beneath the snaking sheet.

The dark and light colors set the canvas aflame under the spotlight hanging above. The alluring image belonged in the grand hallway of an old castle or regal art museum. He was like a pagan warrior or a young king, naked to God but mysterious to man. A moment of doubt plagued her. Maybe it would be considered too "romance novel cover" instead of fine art. She didn't care. He was hers, and on canvas, he would live forever.

Obviously inspired by Travis, the image's likeness was all male. She would be mortified if he should see it. When it dried, she would carefully move it back to storage, but for now, she was exhausted and needed a few hours of sleep before her agent, Marcel, arrived later in the afternoon. He would go through the gallery selections for the show and deal with the shipments. It was up to Marcel to take over and do the work now. She would just be there to let him in and go crazy over her art. He always did.

CHAPTER 4

Ally awoke to Ella panting in her face and Harley licking her toes beneath the sheets.

"All right, all right! I don't understand why I have a dog door if you insist I get up to walk you to it," she complained.

She still wore her clothes from the day before, and her fingers and arms showed streaks of paint from her night's work. Since she didn't go to sleep until six in the morning, the sun was high in the sky. She looked at her cell phone on the nightstand, which informed her it was three in the afternoon. Ally heard the knock at the door before Ella and Harley scattered. The frenzy of barking held friendly tones, so she knew it must be Marcel.

"Oh, crap! I must have slept through my alarm," she complained as she jumped up, stubbing her toe on the hard casing of the empty suitcase by the bed. "Ow!" she grumbled.

Marcel was greeting the happy, tail-wagging yappers when she entered the front room. He was a good friend, and she was glad he felt comfortable enough to let himself in. She wasn't exactly a lock-aholic with her two-dog alarm system.

She smiled at her long-time agent and comrade. "Look what the cat drug in."

"Look at what the cat threw up! O-M-G Ally! What happened to you? You look like you haven't slept in a week." He waved his arms as he crossed the room and wrapped her in a big bear hug. Marcel was a GQ model who turned agent when he reached his expiration date for modeling. He was lithe but very fit and very, very gay. He was her oldest and dearest friend, and she could share anything with him, knowing it was truly safe.

"Oh, Marcel, I have missed you." She smiled up at him as he pulled back to look her over. "I know I'm a mess." She sighed with fatigue. "It was a late night."

"Oh, do tell! Do we have a lover, finally? Did you get your divorce cherry popped?" He put both hands over his mouth like the words had slipped out by accident, but Ally knew they were absolutely intended. He scooted onto the nearest bar stool as she rounded the kitchen island to make tea.

"No!" She laughed, swatting him playfully with one hand. "Nothing like that—although I did meet a new friend. He helped me with Harley, the little guy at your feet." She peered down at Harley, who had two paws on Marcel's pant leg. Her friend bent down to scratch the fluff, who wagged its mangled tail in appreciation.

"Looks like you both had a rough night. Ruff, get it?"

She let Marcel tell her about all the gossip in New York as she made tea.

"So—tell me about your mangy pup, and why you look so well-worn." Marcel raised his eyebrows over the steaming cup of jasmine she handed him.

"I was painting last night. Nothing to do with Travis. We went cruising on motorcycles yesterday and had lunch, nothing more."

Marcel held his mug with two hands, savoring the floral scent. "Travis, hm? Do go on."

"The handsome police officer that helped me get Harley home. I found him out in the middle of nowhere while riding my motorcycle last week."

"Which one, the cop, or the canine?"

"Both, actually. Travis gave the pooch a ride here since I couldn't carry him on my bike, hence the name Harley."

Marcel stuck his full bottom lip out a little. "How sad." He then put a hand to his cheek. "Clearly, I have been loitering in the wrong places. Maybe I should get a bike?"

Ally snorted at the image of Marcel on a bicycle with an egg-shaped helmet on his head. "A bicycle or a motorcycle?"

Marcel's eyes searched the beams of the cottage ceiling, then he challenged, "What, you can't see me decked out in leather, stretched across a Harley?"

Ally giggled, shaking her head. "Not really, but if you do decide to ride, please tell me so I can stay off the road."

"Oh, well, that hurts, Ally."

Ally touched his arm. "Sorry. The whole thing was nothing, really. Just a nice officer, helping a damsel in distress."

Marcel did his best Bogart impression. "Maybe it's the beginning of a beautiful friendship." Getting bored by the lack of juiciness to her story, he turned back to work. "So, show me this painting. Will it *redefine* the gallery showing?"

Apprehension shot through Ally. "Oh, no. I mean, I didn't paint it for the gallery. It was just something I did for me. A little creative energy that needed to be let out. I finished the series for the gallery last week. Those paintings are ready to be picked over and shipped." She walked out the back door of the kitchen and motioned for Marcel to follow.

Ally hadn't thought about the evidence of her lust sitting in the middle of the studio, beckoning all the world to see. She opened and quickly shut the door. Marcel stared at her, first startled, then curious.

"Oh, uh-uh, girlfriend! Now you *must* show me!" He pushed past her, to her dismay.

"I know it's not what I usually do. It's totally not meant for the show. It's just an exercise I was doing—to relieve stress," she babbled.

"*Oh, my God.* This is so—I don't have words for it." He walked in an arc around the canvas, staring at it with his mouth agape and his hands on his hips. "It's yummy, wonderful, elegant, delicious." Marcel licked his lips in obvious lust before declaring, "It's elitist porn." He laughed as Ally slapped his arm.

"Oh, —stop teasing me! I haven't been laid in a while, and I just needed to release a little pent-up energy. When I started, I had no idea it would be him, I just couldn't stop myself, and by morning I felt like he was—imprinted on my soul." She sighed. After the giggling subsided, she stared at her work, analyzing Travis's likeness and wondering how terrific he might really look naked.

"All kidding aside, he is fabulous. Like the statue of David, or may I guess, Travis?"

"No! I mean, maybe inspired. Not actually him. I—I've never seen him that way. I barely know him. It just happened," she ended lamely as she flopped into an oversized, white fuzzy bean bag chair.

"Well, tell him to come back over, please. We could do a whole show of paintings inspired by him. Is he really that perfect?" Marcel put a finger to the corner of his mouth, pretending to wipe off drool.

"I don't know. I've never seen him outside of his uniform or riding gear. It was his energy and kind heart that inspired me. He has a chiseled Marlboro-man-meets-Hugh-Jackman look. He isn't really pretty, but what did you say earlier?" Ally paused, looking up at the ceiling like she was star struck. "Yummy." She laughed as Marcel chimed in with the same word at the same time.

"Pinch, poke—you owe me a super big margarita with extra Don Julio."
Pointing at him in agreement, Ally exclaimed, "Done."

The paintings were tagged, and the shipping guys arrived shortly after Marcel.
He begged her to let him show the painting he now dubbed, *David Reborn*.
After much cajoling and begging, Ally finally let the painting be tagged and
shipped with the others. She would let them deal with the wet paint issue.
Ally sighed with exhaustion and a little relief for it to be out of the small
studio. She needed a breather from its overwhelming presence.

Marcel asked her to lunch, but she had seen him peer at his watch one
too many times over the course of their visit. She told him she had a meeting with the supplier for more canvas frames and would take a rain check
for next time. She had no doubt he was busy planning the opening of the
show, but Lambert was in New York for two days, and she knew he would
want to be back there to drool over him. Lambert was Marcel's one that
got away. He was actually the one he never had, so that made him all the
more desirable to Marcel.

The house was quiet after everyone left. Ella and Harley slept on their
beds by the small hearth in the front room. Its simple wooden mantle,
ornamented by columns on each side, was topped with an elaborate mirror
framed in gold-leaf. Depression glass candlesticks complemented the setting. Ally had a shabby chic style, steeped in a Louis the fourteenth fashion.
The antique pieces in the room were sanded with streaky, uneven paint. She
loved to ornament cabinets with glass knobs or golden treasures. The entire
feeling of the house was rustic elegance. Everything was beautiful, yet comfortable. She didn't want people to be afraid to touch anything. Ally wanted
a home that was inviting, one where she could prop her feet on the coffee
table without thinking. Accent pillows generously graced the couch and
chairs, and white linen drapes puddled on the floor below every window.
They were fashionably worn, and she tossed them in her washer when needed.

Ally picked up a broom to tidy up around the kitchen dog door. Ella
had brought a few mud clods back from her afternoon romp with Harley,
and a path of paw prints dotted a trail to the living room where the dogs lay.

She stopped and listened, curious, as she heard her phone vibrating from the counter. The text was from Travis. He was playing downtown with his band tonight and asked if she wanted to come.

Soledad hovered patiently all day, taking in Ally's activities. She hushed the dogs and sent out soothing energy so Ally could rest until her agent arrived. She smiled at the friendly banter between the two friends. When Marcel saw the amazing Adonis painting and insisted it be in the show, Soledad cheered with excitement. Now, as the phone vibrated with a message from Travis, she jumped up and down channeling to her ward. "Go! Go! Go!" The energy flow woke the dogs, and they stared up at Ally in askance.

Her ward stood immobile in contemplation for a few moments, then wandered around the island with the cell phone in her hand. Finally typing yes, she reasoned aloud, "I'm free of responsibilities here since Marcel took the paintings. Besides tying up a few loose ends around the house and packing my luggage, there isn't much to do." Ella and Harley tilted their heads in unison as if agreeing.

Ally took the dogs down to the lake in her Jeep for a good romp and let them play in the water. It was too cool to swim for most people, but Ella was a water dog and swam year-round. Harley skirted the lake's edge, barely getting his paws wet until Ally threw the ball into the water. Ella launched herself after the toy, and Harley dove in, forgetting his water phobia. His white checkered fluff was now a wet mess, and he looked no bigger than the tennis ball he held clamped between his little teeth. He was so adorable and spirited that Ally couldn't imagine how someone could have dumped him. At least he was now safe and well-loved. Ella had needed a friend to keep her company while Ally traveled. She loved Maria, the cleaning lady, who came every day when Ally was gone, but it wasn't the same kind of twenty-four seven attention the lab normally received when Ally was home. She would miss them dearly when she flew to New York.

CHAPTER 5

Ally took extra time with her long, dark hair to make sure it was straight and shiny. She put on a pair of her dressy jeans and black V-neck shirt with three-quarter sleeves. She wasn't big on jewelry, so she chose a simple chain necklace with a small stone that dangled at the base of her neck and a pair of matching earrings. She adorned her complexion with a hint of blush and deep red lipstick. Mascara was all she needed around her turquoise-colored eyes. She stood in front of the mirror, surveying her reflection. The green suede calf-high boots with black lace-up backs made her legs look long and sexy. Ally appeared casual with a fashionable flair. Sighing, she said to herself, "It'll have to do." She turned to leave, and a breeze flowed through the room, reminding her to shut the open window.

Soledad pushed the air around Ally, trying to remind her to lock up. She also moved the small bottle, sending it over the edge of the vanity as Ally leaned forward to shut the window. Ally retrieved the fallen bottle, plopping it into her purse. Soledad knew her ward had purchased the fragrance from a boutique in Paris. It was apparent Ally didn't want to come off as trying too hard, but Soledad wanted her to make an effort. Ally argued with herself for a few moments before pulling the bottle back out, squirting the perfume on her wrist and neck. "What's the use in buying such things if you never use them, right?" Ally said to the dogs. Harley lifted his ears but didn't move from the pillow where he lounged. Ella stood on the bed, made a turn, scratching the covers with one paw, before flopping down with a humph.

Soledad sighed at her ward's words, wondering about the evening ahead. She had her work cut out for her.

Ally patted each of the pups on the head before leaving, telling Ella to watch the place while she was gone. The area by the lake was safe, but transient people came through every now and then to use the park. Soledad floated between the pups as she followed Ally, touching them lightly across their backs. Both pups' tails thumped. They had recognized her presence as soon as she arrived, and both seemed to know she cared for and protected Ally as they did.

Soledad was determined to do her job right this time. She was sure Travis must be a piece of the puzzle in Ally's life. There had to be a reason Soledad was given the option to come to this specific place in time, and it was important that she didn't screw it up. If she failed, she could stay with Ally for a lifetime, haunted by both her own and Ally's regret. If Travis didn't have the patience to deal with Ally's skittish-colt personality, then all would be lost. To live a life without your soulmate was okay if your soulmate wasn't embodied at the same time. A soul complement might fill that gap by adding peace to the heart, but to miss a life you could have had—Soledad couldn't contemplate that failure right now.

Even a life alone could be rewarding if it was geared to help other souls. Fulfillment was a gift when a life of service was chosen, but to have a soulmate so close and miss the opportunity to live in unity together would drive most spirits to vices beyond redemption. She didn't see Ally as the crack-addict type, but she did see a reflection of herself. A suicide sentenced to repeat life until all lessons were learned.

Parking was easy downtown, but as the city grew, so did the prices. Ally gave the guy a twenty-dollar bill and told him to keep the three that he offered her back. One thing Ally believed in was karma. The more generous she was with others, the more life gave back to her in success and fortune. When she waited tables through college, she was more conservative and even a little tight-fisted with her earnings. Having worked in a tipping industry before, she now knew how much each dollar counted for people living on a budget. When she stayed at a hotel, she always left money for the maid and tipped the valet. If she was short of change, she would procure the proper amount at the front desk, even if it was an inconvenient trip down the elevator and back up to the room. She felt it was bad luck not to show gratitude, and every year she saw her success and monetary security grow because of it. She imagined the cleaning lady with so many mouths to feed or the valet working to go to school. She felt like she could help in this small way, and it made her feel good.

The walk to the bar was just a block from the garage. The downtown area was compact, and the most popular bars covered about a four-block area. Smoking had been banned some years ago, so she didn't have to worry about her allergies making a mess of her mascara, but the bar air was stale with the smell of old beer and a mustiness from the freezing air conditioning. She was thankful for the black cotton wrap she had tied to her purse. Ally never went anywhere in the South without one. The temperature outside could be boiling during the summer, but indoors was always ice cold.

The crowd milled around the bar as the band finished their set, saying good night. They were obviously opening for the feature act. She imagined Travis played guitar, or maybe he was a drummer kind of guy. She was surprised he had never mentioned being in a band while they talked at lunch the day of their ride.

Ally had wanted to play an instrument, but the few times she picked up a guitar, it was awkward. The passion didn't stick. She supposed she might have tried a lesson, but art took up most of her creative energy, and she wasn't sure she had time for more hobbies. It was on her list of things to do, along with a hot air balloon ride, learning a foreign language, and seeing the pyramids. The bucket list was ever-growing and changing. She used to want to live in New York, but that was no longer her thing. She had no desire to climb Mount Everest but had hiked many tall mountains in Colorado and California. She could see the allure but didn't see the need to go through such extremes to find satisfaction. Skydiving, she would leave for the birds and her friend Amy. If Ally never had to get on a plane again, that would be fine by her. Some people were just meant to be on land. She was one of them.

Ordering a Sprite and cranberry juice from the bartender, she moved through the throng of people to a small table with one empty chair. The guy sitting next to it motioned that it was vacant, so she settled in. Ally learned a long time ago that it made others uncomfortable if you didn't have a cocktail in your hand. She always ordered something that looked like an alcoholic drink, and everyone was happy to leave her alone. She loved wine and champagne, but the laws on drinking and driving had become very strict in the city, and she didn't like the idea of phoning someone to bail her out of jail. The way the county had cracked down, two drinks was too much. It was too much government interference when you were afraid to have two drinks in an evening, but it didn't do any good to think about that now. She quickly turned her mind off politics as the band took the stage.

The lights were bright, and she saw Travis trying to see past their brilliance into the crowd. She wondered if he was looking for her. The drummer was black as night with a red do-rag tied around his bald head. He wore baggy cargo pants with a loose button-down shirt. His teeth glowed in the black-light of the bar. The guitarist looked like every girl's rock and roll dream. He wore faded jeans with a well-worn, orange T-shirt. The light cotton stretched taut over his muscular pecks. His soft brown hair was styled fashionably short for a rocker, but she couldn't imagine him any other way. At the keyboard stood a similarly dressed younger kid, who looked like he might be in college. One thing she could say was that the sum-total of the group was very appealing. Every band member was fit, and it explained why most of the bar was filled with young women. Ally felt a little too old for the bar scene, and it was rare she traveled downtown for a night out, but the energy was good tonight.

Travis picked up his instrument, and Ally studied his strong hands against the sleek finish of the wood. Not many bands boasted an electric violin. In truth, she wasn't sure she had ever heard one. She did a short rendition of "The Devil Went Down to Georgia" in her head, smiling before they started to play. Travis wore a cotton pullover that flattered his lean build. The fabric clung to his muscular arms as he flexed the bow over his violin. With a booming start from the drummer, the music blared, and the audience went wild.

Ally couldn't restrain her own excitement as the band played through its first set. They were amazing. They played cover music from other popular bands and nestled a few of their own songs in between. Travis played the violin like it was a part of him, but for one slow country ballad, he stole the stage with his amazing, sultry voice. Ally had never been a fan of country music, but she did love old Patsy Cline and Johnny Cash songs. Travis would be added to that must-hear list. She couldn't get over how good they were, and that she had never heard of, Hell's Not That Hot, before tonight.

As they cleared the stage, and the house DJ filled the void with a popular top-forty song, Ally fidgeted with the ice in her glass. Should she go say hello, or wait for him to come to her? Should she go to the bar and play it casual? This was exactly why she avoided dating. She had been off the market for so long, she was sure her expiration date had come and gone. Ally felt clueless about current dating rules.

Deciding to return to the bar, she turned quickly and almost collided with someone.

"Hey, I was looking for you. Glad you came." Travis smiled with sincerity, soothing Ally's insecurity. Her heart was still pounding from almost running him down. She smiled dumbly, twirling the rocks in her glass. "Need a drink?" His voice rose over the music, as he leaned closer. "Umm, you smell nice."

His head lingered inches from her neck. Ally's heart began to race. With his proximity, she found herself taking in his own scent of fresh laundry mixed with perspiration and light cologne.

"It's ah…something I brought back from Paris. Is it too much? I always worry I'm overdoing it…" She trailed off, realizing she sounded as insecure as she felt. "Hey, you guys are great! And you—I never would have pegged you as an electric violinist. Amazing!" Her voice bubbled with excitement, causing Travis's grin to widen.

"Why, thank you, ma'am." He winked. "Let me buy you a drink?" he insisted.

He waved in the direction of a cocktail waitress. The busty blonde with a tray practically ran over three tables trying to get to him. Ally smothered a laugh. She ordered a glass of Prosecco, and he ordered an O'Doul's.

"It's hard to play if I get too lit up," he said, gesturing back to the stage.

"I know, I'm driving, so I'll only have this one glass myself," she confessed.

"Good girl." He winked. "Though I'll be happy to drive you back if you want to relax and kick back a few tonight."

"Thanks. I've got a few things to do tomorrow. I thought I would still be busy preparing for my trip, but we finished up most everything already. Another night, though." She raised her eyebrows in interest. "You guys are great, but I don't think I have ever seen a band quite so…clean cut." She smiled, unable to come up with another adjective.

"Just guys from the station, except for Mike, there. He's a volunteer fireman. Computer programmer by day. We started playing in Eddie's garage a few years back, and…well, this all just happened. Ross has a gal he sees in band promotions, and she got us into a gig at South by Southwest. Next thing I knew, we have a steady gig. Just once a month, though. I wouldn't want to do it any more than that. It's fun. It frees my mind." Travis took a long drink from the beer and placed it on the table. Ally thought back to the conversation they had had over lunch. She got it. "I have to get back to the stage, but I'd really like to chat some more. Stick around?" He nodded as he asked, waiting for her to confirm.

"I don't know." She paused, looking around the bar. "I'd love to, but it's late and I really should get back to Ella and Harley." Ally checked her cell phone for the time.

"Okay, then." He nodded. "If you take off before the band quits playing, just promise me you'll be safe getting home. Let me take you out to dinner Friday night?" He was already backing toward the stage.

"Maybe." She smiled and grabbed her small handbag to go to the ladies' room. She would watch a few more songs and then head home. The road was dark and winding, and she didn't like driving home with the two a.m. crowd. She also didn't want to give the local police chief, Collin, a reason to pull her over and chat her up. He was nice enough, but it was late, and she felt like being home with her dogs and a good book.

CHAPTER 6

Both dogs were lying by the hearth in her favorite beanbag chair when Ally returned home. It was a throwback from the seventies, but bigger, with a plush, cream-colored cover. It had become their favorite bed. Harley was laying above Ella's head, sprawled out like a dust-mop, belly up. The duo was so cute that it was amazing she could ever leave them.

"Hey, you guys," she called softly to them, closing the door behind her.

Both pups bobbed up and bounded toward her. Yawning, stretching, and wagging followed. Ally did her usual night-time routine, making herself a cup of chamomile and setting a bottle of water by her bed. Both pups jumped in, burrowing under covers and finding their usual spots. She slipped on her softest, most threadbare T-shirt and snuggled in close to her furry bed partners. She opened her e-reader and picked up where she had left off a week ago. Things were busy lately, and life never seemed to slow down.

An indescribable energy surrounded her. She couldn't explain it and presumed she might be fanciful for thinking it, but she noticed Ella and Harley thumping their tails and staring into space on many occasions. This feeling she picked up last week inspired her guardian angel portrait, and she was thrilled with the outcome. She didn't believe in guardian angels, but it also didn't hurt to hope. With that last thought, she reached up and turned off her reading lamp. She was too tired to read after all.

Bang, bang, bang!

Ella jumped up first with Harley on her tail. They raced toward the front door at lightning speed, barking non-stop.

"What the—" Ally blinked, trying to see the numbers on the clock.

She reached for the HK45 pistol she kept tucked under the pillow beside her and hurried toward the front door. She had learned to shoot in high school. Hunter safety was mandatory back then. A few safety measures were required when living in the country, though she never had to use them. The dogs barked excitedly, which confused Ally. If there was a threat, Ella would be snarling in the bay window, but Ella was thumping her tail and scratching at the closed doggy door to go out. Harley, of course, followed her lead. Ella whined, pleading for Ally to raise the plastic latch, but Ally cautiously looked through the peephole. Sighing with exasperation, she opened the front door.

"Justin, what are you doing here? It's three in the morning!" Ally set the firearm on the console table by the door and assessed her ex-husband. Yep, he was drunk.

"Now, that ain't no way to greet the man you were married to half your life," he slurred and swayed a bit. "You getting too big for your britches, aren't cha? Think that all them fancy paintings gonna get you rich? Hell, you already have everything, and look what I got. Nothin'." His voice rose. "You left me and took it all, and now you're living the high life! You stole the best years of my life, and now it's all wasted because of you," he sneered. "You left me!" Justin pointed an accusing finger.

Ally was careful not to open the door more than a crack. He had never hit her during their marriage, but she didn't know him well anymore. He dropped by about once a year to complain about his finances and cause a scene. She had hoped the last check she wrote would keep him off her back for a while. She did have money, and he didn't, but it wasn't because she had taken it all. It was because he refused to live within his means, and the alcohol made his spending habits loose.

"Justin, you need to go on home or down the hill to Doreen's and sleep it off. If you want to talk, just call me in the morning, and we can arrange something."

Bright red and blue lights lit up the blackness in front of Ally's house, and she cringed. The neighbors must have heard Justin's outburst. She would apologize to April tomorrow. She knew it was late.

"Fuck, Ally! You know I'm on probation. I'm still fighting the DUIs, you little bitch!" He turned back to her, eyes glaring.

"Everything okay?"

Ally looked around Justin to see Travis walking up the drive. Relief flooded her senses, then pure embarrassment. Justin knew the gate code and had apparently left it open. She really needed to figure out how to reprogram it.

"It's fine—we're all good. Justin was just leaving."

"What's it to you, asshole?" Justin popped off. "A husband has rights to talk to his wife." He pointed his finger at Travis while hitching his jeans up with his other hand.

Travis's hand rested on his hip. He was in the clothes he wore from the bar. Ally noted that he wasn't wearing a gun. "Husband?" Travis's eyebrows rose as he paused. "Well, husband or no, you better show some respect."

"Ex-husband," Ally corrected. "Justin was just heading to his girlfriend's place down the hill. She'll take good care of him. I think he is just a little lost tonight." Ally hated that she covered for Justin, but it had been that way their whole life, from high school to divorce court. She had bailed him out more times than he deserved, but at this point, he was like bad family. He never truly went away, and she felt sorry for him. He didn't have a good life, though it was his own fault.

Justin glared at her once more, then sized up the bulk of the officer's form blocking the streetlight. Resignation made his shoulders droop. As he staggered down the drive, he called out, "Yeah, I got better places to be anyway."

"You okay?" Travis asked more specifically this time.

"Yes, I'll be fine. His untimely appearance just rattles me is all." She shook her head, wondering how she must look. "How did you know…" Her words trailed off as she looked at his car in the distance.

"Don't worry, I'm not stalking you. I was giving Ross's gal a ride home. She's about three blocks down off Angie Street, but I'll admit I back-tracked just to see if you made it home okay. I saw your Jeep in the drive, but then I saw the truck parked out front and someone entering your gate. I wouldn't have thought much, but you said you weren't seeing anyone, so I was worried about the late visitor. When I heard him getting riled up, I just thought I'd make sure you were safe." Travis dipped his head, and the muscle in his jaw flexed.

Ally smiled. He seemed honest enough, and it was nice that he'd checked on her. She couldn't trust Justin in his current condition, and even Ella had her hair up. The yellow lab loved Justin, and he generally loved all animals, but he could be unpredictable when under the influence.

"Well, thanks. You want a cup of tea for your effort? I know it's late, but I'm not going to sleep anytime soon, and I have some chamomile that's soothing."

Travis smiled, nodding, and Ally motioned for him to follow her in.

He held up a finger. "Give me just a minute." He went back to his vehicle to grab his keys and turn off the flashing lights, then returned. She showed him into the kitchen, and he leaned against the counter, watching Ally pour water into the kettle before plugging it in.

"I've never been much of a tea drinker, but that's because most of us drink strong coffee down at the station. My mom liked tea. She would have liked you." His smile was whimsical.

"What was she like?" Ally asked curiously.

"She died young. I was only ten or so. She had long, dark hair and a sweet, soft smile. She sang like an angel. My dad remarried pretty quick afterward. Liz Anne was nice, but she wasn't Mom. I feel bad about all the grief I gave her back then. I buy her the biggest Christmas gift each year and try to make up for my bad behavior." He sat on one of the stools by the island, and Ally smiled at his boyish guilt. He made her counter look small and the stool beneath him spindly.

"I'm sure she understood, and it's all water under the bridge now, right?"

"Things are good. She has more to worry about with my half-brothers' children now. Being a grandma is a full-time job, and she takes it seriously." He took the mug she offered and added two spoons of sugar from the dainty, pink porcelain sugar bowl.

"Half-brothers? They have children already? They must have started young."

"The oldest is thirty-five, and the youngest is twenty-eight. There are two more in between." He laughed. "Dad was busy. I'm forty-seven if you're guessing."

"Oh! Sorry, I didn't mean to pry." Ally ducked her head and took too-big a sip of her tea, burning her tongue, "Ow!" She dribbled a bit down the front of her nightshirt, making it stick to her bare skin.

"Easy there, killer," he teased. "I know there's probably a decade between us, but I'm young at heart, and you seem like an old soul to me." His careful words brought Ally's eyes to his.

"I wasn't fishing for your age. As you can see, my ex had Peter Pan syndrome, and it would be nice to hang around an adult for a change." She tried keeping her words light.

The conversation was getting sticky, and she didn't want to get stuck. She was having trouble stamping down the physical reaction she was having, standing so close to him in her small kitchen.

As if he felt it too, he reached out for her, tugging at her well-worn T-shirt, pulling her toward him, resting his arms on her waist. "I'm no Peter Pan, Ally, and I'm not the kind of guy who dates around. I am interested in you, and I think you might like me a little, too." His eyes searched hers. Hearing no objections, he continued. "I don't want to scare you off, but I want you to know I'm here. Waiting for you when you're ready."

Ally felt a sizzling vibration shimmy down her spine and into the pit of her stomach. She was paralyzed by sudden lust and didn't know what to say. She couldn't say what she was thinking. *I haven't been with anyone for so long. You're gorgeous, and I would like to see you naked. I want you so bad that I wish you would throw me onto my kitchen counter and have your way with me now!*

He must have felt her thoughts, because he pulled her closer, bringing his lips to hers, caressing her lower back with one hand as he wrapped his other in the thick strands of her cascading hair.

He tasted lightly of chamomile tea and mint. His tongue was tentative at first, gliding across her mouth, lingering in the crease between her lips. She was startled by the amount of electricity between them as heat pooled in her lower extremities. All hesitation was reasoned away. She was a grown woman of thirty-six. She had been married half of her life and hadn't slept with anyone besides Justin. She deserved to have sex with someone else before she died, and this man was the sexiest man she had ever seen in real-life. Travis was all male. Pretty men on the cover of GQ magazine didn't do a thing for her. She had seen a few of those at the gallery in New York. Shaved, sculpted, dressed in the latest fashion, and slathered in designer fragrance. Most of them were more into Marcel than her.

A sweet-smelling soap mingled with an earthy scent on his warm skin. His light blond beard was trimmed around his jawline, emphasizing the cords in his neck. It was more of a groomed, after-five shadow than beard. His cobalt blue eyes set off his tan for as far as she could see, making her wonder where his tan lines were hidden. He moaned as she kissed him back and leaned into his muscular frame. Her hips came to rest between his thighs, and the wooden stool groaned from their combined weight. She felt his hardness press against her stomach, and her breath caught.

Slowly breaking away, he grinned. "I think your stool is telling me it can't handle much more."

Ally flushed then squared her shoulders as she looked him in the eyes.

"Maybe we should move to a bigger chair." She smiled, leading him into the cozy living area with the beanbag chair made for two. "Give me a minute."

She hesitated, gauging his interest level and the heat potentially lost by her next action. She lit the fireplace, shooed Ella and Harley to the bedroom, and brought in the remains of their tea. He had already made himself at home in the chair, and she cuddled in beside him with the two teas. He took the cups and slowly placed them on a side table and then picked up a wisp of hair to tuck behind her ear.

"You are so beautiful. When I saw you in the bar tonight, you had an aura that glowed around you." He studied her features, mapping out the angles and planes of her face.

"That's my guardian angel," she mused.

"Lucky girl," he said, as he shifted onto his side and resumed the kiss he had started in the kitchen.

Ally wasn't sure if he was talking about her or the angel, but right now she felt like the most fortunate woman in the world, and it had been a while since she had gotten lucky.

His hands danced over her soft, bare skin, lifting the night-shirt over her head. Ally couldn't suppress a shiver of excitement that danced havoc along her spine. He pulled her close and embraced her in his warmth. She nipped at the cords of his neck and brushed at the tendrils of hair curling at the edge of his ear.

"It's been a long time for me. Since I've been with someone, I mean," she confessed.

His voice was laced with desire. "It's okay. I promise to go slow."

The scent of his warm skin brought images, flashing through her mind, of their bodies twined together from an aerial view. She knew she would paint it as soon as he left. Her stomach tingled as he dipped his head to her breast and took one nipple between his warm lips. The heat of his tongue swirling around her areola made her gasp with pleasure. Moving from one breast to the other, he gave each peak his ardent interest. Ally couldn't take much more of his teasing. She laced her fingers through his hair, pulling him back to explore her mouth with the warmth of his kiss. His hand sought out the elastic band of her boxer briefs. Delving into her molten heat, he spread her woman's flesh, pushing his fingers inside to explore her inner depths. She bit down hard on his shoulder, spreading her legs and yearning for more. His fingers dipped and swirled, playing her as well as the instrument he'd stroked earlier, and it made her dizzy with passion. Ally couldn't help herself. It had been far too long. She cried out in an almost-too-quick orgasm that wracked her body with heavenly pleasure. His expert caresses sent her entranced form drifting on a cloud of ecstasy.

She felt warm and bubbly, barely suppressing the hysterical giggle that welled up inside as he kissed her. Ally pushed at his shirt, helping to strip it off. She reached between them to unclasp his jeans and encouraged Travis by closing her legs tightly around him. Starting an exploration of her own, she released his hardened member. Her hand between them, she found the smooth skin of his engorged flesh hard and ready at her touch. Pushing at the stiff denim jeans, she pleaded with him to find a home in the cradle of her warmth. After a few seconds of fumbling with the foil wrapper he had pulled from his wallet, he filled her tight sheath with a guttural groan. A rhythm built between them, escalating until they lay spent in the afterglow of their dual crescendo.

Ally didn't know what happened next. She awoke to sunlight streaming across her face and a wet nose reminding her to open the dog door. A light throw lay over her naked form, and the fireplace was cold. She was alone except for the dogs. A moment of fear squeezed her heart, reminding her she was vulnerable. Sitting up and looking around, she saw a note weighed down by a drink coaster where their tea mugs still graced the table.

I never kiss and run, but my shift starts at 6 a.m.

Call you when I get off later, and maybe we can have an early dinner uptown on Friday.

You are truly an Amazing Woman!

Travis

CHAPTER 7

The next few days raced by. Ally was booked to fly out on Sunday, and she spent most of her time painting or on the phone working out the details for the gallery showing. It was suddenly Friday, and Ally was painfully aware that she had never heard from Travis. He seemed so interested in her company until she slept with him. *So typical!* She'd heard most men lost interest once they got what they wanted. Ally didn't like the sticky feeling that clung to her throat, making it hard to swallow. Besides her art, he was the only thrill she'd experienced in the last three years. She admitted she had closed herself off to deter from being hurt by the opposite sex, but Travis seemed genuine and different. The special energy she'd felt with him had made her look forward to their date. Apparently, her perception of his interest was wrong. He was just an average guy, and she'd been an easy conquest.

Marcel handled all the show's business aspects, but she still had a few tasks to take care of. She never worried about the details when he was in charge. He was like a pit-bull dealing with her art. Ally contemplated taking a motorcycle ride through the hill country or calling her sister to touch base. She wanted to make sure they had plenty of time to set things straight once she arrived in New York.

Soledad twiddled her fingers and waited for Ally to go through her normal routine. She had stood back observing her ward most of the time since the night at the bar. Travis had been free of the vampiric energy that haunted him, and his mood with Ally was light and fun. There had been no reason for Soledad to send any channeling of encouragement or warning. Ally seemed to play it all just right.

Everything had been rather dull since the one night with Travis, except for the electric tea kettle incident. The ancient appliance had been left on and almost burned down the house. Ally had been in the studio, and Soledad tried to channel warnings that would pull her back into the kitchen with no luck. In desperation, she channeled energy to Ella and Harley, getting them stirred into a barking frenzy. She knew her high-pitched warning pierced their ears, but it was the only thing that finally brought Ally back to reality. She petted and doted on Harley and Ella afterward, giving them extra treats and praise. Later, the pups picked up Soledad's presence and thumped their tails in unison. Soledad smiled. *Good puppies.*

"What do you two see there?" Ally asked the dogs, who sat looking in the same direction, tails wagging. Ally looked past the stairs to the loft Soledad lounged on and peered out the window to see if someone was coming. There was nothing there for the dogs to be happy about. "You two anticipating a walk?" Ella barked, and Harley raced to the dog door. His white fluff shot out of it like a canon, then with a hard whoosh of the plastic flap, he returned.

Ally looked at her cell phone for the fifth time. It was almost noon. She grabbed their leashes from the hook and moved to open the door. Both Ella and Harley looked like Daffy Duck, spinning their back paws on the slick wood in their excitement to go out. Their joy was infectious as they bounded out the door and over the property to walk the fence line. Soledad felt Ally trying to clear Travis from her mind, and she was clearly irritated that all her thoughts kept pulling back to his strong, tanned hands, sharp aquiline features, and his backside in ripped denim jeans. His smile seemed so genuine, and the story about his wife had touched her heart. It wasn't a true-love story, but the dedication he had shown by making a commitment was compelling. Why hadn't he called, dammit?

Ella danced in the air, yipped, then sped off like she was chasing an invisible stick. Harley was hot on the yellow lab's haunches. Ally tried hard to see what the dogs were chasing. Static raised the fine blonde hair on her arms, and goose flesh alerted her to a presence occupying her space. The dogs bounded back to her and bowled her over onto the grass.

"Ow! You guys," Ally complained as she landed on a stick that ripped her jeans. "Take it easy," she admonished, laughing at their enthusiasm.

Harley took advantage of her grounded status and wiggled up her torso to lick fervent kisses over her face. She laughed and tried to ward off both dogs' advances until the sun breached a cloud, and a long ray of sunlight pierced the ground. The shadow of a woman stared down at her, and Ally remembered the angel she had painted. As soon as Ally reached out, the image was gone like a disappearing hologram.

"Come back!" she called out to the empty air, but with no luck. Ella and Harley sat calmly, looking up. "What was that?" Ally asked, dazed.

Standing up to brush off the grass and muck, she looked back at the sky. Shaking her head, she led the pups back to the house. She would paint then take that ride she so needed to relieve her pent-up frustration and anxiety about the upcoming flight.

CHAPTER 8

Ally called Jessica on her cell before boarding the plane. There was no answer, but she wasn't surprised. It had been touch-and-go with their relationship lately, and Ally could imagine Jessica hitting the ignore button every time the phone rang. Ally was guilty of that herself when she didn't pick up Jess's call last week.

The takeoff was uneventful and the flight smooth, except for a few bouts of turbulence. Still, Ally's heart sank, and her knees grew weak. She looked at the young Asian man beside her, who typed on his laptop with quick, deft strokes, ignoring her clenched hands. She had a glass of wine, but nothing seemed to help. In a previous life, she must have died in a plane crash. She had no other reason to be so afraid, and knowing it was the safest way to travel didn't help. Ally couldn't get her body to agree with science or statistics. Her palms were sweating, and her stomach lurched. She couldn't wait for the wheels to touch down, *Oh so gently, please.*

She tried to imagine her happy place as the therapist taught her, but her happy place was at home, and she was currently thirty-thousand feet somewhere over Kentucky. Where was her guardian angel? Ally hadn't felt uncomfortable the past few weeks, even though she was sure someone was watching her. It was like she was a film actor in a movie. Her life was surreal, and the mistake she had made in trusting Travis made her feel foolish and used. Ally gazed out at a large thunderhead and tried not to think about the plane. She imagined Ella and Harley anxiously waiting by the door. Poor pups, it would be a long wait.

As she made her way from baggage claim to passenger pickup, her scarf blew away in the wind, billowing high, then low into a stranger's grasp. The handsome man in a well-cut suit smiled and walked toward her.

"Mademoiselle," he smiled and made a small bow.

"Oh, thank you…" Her words trailed off.

Ally was mesmerized by the dimple in his left cheek. She guessed he was several years younger than she, but his charm and manners were years older than what his generation would suggest. His eyes were liquid amber flecked with a shade of ivory-gray, and his accent was incredible. He was the kind of man Marcel would go gaga over, but by the way he was looking at her, she doubted he had a gay bone in his body.

"Pleasure is all mine" He was still smiling.

Ally didn't know what to do, so she turned to look for her ride. She had to get away from this hunk before Marcel spotted her and attacked him. Nodding back at him, she started walking. *What a beautiful specimen of a man*, she mused.

"Um, mademoiselle," he called out to her, and Ally whirled around. "Yes?"

He motioned toward her luggage that she had left at his feet.

Flushing with embarrassment, she silently kicked herself. How could she be so mindless? "Oh, yes. Thank you. I…um, I have a big show this weekend, and my mind is anywhere but here, I'm afraid." She was lying. Her mind was on him, not the luggage. Why did she bring up her art?

She could almost predict the question before it was asked.

"A show? You are an actress? Broadway?" His voice pitched with interest as his eyes searched her features for recognition.

"No, I'm an artist. My paintings will be shown in an exhibit this week-end. I'm just flying in to get organized before the event." She tried to sound nonchalant.

"May I ask where? I love art," he exclaimed.

It was at this moment Marcel appeared and began campaigning for an introduction. Since Ally didn't know the young man's name, she could not grant one, so she smiled smugly.

Marcel gave her a pleading stare, and she finally gave in. "It's in Manhattan. I'll have Marcel give you his card. Call the gallery, and Rebecca will set aside two tickets for you at the door if you are interested." *There, Marcel had his in.*

"I would love to, but I only need one," he emphasized, still smiling. "I am here alone from Paris for a few weeks to see my aunt. I regret she is not well enough to be out at her age. It would be a nice diversion for me and a chance to see some of the city."

"I hope you'll come then." Ally firmly grabbed the roller bag and searched for any other forgotten items.

Marcel began chatting as she started to walk away. Again, she heard the handsome man.

"Louis," he called out. Ally turned, and he supplied, "Louis Lamereaux is my name, for the ticket," he emphasized the singularity of the word. He held up Marcel's card but was making sure she knew his name.

She nodded, "Ally."

Louis was all she heard about the entire drive to Manhattan. Marcel was in love. Ally laughed. "You know he's straight, right?"

Marcel always went for heterosexuals. It must be the challenge of changing them. His good looks had championed more than a few prized virgins that she wouldn't have thought possible, but they usually ended up ill at ease with the venture and quickly closed the proverbial gay closet door, hoping their secret exploration would never come out. Ally stayed out of it. Marcel was his own worst enemy when it came to love, and who was she to judge?

They happily gossiped all the way to the gallery, where Rebecca took over, and Marcel darted out to pick up coffee. It would be a long afternoon of inventory and placement mapping. They were still finishing the program, listing the new art, and updating the artist's bio, not that there was much to update.

There would be an interview with *The Times* that she dreaded, but the hours would pass, and then she would check in on Jessica. It bothered her that Jess hadn't answered any of her calls. Just then, Ally's cell vibrated in her pocket, and she looked at the screen. Travis's number replaced the colorful picture of *David* she had downloaded. She hesitated to answer. It had been almost a week, and he hadn't called as promised. Why should she answer as if waiting by the phone? It wasn't like he was the only guy interested. She had seen the way Louis admired her at the airport. Of course, maybe he was an art junky, and anyone in the business would have made him excited. She returned the phone to her pocket. Travis could wait. She had work to do.

"James Rafferty. Pleased to meet you." The writer for *The Times* introduced himself, and Ally waved him toward the contemporary chrome and white leather chair in front of Rebecca's desk. She pushed the intercom button and asked Christine, Rebecca's secretary, to bring in some water and coffee for them. Christine would bring her tea. It never had to be said. Everyone knew Ally didn't drink coffee.

"Thanks for seeing me. I was excited when I got the assignment. I've been following your work for some time."

"You have a personal interest in art?"

"I'm not educated on the subject if you will forgive my lack of expertise, but I know what I like, and I like you."

His coy smile made her edgy. Ally missed a beat, creating an awkward pause. Was he hitting on her? *Must be the French perfume*, she thought. Maybe it was filled with pheromones. She felt like she was on fire with sudden sexual awareness. Her one-night stand with Travis opened a door that she previously feared was forever nailed shut. She had thought she had given her best years to her ex, but maybe she still had reserves.

"Well, thank you. It's nice to know my interviewer will be kind." She smiled, trying to cover her fidgeting. She hated interviews. They robbed her of her brain. She worried so much about what she would say that she found it difficult to come up with eloquent words to describe her work. "I take it you have seen the current display lined up for the gallery."

"Yes! It's fabulous. The colors, flair, imagination. My favorite is *David Reborn*, and I'm *not* gay," he stressed, looking over his shoulder as if Marcel would suddenly appear.

Ally smiled. She could reassure the reporter that he wasn't Marcel's type, but she kind of liked him being on edge. It made the playing field even. Christine appeared, bringing in two steaming cups, and placed them on the desk.

Ally nodded her thanks and then smiled at Mr. Rafferty's earlier omission.

"I'm glad you liked the display. *David* wasn't supposed to make this showing, but Marcel insisted, so I allowed it to be displayed in the show after a little arm twisting."

"Why did you want to hold it back?" His quizzical tone sent an alert to her brain, making her scurry to find a defense.

"I...um...don't know, really. It was a last-minute piece I had just finished, and I hadn't thought to include it. I hadn't had time to process it, so to speak," she floundered.

"Who inspired it?"

Short comments were always better than elaborations. "I had a vision," she said simply.

Artists sometimes let their vanity get the better of themselves when they nattered on about their work. Ally was shy when discussing her innermost feelings.

"Are you saying you just see images and they come to life in your brushstrokes, or are you a form of psychic who sees messages from another reality?"

She wanted to say, *No, I just needed to get laid,* but instead, she tried to divert his line of questioning. "Did you like *Fog in Mirrored Palace?*"

"Are you avoiding my question?" He pierced her with his unwavering stare. His fingers paused over the small screen of his notebook.

"No, no. I'm just excited about all of the work on display, and my favorite happens to be *Mirrored Palace*. It's a view from a place in Greece that I love. It's by the ocean. *David* was inspired by an intriguing man I met, but it was just a fleeting acquaintance, so I would rather not name him."

"Are you in love with this David? Did he break your heart?"

"Mr. Rafferty…" This was getting uncomfortable. If she had predicted they would land on the topic of David so early in the interview, she would have canceled.

"Call me James. I hate formalities."

Ally nodded, trying to smile. "I confess I'm not great at interviews, and I'm really deplorable at talking about my personal life. Could we get back to the gallery and the exhibit?" she pleaded.

"Sorry, I didn't mean to pry. I was actually wondering if I had a chance at taking you out to dinner later." He winked at her, leaning forward in his chair, giving her what he probably thought was his winning smile. The reporter's confidence bordered on egomania, and she didn't care for Mr. Rafferty's pushy approach. She didn't want to be rude since she hoped to have a successful write-up to enhance the show's success. The writer was handsome, but he gave off a cheesy salesman vibe, and his sincerity was that of a hungry lion. Lucky for her, she had Jessica as an excuse.

"Sorry, but tonight is my only free night before the show starts, and I have plans to see my sister for dinner. We haven't seen each other for a while now, so you'll have to excuse me. In fact, I hope you have enough to write about from the sneak peek because I am late for another meeting with the directors. I hope to see you at the show." Ally rose from her chair and started to show him out.

"Intriguing…" His words trailed off.

He rose and followed her to the door, stopped beside Ally, and turned to face her. His proximity was too close. She could smell the wintergreen on his breath to cover up his cigarette habit. She leaned back into the hard, cold door frame to create more space between them. He stood, assessing her for a moment with obvious interest, then made his exit. Ally sighed audibly after he left. *The gall of the man.*

Ally returned to the elegant glass desk and retrieved her tea. She dug in her pocket and produced her cell phone, scrolling through the contact index for her sister. She tried to call Jess once more, but her sister still wasn't answering. Ally hung up and made reservations at their favorite place on West Grand then sent Jess a text with the address and the time. She would love to take off and go by Jess's apartment, but there really was a lot to do, and it wasn't unusual for Jess to ignore her for days.

Soledad perched upon the sleek, modern desk made of glass and steel. She wasn't always present in Ally's life. There were huge chunks of time she couldn't account for. As between lives, she spent expanses of her existence unaware in the soul-watching world. Her only explanation was sleep. All beings needed sleep, so why shouldn't souls? Of course, hers was a narcoleptic sort of slumber, fading in and out, sometimes without any warning. Soledad knew her ward had flown to New York, but she had no memory of how she herself had arrived. It was a mystery how her luminous form stood in a superb high-rise overlooking Manhattan. Soledad became aware once more during the exit of the awful man who made Ally so uncomfortable. *Who was that guy?*

Ally's hand flittered through her own as she reached for the cup on the desk. Soledad channeled soothing words of confirmation to ease Ally's agitation. Her ward made a call to her sister, then a second phone call that included reservations for two. Ally was distracted by her phone as she tapped at its glass surface. Clearly perturbed, she shook her head, pocketed the phone, and headed toward the elevator. Maybe Travis had called? Soledad wasn't sure if she should sway Ally back into his court. She had to admit the possibility that Travis wasn't the connection she had once hoped.

He was already making her ward doubt herself, and Ally's confidence was fragile to begin with.

Being a soul watcher was not the same as the spirit being in an embodied state. The core of energy was the same, but without ego. Soledad didn't pack value into material wealth or status as a soul watcher since it didn't benefit her in the afterlife. She understood the many levels of human emotions, but issues that plagued embodied spirits had no effect on the soul once released.

An awareness of Ally's hurt, betrayal and vulnerability coursed through Soledad. She took a moment to breathe and floated to the window. Ally had not sensed her presence, and it alarmed Soledad that her ward was suddenly throwing off so many distress signals. When Ally departed, Soledad did not follow. It wasn't necessary for her to shadow her ward continually. Watchers could be drained of their energy from such constant awareness, especially when it was loaded down with despair. Soledad needed a few more pieces of the puzzle to decipher her next course of action. Meditation-fielded plans and a course to navigate. She reached deep within to journey to her sanctuary. She didn't know if the place actually existed, or if it was a plane in her spirit's mind. Soledad stood on the shore of the ocean, staring out at the clear, green-glass waves of water. The gulls squawked above, and fresh sea air swirled around her luminous form, lifting her ivory robes. Here she could think.

Ally's thoughts and recent past events unfolded before Soledad. In a flash, she saw Ally saying good-bye to Ella and Harley, then saw a flicker of a movie that she had watched on the plane. Soledad felt her throat contract in fear as she felt the turbulence her ward must have encountered. A man in a business suit sat quietly beside her, busying himself on his laptop. Finally, rays of sunlight glinted over a beautiful man catching Ally's scarf. Soledad nodded in understanding as her vision world closed, leaving her staring at an empty room of glass. The large framed photograph on the wall beckoned her. A vague memory trickled over her senses. She neared the black and white picture in the minimalist silver frame with black matting. It was a small sailboat with its sails tethered to the mast. *Grey Dawn* was written in faded letters across the bow. In the bottom of the photo was her own prior life signature, Katia Grey. A flutter of excitement, then a hollow feeling eclipsed her energy source. She would have said someone walked over her grave, but it would have been impossible since hers was a watery burial many leagues deep. Temporarily paralyzed by regret, Soledad mourned her lost life. She might have found more to live for if she had tried.

While Soledad stared, transfixed by what could have been, a moving force of energy startled her, whisking her deep into the belly of the high-rise. She found herself in a cold, dry room without windows. Covered canvases filled the area, and shipping remnants littered a corner where Ally and Marcel debated over descriptive tags. Marcel tapped each piece of work into his handheld computer and made notes about the details of Ally's vision for each. Soledad was in the gallery's storage room.

"So, what about sweet Louis? Can I have him? Did you call dibs? I don't remember you calling dibs," he gushed. Chattering, he went through all Louis's assets, "That man has a rear end like a sex god and a gorgeous head of hair. Did you see those pecs?"

Soledad had known more than a few Marcels in her last life. He was Ally's best friend but would leave her hanging in a heartbeat if Mr. Right was standing at the door. Faster if it was Mr. Wrong.

"I didn't call dibs, and I don't own him. If he bites, he bites. Let's just leave it at that." Ally said.

"Seriously, Ally! Didn't you think he was so—yummy? I know Justin left a bad taste in your mouth, but you are still beautiful. Maybe a little old," he teased, popping her on the arm with his stylus. "You need to get out there and explore. What happened to the Adonis who inspired *David Reborn*?"

Ally tapped her chin, "Hmm, David, David. Oh! You mean that?" Ally pointed to the huge canvas the workmen were setting against the adjacent wall. Soledad loved Ally's art. Her ward probably had no clue that her talent came from her great-great-grandfather. It was a gift to be treasured, and no one else seemed to have inherited the great passion for art in their family. Contemplating her past talents, Soledad wondered if she would possess such passion for art in her next existence. The longer she stayed on this plane, the foggier her past life memories became, and even the life of Katia was fading. She wondered again how many years or cycles she would follow Ally before she might be granted a presence with her own soulmate.

"Yes, that would be the one," Marcel sighed appreciatively as he admired the painting.

"He never called me last week," Ally confessed.

Her voice betrayed the regret of something lost. Soledad saw a flash of her ward's recent memory. Travis had called, but it was way too late in the scheme of things to count. Ally hadn't given in to the urge to check her voice mail. What could he say outside of a family member dying that would excuse him for not calling until now? His note said he would call Ally about dinner plans, but he hadn't even sent a text message to reschedule.

"Aw, kitten, don't fret. He was too rugged anyway. Men like that are all sluts. They think you had fun, so no real harm. Now, let's move on." He started walking toward the hall. "You're going to make me give you Louis, aren't you?" Marcel pouted then smiled.

Ally laughed. Soledad was suddenly glad Ally was in New York with Marcel. He lightened her mood, and it was good to see her ward throw herself back into her work. Soledad knew it was how Ally got through her divorce and all other life crises.

"The one night with Travis was fun, so I guess I shouldn't complain. It's like you said, I got my divorce-cherry popped. Yes, let's move on." She shrugged her shoulders and tried to smile. Soledad felt the pulsating waves of longing Ally radiated for the sexy man who knew every inch of her. "And don't think you are *giving* me anything!" Her ward noticed Marcel texting someone named Yummy Louis. He was sending the address of a swanky lounge to the new contact.

Marcel reacted to her opened-mouth disbelief. "What? He wants to pick up the ticket."

Ally smirked at the quick text Louis sent back, asking if she would be there.

Smiling conspiratorially, her smug voice chimed, "The man is yummy, heterosexual, and apparently has eyes for *me*."

As she had told *The Times* reporter, it was a long day. Ally exited the high-rise yawning and checked her cell phone. Two missed calls from Travis and a text that simply said, *I know you think I'm a jerk, but call me and let me explain.* She put up a mental block to keep her mind from racing to her heart. He could wait. She would hear him out later, but right now she had more important things on her mind, like finding her sister. There were two unknown numbers and another voice mail, but Ally ignored them. Instead, she tried Jessica again. No answer.

She hailed a taxi and gave the driver her sister's address. If Jess wouldn't pick up the phone, Ally would ambush her at the apartment. The arguing had to stop. They were sisters, and they were grown now, for God's sake. It annoyed Ally that Jess treated life like she was still a teenager. Ally needed to stand up to her emotional sister. Lord knew, no one else had the guts. Jess had always run hot and cold, a hot-tempered drama queen. She was also an elitist, complaining about her ignorant students, who didn't know what a prepositional phrase was. Jess stayed on Prozac but self-medicated as well. Ally wasn't shocked by the roach clip she saw on Jess's nightstand her last visit, but she worried about how the recreational use affected Jess's health.

The brownstone in Harlem glimmered like champagne in the setting sun. The day grew shorter, and the shadows of larger cityscapes eclipsed its stone base. Ally had visited before, but Jess was famous for moving every time the lease was up. She fantasized about moving to Tibet to teach English and talked about going to Seattle a few semesters to teach playwriting. Her whimsical spirit kept most people guessing, but Ally knew she would always be here. Jess loved the hustle and bustle of the city. More important, she loved the people that provided an audience for her theatrics. Her friends would fawn over her writing and lectures about politics and grand adventures. She had once told a group of strangers she had interviewed Loretta Lynn for a piece she was writing on the oppression of women through country music. Ally's mouth had dropped at the blatant lie, but the group excitedly praised Jess over her talent. When Ally challenged her, Jess shrugged her shoulders and said, "Don't judge me. You don't know where I am twenty-four seven, and I could have interviewed Loretta." Then she went on eating her popcorn doused in butter and salt, turning up the TV.

Ally pushed the button that rang Jess's apartment several times, but there was no answer. A lady with a stroller started toward the outside door, and Ally helped her hold it open to get the child through.

"Excuse me. Do you know Jess in three-B?" Ally asked, hopefully.

"The woman who teaches at the university? The one with brown hair?" The lady's British accent was delightful, as was her smile. Good, she must like Jess. Jess could be an awful bitch sometimes.

"Yes, she's my sister. I'm in from Texas, but she hasn't answered my calls."

"Oh, no. I haven't seen her, I'm afraid. Maybe she's on holiday?" she said hopefully. Ally smiled and looked out at the street as shadows crawled farther across the city, shading the woman's brow as it furrowed in concern. "If I see her, I'll be sure to tell her you've come 'round."

"Thanks." Ally turned and started walking without knowing where to go.

It didn't look like taxis frequented this street, and she would have to walk a few blocks to catch one. A lady with a cleaning basket passed her, and Ally looked back to watch her climb the stairs of the brownstone. Ally quickly called out to her, asking if she knew Jess, and if she had seen her. A wary look crossed the woman's features as she nervously looked back at the door.

"Um, yes. She's been ill. Are you family?"

As Ally approached, admitting she was Jess's sister, she didn't miss the look of loathing. She had seen the look before from friends of Jess. Who knew what stories she told them, but Jess was Jess, and dramatics were her life.

"Well, she's been at Liberty Memorial for over two weeks. I'm just here to clean her apartment and gather a few items she requested."

"Jess is in the hospital? She never told me—she never called," Ally said with dismay.

Jess might be mad at her, but she would always call if things were bad. Ally couldn't imagine her sister would hold their last row against her when the illness drove her to the hospital. The girl on the steps looked away in discomfort. Who knew what she was thinking, but after Jess posted all over her social media accounts, that her sister was not going to give her a kidney, Ally knew it wasn't anything warm and fuzzy. "Do you know what room?" Ally said, hoping the friend might share.

"They are moving her out of ICU today, so I don't really know. Her girlfriend's been MIA too. Poor Jess. She works so hard, and no one but her colleagues to help. I honestly thought she might be an orphan making up stories of having a family."

Ally's cheeks were scalding in the cool air. "She has family. Family that *does* care for her no matter what she might say," she said calmly then turned to leave. When Jess got better, they were going to have a serious talk about her stories.

The hospital was near the hotel where Ally was staying. In the cab, she called and canceled the dinner reservations. The information desk at the hospital directed her to the third floor, where she found Jess's room empty. Ally's heart lurched with fear. Where had they taken her? A nurse saw her standing in the empty doorway and asked if she could help. She informed Ally that Jess was fitted with a port for dialysis and was now being dialyzed on the fourth floor. It would be after visiting hours when Jess was finished.

"Would you like to return tomorrow?" It was like she was hearing the nurse's voice from another room. When she visited Jess before, the doctor had warned that dialysis was the next step. Her kidneys were on their last leg, and Jess had been desperate to sign Ally up to be her kidney donor.

It wasn't that Ally couldn't live without one kidney, but she didn't think giving it to Jess would save her sister's life. Jess smoked, drank, and ate most of her meals through the drive-through. She used recreational drugs with her professor friends and thumbed her nose at the health-conscious yoga girls she knew. Jess spent her whole life in denial of her own mortality, even after suffering some of the devastating consequences of her disease. She never believed diabetes would be her end.

Ally tested to see if she were a compatible donor months ago. She was a match. She could donate her kidney and possibly save Jess's life, but the question was, even if Jess could qualify for the transplant, could she survive the gift? It took fifty pills a day or more after getting a transplant to help the body to keep from rejecting the organ. Jess couldn't change her lifestyle before to save her own life. How would she take care of a donated kidney?

Returning to the hotel, Ally called room service. She felt rather unhealthy herself, so she ordered a hamburger and fries with a bottle of soda and a half bottle of champagne. She knew if she ordered a whole bottle, she would finish it, and she needed to be at the hospital first thing in the morning. Marcel had left several messages about the show, and Travis had called several more times but didn't leave messages. She didn't feel like dealing with work or men right now. Travis had his chance, and she wasn't sure she wanted to put herself out there again to be hurt. She didn't want to deal with romantic disappointment again. There were more pressing issues to contemplate at the moment, like helping her sister.

CHAPTER 9

Ally spent the night wrestling with the high-thread-count white cotton sheets. The bedding might be *Heavenly*, but there wasn't a bed in the world where she could have slept peacefully, knowing her sister's life hung in the balance. When she finally fell into a slumber, her cell-phone alarm blared ACDC's "Shook Me All Night Long." Ally peeled herself from the bed, stumbled to the shower, and stood under streaming jets hitting her from three different directions. It was enough to revive her, and after consuming half a pot of earl grey, she would be almost human again.

The hospital room was brightly lit with fluorescent lights. Jessica lay pale beneath the greenish reflection of the blanket pulled up to her chest. Her eyes were gaunt and her body listless. Tubes ran from her arm to an IV bag hanging from the metal rack with wheels. The TV was barely audible through the bedside speakers, and Jess watched the program with disinterest. Ally wasn't sure if Jess sensed her presence and chose to ignore it, or if she was tuning out the ambient murmur of the ward. The beeping of other patients' monitors was enough to drive Ally insane.

"Jess, hey. It's me, Ally. You awake?"

"I've got my eyes open, don't I?" That answered her question.

"Yeah, well, I went to your apartment..." Ally's voice trailed off.

In the mood Jess was in, Ally knew anything said could trigger an argument. Jess probably blamed the dialysis on Ally for not jumping up on a table and insisting they do the transplant right there and then.

She tried to tamp down her irritation, reminding herself that Jess was very sick.

Ally contemplated how she would feel if she needed a transplant. It's not like she would expect Marcel or Rebecca to throw their lives to the wind and donate a body part. In truth, she didn't think she could ask anyone. She would probably wait for a cadaver or die. It didn't mean Jess was wrong to ask, but it irked Ally that Jess was so angry at her. Ally hadn't refused, after all, but Jess was doing her best to disown her, and it wasn't fair.

A nurse entered to check Jess's blood pressure and temperature, relieving them from the awkward silence for a moment. The pretty blonde, in blue scrubs, made some idle chit-chat about the weather and smiled. Ally appreciated the short reprieve from Jess's disapproval but only managed to pinch her lips together and stare at the floor. Jess huffed, batting the controls on the hospital bed.

"Easy, Jess. What are you trying to accomplish? Maybe I can help." Ally came to the side of her bed and pushed the button, lifting the head of the bed and bringing Jess to a more upright position.

"What are you doing here, Ally? I didn't ask you to come."

"I know. You haven't returned any of my calls." Ally stared down at her sister, who was only a couple years her senior but looked a decade older in the fluorescent lights. "I came to take you to dinner last night. I've been worried, and now I find out you've been here alone. Why, Jess? You have family."

"You are not my family! You made it clear the last time you visited. You said you wouldn't help, so why are you here?" Jess demanded. It was the same accusation that haunted Ally after her last visit.

"I never said I wouldn't, Jess. I said I wanted to learn about it first. You can't expect me to go diving into something I know nothing about. You're not being fair." Ally shook her head. It was like they were children again, arguing over some childish board game. The gravity of Jess's health gripped at Ally's stomach. It wasn't a game. It was Jess's life.

"I asked you before, and I'll ask you again. If you aren't here to give me a kidney, what are you here for?" Jess's face was contorted with anger. Lines formed around her mouth that Ally had never noticed before.

"Geez, Jess. You kill me. Is that all I'm good for, to sustain your life? Without my commitment to do your bidding, I'm nothing to you?" Tears choked her voice, and she stopped before she said something she'd regret. They had both gone too far down a road that was forever forcing a wedge between them.

"Just go, Ally. I don't want your company, and I sure as hell don't want your kidney." Jess's bitter words melted the last of Ally's resolve.

"I know. I read it on your blog to the world." Without pausing for Jess to explain, Ally turned to leave. She stood just outside the door, waiting for

Jess to call her back, but wasn't surprised by the silence. Ally had always been the first to apologize, even when she wasn't wrong.

She leaned against the wall by the elevator, going over the awful dialogue in her mind. How could she have made it different? What could she have said to defuse the situation? This isn't how she wanted things to go.

"Do you have a moment?" A tall, thin, black woman with hair curling just above her shoulders and a smart tangerine-colored suit glided up to her. Ally looked for any indication that she knew the woman since she wasn't wearing a nurse's uniform. "I'm Louetta Johnson, hospital social worker. You are Jessica's younger sister?" Louetta held out her hand and offered a smile. Her eyes were kind and all-knowing.

Ally cringed with embarrassment. Had she heard the whole exchange?

"Um, yes. I'm Ally. Jess is the oldest. We have a younger sister, too." Her voice sounded strained to her own ears. She had never been good at sharing feelings, but covering them up was difficult as well, and right now, she just wanted out of this place.

"Can I buy you a cup of tea? Maybe we could talk downstairs in the café?"

The woman's kind eyes didn't allow Ally to brush her off. She couldn't be rude to someone who seemed to have good intentions, and she wasn't due at the gallery for another few hours. Stepping into the elevator with Louetta, Ally asked, "How did you know I like tea?"

Louetta smiled. "Jessica told me. She said when you came that you were going to do high tea at the Garden."

"So, she *was* expecting me."

"Oh, yes. She was looking forward to it, but after the difficulty with the port implant and dialysis, her mood is a little down. I imagine it might be difficult for her to get back on track right away. I was hoping to go over her hospital exit plan and wondered how long you might be staying to help with the transition?" The elevator doors opened, and Louetta led Ally the short distance to the chic hospital café. It was newly remodeled and very nice. The thick green weave of the fabric couches and reclining chairs created a cozy atmosphere to help long-term visitors feel more at ease. There was also a reception area with docking stations for laptops and other electronic devices.

"I don't know how to say this, but Jess doesn't want me here right now. We had a falling out my last visit, and clearly, she hasn't forgiven me." Ally blinked back tears. She hated sharing family matters with a stranger. She didn't want to be analyzed.

"Oh, I'm sure that isn't true. Jess is at a difficult point for a type-one diabetic. She needs someone to blame, and right now, it may be easier to blame anyone but nature or herself. From what I see in her chart, she hasn't taken her health seriously for quite some time, and maybe she's feeling guilty for not trying harder. It will be a hard road ahead, but if she does what the doctor tells her, she could have some very good years left." Louetta's smile was encouraging.

Ally wondered how she did this job every day, helping sick people who were dying, or guiding their family members through the five stages of grief.

"I want to help Jess. I'm her sister. But we have another sister with special needs. How am I supposed to take the risk to help one when it may leave the other without either one of us?"

"I'm not telling you to donate your kidney. No one can tell you that, or make you feel bad if you don't. That is between you and God. I'm just hoping you might consider being here tomorrow when she is released. Help her get home, and maybe start making some plans. Jess won't be able to teach as the kidney disease progresses, and she tells me the apartment is on the third floor. That will have to change. Diabetes is a terrible disease, but with the right decisions, things can be tweaked and adjusted, and a number of lifestyle enjoyments can be saved."

"She gets out tomorrow? What time? I'll pick her up, but I'm not sure she will let me take her home. Jess isn't speaking to me at the moment," Ally confided.

"I'll see what I can do. You go get some rest, and if you need to talk or have any questions, feel free to call me. My number is on the card." She slid the business card across the table. "This is a challenging time for both of you, and there isn't much I can say to make things better. My advice is to take some time and solve your issues before it's too late. Life is short. Trust me on this one," she said solemnly.

They parted ways at the elevator, and Ally thanked her for the advice and the tea. Louetta smiled and hugged Ally like she was an old friend. It would have made her uncomfortable if it had been anyone else, but Louetta had a positive, motherly feel. Ally wasn't sure why, but she did feel better after talking to the kind woman.

Soledad hovered near the hospital bed, reluctant to follow her ward. Jess was equally Katia Gray's niece. She had once loved them both with all of her human heart. Where was Katia's sister now? Had she passed as well? The girls weren't that old. Why was Jess all alone? It wasn't fair that she held Ally responsible for her failing health. Even if Ally gave her the organ, Jess wouldn't survive. Soledad could feel Jess's energy, or the fading of it, and knew she would never endure the surgery with success. It took a dedicated health regime to keep a transplanted organ. Ally was a match, but it wouldn't help keep Jess alive. Jess's years were numbered. Soledad sighed with regret for her two young nieces, but they weren't *her* girls anymore. They were just souls to be watched, and Jess was not hers to guard. If Jess had a soul watcher, Soledad couldn't feel them. What she could feel was that Jess was cold and alone in her own heart. Soledad wished she could channel warmth and understanding to her, so the sisters might find peace in the time they had left, but it was not for her to give peace or love to anyone but her ward. Soledad walked a fine line just by staying in the room.

A thing as black as night shrouded itself beyond the alcove of the in-room bath. Soledad pricked with recognition. Such entities were soulless beings that she did not understand. She had seen them stand over men on the battlefield and leach the life's spark from their mangled forms. They were older than her own existence, and even Alekeen knew not of their origins. He had warned her to avoid them at all costs, except in the event they endangered the soul she watched.

They preyed on the weak, young, old, misled—they were all she knew of darkness, and she didn't know what happened to the souls they leached. It was a mystery to her whether Jess was trickling away into disease and sickness, or if because she was ill, she was being drained of her existence. Jess had been spoiled as a child and grew demanding and thoughtless throughout her life. Karma was a real thing. Maybe her bad temper toward others brought this creature of the darkness to her side. But it was just as possible this evil entity transformed Jess by depression and negative energy.

She was a young soul who had made many mistakes. Jess was suffering due to prior mishaps and was thus failing again in this short life. Soledad wanted to help Jess, but she couldn't step outside of her role again. Helping Ally was the only way to do anything for Jess without paying once more for helping a spirit outside her charge. As a soul watcher, Soledad felt tortured seeing life slip away into darkness without protest, though she hadn't fought for her own embodied existence. She would try her best to have Ally help her dying sister. Jess's soul depended on it.

Soledad stayed a bit longer watching the alcove, but the blackness retreated and never reappeared. She felt the cold, dark blanket of narcolepsy slipping over her, stamping out any further thought. She would return to Ally's present. That was her purpose.

CHAPTER 10

Ally walked through the gallery, examining the paintings and the descriptive plaques placed at the side of each piece. The gallery showing was a success. The evening swirled by like the champagne in her glass as shrimp cocktails floated by on silver trays. Bubbles tickled her nose as she tilted her third glass to her red-painted lips. She couldn't shake the confrontation she'd had with Jess earlier and worried about returning to pick her up. Ally wasn't ready to go through the argument again, yet she couldn't *not* be there for her sister.

As she assessed the angel portrait, a familiar voice whispered in her ear. "It reminds me of something from my childhood in Paris." Louis looked debonair in his black evening jacket with a gray silk shirt open at the neck. Ally liked that he didn't wear a tie. He was cultured, handsome, and sexy beyond belief.

She smiled, clinking her glass to his. "Glad you could come."

"I wouldn't have missed it for the world." His smile made the dimple on his left cheek deepen.

"And your aunt?" Ally learned long ago that it was not only polite to ask about family, but it also served as a diversion from conversation about herself. She didn't care to be in the limelight.

"She is well, thank you for asking."

His eyes sparkled as he appraised her lavender silk cocktail dress. The strapless concoction showcased her shoulders and long neck. She wore her hair in a simple chignon with pearl and diamond earrings. A single pearl on a dainty white-gold chain lay at the base of her throat. She was self-conscious as he openly appraised her. Ally's eyelids fluttered when he told her how beautiful she looked.

"Um, thank you," she muttered and looked for another tray of champagne.

"Allow me." Louis motioned to a passing waiter, placing the old glasses on the tray as he retrieved two fresh ones.

Ally relaxed. The world was a safer place with bubbles in hand, and without having to drive, she could indulge. She appreciated the tight string of effervescence streaming to the top of her glass, watching the lines swirl in a double helix of festivity. She sighed, relieved, as she sipped from the thin crystal flute.

"Is it nerve-racking, having the world size you up in one glance?" Louis looked truly interested and concerned for her.

"No. Yes. I mean, it was at first, but I have been doing this for years. I don't really care what people think when I paint. I paint for pleasure. I'm just lucky that they buy it." Ally tipped her champagne glass toward the gothic angel before them.

"Did you see her in a dream? She looks so majestic and good. I would love to know this angel was beside me, watching over my family and me." His eyes were kind, and she felt the sincerity of his words.

Ally side-stepped the question, remembering where it led *The Times* reporter. "Do you believe in angels?"

"I'd like to, yes, but I don't really know much about that sort of thing. My family is Catholic, but not the kind that goes to church often. My aunt is a different story. She never missed a Sunday before she became ill. I'm afraid her arthritis keeps her home now. I'm positive she would like this painting." He smiled, nodding at the canvas showcased by the gallery lights.

"I'll have to make a miniature for you to give to her," Ally offered.

"That would be very kind, but I cannot accept. Let me buy the painting for her," he suggested politely.

"No, I insist." Ally didn't usually involve herself with the financial side of pricing the canvases, but she knew the angel was several thousand dollars, and Louis was several years younger than she. She didn't know what he did for a living, but the price would be shocking to a lot of younger people on a budget. "My aunt was an artist. She drowned when I was young, and I miss her very much. It would be my pleasure to do something nice for your aunt."

He conceded, nodding, "Okay. If you insist, it would be an honor. She will love it." Louis put his hand to the small of her back and guided her to the next room of art. They stood before the picture of *David*. Ally pretended to study the plaque description. She didn't want to look at Travis right now. She was enjoying talking to Louis. "This is really passionate. The colors, vivid. Someone you know?"

There was no way out of this one. She didn't know if she would ever see Louis again, but something in the energy between them made Ally want to tell him the truth. If there was ever anything between them, she wanted there to be honesty. "Yes, someone I knew," she said simply.

Louis nodded, understanding that she didn't want to elaborate.

"Sometimes a broken heart can burn new paths," he suggested with a smile.

Tilting his glass forward, he moved to the next landscape of the Napa Valley. A tall man stood before the canvas, appreciating its beauty. His broad shoulders and tapered waist seemed familiar. His golden hair shimmered under the circular lighting above. Ally's heart lurched as he turned, and they came face to face with David in the flesh.

"Hi, Ally," he said simply. A smile lit his suntan features.

"Hi," she replied softly, then remembering Louis, she cleared her throat. "Ah, Travis, this is Louis. Louis, Travis."

Louis smiled politely and shook Travis's hand. "I recognize him."

Travis looked surprised. "You do? Have we met?"

Ally internally sighed with relief. He hadn't seen the portrait yet, which meant he also hadn't encountered Marcel. Now how would she distract him and get him out of there before Louis answered? It was too late. She saw people gathering at the outskirts of their small circle gawking at Travis's likeness to the painting.

Marcel could be heard from a mile away as he spotted Ally. She cringed. *Here goes nothing.*

"Darling! You didn't tell me David was coming! You little devil, trying to hoard them all for yourself." He snapped his fingers in the air, appearing not to know which man to devour first. His eyes glinted playfully. "Call dibs quick, before I dib them both."

Ally tried to ignore the rush of heat climbing from her shoulders to her cheeks. Both men looked confused and wary of Marcel's proclamation.

"Marcel, this is Travis, and you remember Louis from the airport?" Ally tried to cover her discomfort by taking a long sip of her champagne.

"Travis, hm, well, I like David better. Mind if I call you David?" Marcel batted his eyes and linked arms with Travis playfully.

Ally almost sprayed her champagne onto the floor when she saw Travis's blank look. She could tell he was uncomfortable but trying to be polite. He didn't know the dynamics of the group, and his eyes pleaded with Ally to save him. She let Marcel whisk him off to the room where

David was displayed. If she was uncomfortable at his sudden appearance, then he could be uncomfortable with Marcel. She hated that the jig was up, and now Travis would know exactly how he had plagued her sleep.

Louis cleared his throat then let out a small laugh. "I fear your Travis is in for two surprises." He tipped his glass toward the departing duo.

Ally giggled a little too hysterically. Maybe she should cut herself off. Yes, it was definitely one too many, and it wasn't the champagne she was referring to. She spied Mr. Rafferty across the cream-colored carpet spanning the hallway to the main room. Cringing, she took another long sip of champagne, forgetting that she had just cut herself off. He was headed directly toward her.

She warned Louis, "I'm afraid the surprises are never-ending tonight." As the reporter from *The Times* approached, Louis excused himself to the men's room. Ally wasn't sure if she felt relief or regret. She needed a buffer. Something about the reporter was off-putting, and she didn't want to be in close proximity again.

"So here is where you have been hiding," Rafferty smiled appreciatively at Ally. His eyes lingered too long at her cleavage.

Ally rolled her eyes, but the daft man never noticed. "I'm up here." She wiggled her champagne glass by her face, one arm clutching her midriff as she looked him in the eye. He wasn't worth going toe-to-toe with, and she didn't feel up to par after her row with Jess earlier. She scanned the room for Louis. Maybe he wouldn't return. The awkward moment with Travis and Marcel might have been enough to send him running for the door.

"You can't look like a million bucks and not expect a man to appreciate the assets on display. Come on." He laughed at his own disclaimer as he leered at her with a sideways grin.

She supposed most younger women found him attractive. On a scale from one to ten, his chiseled features, athletic form, and designer attire made him aesthetically a nine, but his energy put her off. He was cheesy and inappropriate on so many levels.

"Our interview ended earlier today, Mr. Rafferty. I hope you will stay and enjoy the show." Ally turned to leave. His arm shot out and he grabbed her elbow. She felt a jolt of shock, then fury.

He held her firm. "Hey, what's the rush? No need to be rude."

How dare he manhandle her at her own show? Good review or bad, she didn't care. She was about to let him have it.

Travis reappeared, towering over Rafferty.

"You heard the lady. Interview is over. Now move along before you lose that arm." Travis's deep voice was firm, but he never raised the decibel. The smooth Texas drawl let Rafferty know Travis meant business. No one around them seemed to grasp there was any issue, except for Rafferty, who looked incensed, then angry.

"I think it's you who needs to move along, cowboy." Rafferty had had one too many free cocktails. His drunken slur rose above the steady hum of the crowd. Movement immediately halted around the trio as patrons sensed there was another show about to ensue. Ally wasn't the only one who had imbibed too much. The reporter suddenly seemed inebriated, and if she didn't intervene, there was going to be a brawl.

"James—" She calmly appeased him by using his first name. "Why don't you catch Marcel in the next room and get an invitation for the after-party. After the show," she emphasized.

Rafferty stopped, and she could see the gears turning. Alcohol had made him slow. Travis glared down at the city slick reporter without budging. The invitation gave Rafferty time to rethink fighting with the cowboy, who was twice his size. He was deciding if the after-party was worth giving up this bit of entertainment, and Ally worried the reporter didn't look like the type to entertain a fair fight. His hand groped in his pocket while he sized up the competition.

"Okay, I'll go find Marcel, but I want to see *you* at the after-party." He pointed at her and winked.

Ally inwardly groaned. She awkwardly thanked Travis for coming to her aid after the drunk reporter left, but her balloon of relief deflated when she remembered she had to face whatever it was he wanted to discuss.

"Ally, can we go somewhere and talk? I wouldn't have bothered you here, but I didn't know where else to find you when you didn't return my calls." His voice was soft and pleading.

She thought about rejecting his offer, but she had had enough of the show, and the idea of running into Rafferty again was enough to make her agree. "Just give me a few minutes to say goodbye to a few people, and then I'll meet you around the corner at Bix for coffee." She turned and joined another nearby group. "Order me a tea," she called back to him as she disengaged and walked toward the opposite end of the room.

"Yes, ma'am," he said, tipping his invisible hat with a wide grin.

Ally found Rebecca and informed her she was leaving. She quickly filled her in on Louis's MIA status and *The Times* reporter looking for Marcel.

"Tell Marcel I am sorry for diving out, but truly—I can't take any more hobnobbing tonight. I promise to stay longer tomorrow." Ally waved as she grabbed her wrap and bag with the diamond clip. Her heels clattered on the pavement as she hurried down the sidewalk to Bix. She half-heartedly thought about hailing a cab and going back to her room, but as she stopped and looked down the empty street, no cabs were in sight. Her thoughts of escape were squashed by a very live version of the handsome David leaning against the brick wall outside of the familiar pub.

Bix was drawn out in bright red letters with gold trim. The plaque swung from a high beam jutting over the doorway. The wood creaked in the cool breeze as a steady thump of music from the bar poured out onto the mostly empty street. It was too cool to stand outside, and Ally hadn't brought more than a light evening wrap to cover her bare shoulders.

He saw her hesitate and straightened to meet her. Ally wrangled up her nerve, along with her injured ego, and crossed the gap to her one-time lover, now-estranged enemy. Something about that word didn't seem right. He wasn't her enemy. Maybe he lied to get her into bed, but she was a big girl, and she enjoyed their night together. Ally hated to admit it now, but she would have slept with him even if she knew it was a one-night stand. What she was really mad about was that he didn't want to see her after.

"You thinkin' of bolting?" he teased her as she approached the pub.

"You were supposed to order tea," she said.

"I wasn't sure you would show up, and then what's a man in western boots going to look like in a New York pub, sipping tea?" He smiled, and they both laughed.

"You do stick out like a sore thumb. Why did you wear those things?" she admonished, looking down at his boots.

"Hey, these are Luccheses, hand-tooled leather, and I special-ordered them for special occasions. How was I supposed to know that the only thing people wear in this city is black?"

Ally giggled as they wandered inside to find a corner booth.

"Haven't you ever been to a big city? Everyone wears black. It's the urban uniform to blend in so you don't get mugged."

He smiled, nodding as he made a clicking noise with his tongue. "Then why are you wearing purple?"

His smile was infectious.

"It's lavender, and I hate to blend in during a show. I'm an artist. I love color."

They ordered tea with two cognac shots. The blonde waitress smiled flirtatiously at Travis and gave the *you are so lucky* look to Ally.

"So, you aren't mad at me anymore?" he asked, smiling.

"Hell, yes, I'm still mad!" she teased, then her playful humor turned to serious accusation. "You stood me up."

"I know, and I'm sorry. I have a good excuse, but I hate using it. Because even though Josh got hit by a car while riding his bicycle, I still should have called."

"What? Your half-brother Josh? Are you serious? Because if you are making up this lame story so I'll forgive you—" She paused, searching his face. "I will never forgive you." She sat back in the booth dazed. Had he really come all this way to tell her that?

"Yes, he was hit riding his bicycle, but he's okay. I got called to the hospital the night after I left your place, and it rattled me. His leg was broken, and it was pretty serious, but I still could have called. I don't know why I didn't." He paused, staring at the green and red stained-glass lantern overhead. "I felt like I was in a fog. It messed me up being at the hospital again. I know it's been a long time since my wife died, but it brought back all these feelings. Ones I had buried, or so I thought. I liked you. I *like* you." He corrected. "It scared me to think of falling in love, even though I was never really in love with my wife. I told you we married because of the pregnancy. I never left her, and when she died, I had all of this guilt." He paused, looking at his hands clasped together on the thick wooden table. "It was painful to lose her, even though I never really loved her like I should have." His large frame slumped in the booth as the waitress delivered the tea and cognacs. "I thought you were what I was waiting for. In all this time, I have never thought about any woman the way I think about you." His eyes lifted to hers. His thumb absently caressed the brandy snifter that held the fragrant aged cognac. "So, I freaked out a little, and I didn't call you right away."

Ally sipped her tea. She hated going into a pub and ordering a non-alcoholic drink. It made the staff think she wouldn't tip, so she always ordered something to look like she was a drinking patron. Right now, she needed to sober up so she could think. Travis was winding his way around her vulnerable heart, and she needed to be strong to keep him out. She didn't have time for men between her art and her family. He was dangerous.

"I forgive you," she said simply as she stirred another packet of sugar into her tea.

"You do?" He seemed surprised. "That easy, you're letting me off the hook?" Suspicion tinged his voice.

"I said I forgive you, that doesn't mean I'll forget. Look, I enjoyed that night too. It is what it is. So, if you came all this way just to say you're sorry, okay."

There was no need to drag this out over a long conversation. He felt guilty, and he wasn't ready. She of all people understood that. She wouldn't rake him over the coals. He wasn't ready to fall in love, and she wasn't ready to take a chance that he could break her heart.

"Ally, I'm an idiot, and I know it. I haven't flown a hell of a long way just to walk away. I know what I want now because after the dust settled, I knew I had to see you again. I knew I didn't ever want to lose you, and that's what scared me."

He reached across the rough wooden table and touched her hand. She felt the energy that surged between them, and she wanted to believe what he said, but she couldn't afford that kind of heartache right now. She couldn't deny the zing of excitement she felt in his presence. He was beautiful and rustic. His honest charisma lit her hormones on fire, and despite her real fear of being dumped, she decided to let her hair down.

"I appreciate your coming all this way just to explain things, and I get that you're not ready—" Travis started to speak, but she held her hand up to quiet him, letting a finger fall slowly forward to touch his lips in a signal to hush. "I'm not either. I was really hurt when my marriage failed, and I might have overreacted when you didn't call. I don't know where this thing between us might go, but I do know you shouldn't leave empty-handed." Ally couldn't suppress a wicked grin. She wasn't much for hate or holding a grudge, and she reminded herself that it was why she still had to deal with her ex. She had a soft heart, and it got her into trouble, but it also made her human and capable of enjoying the moment.

After Travis settled their tab, she walked with him to the curb, where they caught a taxi back to her hotel. Tomorrow she might feel like a sap, but right now, she was a woman with needs. He was her beautiful Adonis. The portrait of David in the flesh. She would enjoy this moment of physical pleasure in the real world, in real-time. She wouldn't worry about tomorrow or the commitment she thought might accompany their relationship. If she could enjoy the small moments of pleasure that life brought, then maybe life would be more worth living.

Wrapped in white, brushed-cotton sheets with his tawny hair tinged in the golden light of the morning sun, Travis looked very much like the portrait of perfection she painted only a short time ago. She longed to take up her brush and begin again. She longed to go back and start over, even as new as their relationship was, but that was not reality. She needed to meet the social worker at the hospital and take Jess home. She scrawled a note at the bottom of the sketch she had finished of him sleeping.

Things to do. Have a safe trip home.
Ally

CHAPTER 11

J ess remained surly when Ally arrived, but the social worker must have
convinced her to accept Ally's help. Jess filled out all the necessary paperwork, and she was released with a folder of papers detailing what she
was supposed to do next. A plastic bag filled with medical supplies from
her room hung off the back of the wheelchair. Ally was relieved a home-
health nurse would check in on her tomorrow, but for now, there were
prescriptions that needed to be filled. She took care of that at the hospital
pharmacy while Jess waited silently with the attendant. They caught a cab
back to Jess's place, and it was only then that she spoke to Ally.

"I didn't ask you to be my nursemaid."

Thorns of anger from Jess's comment pricked Ally's patience. She
reminded herself of the trauma her sister had been through and used her
empathy to fan her temper. Jess was dying. Without a kidney transplant,
there would be no saving her. She would only have a few years at best. Still,
she had to put things straight.

"I'm not here to be your nursemaid. I'm your sister, and I love you. I didn't
even know you were going in to get the port, Jess." Ally paused, watching
her sister fiddle with her cell phone, ignoring the conversation. "I don't
want you to go through this alone. We'll consult more doctors. We'll seek
out alternative treatments. There are renal diets that can help, and I have
heard that yoga can reactivate the body. It may not be a cure, but it could
slow down the process until we find a…" A what? Ally asked herself. An
antidote? That was like saying until we find a cure for cancer. Diabetes could
make its victims suffer a long, slow demise, taking bits of their lives one piece
at a time until they ended up on dialysis, lost parts of their body, or both.

Ally unpacked the plastic hospital bags, sorting out the socks, toothbrush, nightgowns, and other paraphernalia they had sent home with her

sister. She held up a plastic contraption with a ball inside a gauge, "What is this?"

Jess replied blandly as she stared stone-faced out of her apartment window. "A breathing tube. It's to keep my lungs working so I don't get pneumonia."

Clothes trailed across the floor to each room. Syringe needles littered every flat surface. An odor plagued the apartment from unwashed dishes and garbage that had piled up for God knew how long. Ally guessed the friend who had come to clean had chickened out. Who wouldn't have under these conditions? The apartment was a biohazard.

Ally looked around in wonder. "Geez, Jess. How can you live this way? You have always been a slob, but this time you have reached a new level."

"Sorry it's not up to your standards. I didn't know the clean police were coming." Her voice dripped with sarcasm.

Guilt gnawed at Ally for her stupid comment. How could Jess clean the apartment when she didn't have the energy to care for herself? "I'm sorry. I didn't mean to pick on you, but it's like you don't care anymore, and that worries me. It's like you've given up…" Ally's voice trailed off as realization crawled over her. She saw a single tear sliding down Jess's cheek. "Are you giving up, Jess, or are you going to fight this thing?" she asked softly.

"You can't fight diabetes, Ally. You just live with it. It takes a little piece away from you every day, until one day you wake up in the hospital alone, and you realize that it's all—" Jess stopped midsentence as if she couldn't bring herself to say it out loud.

"What, Jess, all what?" Ally held back her own thoughts, knowing the obvious. She wanted to hear her sister speak to her as an adult. A real moment of truth with real emotion. They weren't teenagers anymore.

Ally remembered when they were little girls, playing in the sand and pretending they were the three princesses. They said they would live in a castle with three handsome princes when they married. It was glorious to be so naive. Back then, they thought everyone would live happily ever after.

Tears pooled in Jess's eyes as she finally spoke. "That it's all going to go away, one thing at a time until everything is gone and there is nothing left of me to take." Jess's voice shattered. A sob poured forth. Not the kind Ally heard as they were growing up when Jess pretended to be hurt, but the real kind that broke Jess's spirit and cracked Ally's heart. Forgetting all the stones between them, Ally rushed to her sister and threw her arms around her. She would not let this disease take her sister's dignity away, and she would not let it destroy the relationship they once knew. Determined to bridge the gap, Ally promised herself that she would make them all a family once more.

"Oh, Jess." Ally held her sister tightly, rocking her back and forth. Ally was the middle sister but had grown a head taller than Jess after she reached fourteen. She had felt older, too, since their father deserted them, and their mother raised them on her own. Ally had been the head of the family since she was just ten years old. No one ever argued her position. Ally had always felt it her duty to fix what was wrong, but how could she fix this? How could she fix Jess's kidneys?

Soledad appeared in a room she did not know. Ally held Jess tightly as they both shed tears. In her last conscious moment, Soledad saw Travis and Ally enter the hotel together. Deciding she didn't need to guide Ally, Soledad had lingered outside. Some things were better left private.

She now assessed the apartment, noting that the surroundings belonged to Jess. Pictures of billboards, Broadway pamphlets, and a college graduation photo graced the walls. Ally must have escorted Jess home. Warmth surged through Soledad as she picked up the rhythm of Ally's caring emotions. She also felt a cooler current that was not at all Ally's. Waves of fatigue, frustration, and hurt washed over Soledad's senses. Was it Jess? Soledad had never experienced the vibrations of a soul she wasn't watching. This was a first. Her intuition about embodied souls was helpful in guiding her ward, but up until now, she had never felt others' emotions as they were feeling them. Jess was tired, not just the normal fatigue of coming home from the hospital, from having her first dialysis treatment, or too many sleepless nights. Jess was tired of living. Soledad could feel the quiet acceptance of death settling over Jess's young spirit. The defeat felt too great, and Soledad worried about how much time was left.

Her positive energy could only be for Ally, and though Soledad's heart ached, she could not breathe a morsel of encouragement for the sister Ally loved. The channeling for forgiveness, strength, love, and acceptance would help her ward accept what she could not change. Emotions took their toll, causing Ally to wobble as she stood. She laughed lightly as she made a joke about her aging knees and that she might have been on them too long last night. Jess took the thread, and the girls giggled like teens as they explored the evening with Travis. Ally started with the gallery show, brushed over the handsome French Louis before moving on to Travis discovering the portrait of *David*. She railed over the rude *Times* reporter, blazed over the juicy tidbits from the hotel, and then returned to discussing the art from the exhibit. Ally's cheeks turned pink as Jess teased her, begging for more. The sisters dissolved into laughter, sipped tea and then settled onto Jess's futon couch to watch a marathon series of *Rapper's Dream*. The siblings had very different television tastes, but Ally never complained or even changed the channel once Jess succumbed to slumber.

A single candle glowed as Ally sat staring into the night, Jess's head cradled upon her lap. Soledad watched her ward rise slowly, adjusting a pillow to support her sister's neck in her absence. Soledad followed Ally into the kitchen, where she filled the sink with hot water and dish soap. Cups with molding tea rings, egg yolk-cemented plates, and forks that were blackened with something undefinable were stacked in the sudsy water. Ally found the garbage chute and made ten trips to deposit refuse that had sat for so long, the floor in the apartment was permanently stained from leakage. The place looked like it belonged to a hoarder, though she knew Jess was not.

Soledad watched Ally shake her head as she peered into the bathroom. Jess had been sick, very sick, for a long time, and she hadn't asked anyone for help.

"How did you even make it to teach your classes?" Ally whispered to herself.

Who knew what damage Jess had done to her body or how much she was suffering? Empty Oreo Double Stuf cookie packages mixed with sausage, egg, and cheese biscuit wrappers were strewn across the small kitchen island and coffee table.

Ally started a load of laundry. "Thank God you have an apartment-sized washer and dryer. I'm too beat to journey down to the basement to clean clothes." Soledad wasn't sure why Ally was suddenly talking to herself except maybe to keep her mind busy *not* thinking.

After picking up all the syringes and plastic caps that created a biohazard, Ally put them in a plastic container to dispose of safely. She then scrubbed away at the moldy tile and stained basin in the bathroom. It was beyond gross, and she knew Jess would be upset by her cleaning, but her sister had created a hazard that even the EPA wouldn't touch.

Soledad couldn't see Ally leaving her sister in this mess. She watched as her ward sighed and leaned against the doorjamb, taking a short break. "Maybe Jess could move to Texas for a while."

Soledad knew Jess would balk and stand on her democratic political soapbox, but who cared what party ruled the state you lived in when death knocked at your door?

The social worker mentioned that people with type-one diabetes lived about four years on dialysis, but Jess had already had bypass surgery, and the cardiologist at the hospital had told Jess her heart wasn't strong enough for a transplant. He warned her she would wind up a vegetable if she attempted it.

The time for her ward to mention she had been tested and was a match to give a kidney had passed. Soledad knew that Jess would just fly off on false hope, putting more pressure on Ally. Denial was a strong suit of Jess's, and it wouldn't be healthy for either of them to dream when a transplant wasn't a probable solution. As she watched Ally fold clothes in the living room then fall asleep across the laundry basket, Soledad's consciousness began to fade. *Sleep comes for us all.*

CHAPTER 12

It was her third week with Jess, and she missed Ella and Harley so much she thought of shipping them to New York, but the poor things would have to ride as cargo. Even if they could fly, there was nowhere to keep them in Jess's small apartment. Ally hadn't convinced Jess to come to Texas, and she couldn't stay in New York indefinitely. Sleeping on Jess's futon was killing her neck, and she was in a permanent state of pain. What she needed was a good massage. Deciding to indulge herself, Ally called the spa at her favorite hotel to book something later in the day.

Travis called and texted often, but she kept matters light. She explained her sister's health situation, and he had been more than understanding and supportive. Already three vases of assorted blooms graced the living room. A funny-looking stuffed bear sat on Jess's barstool attached to a plethora of helium balloons. Ally and Jess sucked on them endlessly to entertain each other. "Follow the yellow brick road," Beastie Boys songs, and scenes from *Romeo and Juliet* were some of their favorite helium material. Ally even left a high-pitched voicemail for Travis when she knew he was working. The two of them sang "Happy Birthday" to him, sounding a lot like two chipmunks on crack. She didn't know him well enough to send a gift, so she put an order in at her favorite bakery and had a cake delivered to his work. She worried if they left the decadent chocolate concoction at his doorstep, Jake might eat it first.

When Jess's friends dropped by with pizza, Ally frowned. It was a battle she would never win, and if Jess was going to die in four years regardless, maybe Ally should stop harping. The nephrologist had warned Jess about her eating habits years before her kidney failure. If having quadruple bypass hadn't stopped her from smoking, going on dialysis wouldn't stop her from eating pizza. And Ally trying to control her eating habits wasn't helping their relationship.

Ally let herself out of the apartment, quietly shutting the door on the impromptu party. She caught a taxi and made her way to the hotel but she was a bit early. The lounge was cozy, and she ordered a glass of her favorite boutique champagne that she could only find by the glass in New York. She settled into a soft leather chair near the gas fire and stared into the meandering flames. The blue light intermittently mingling with orange and red strands of heat mesmerized her.

"Fancy seeing you here."

The familiar voice startled her. She looked up to see Louis holding a snifter of something amber in a crystal glass.

Her voice was bright with elated surprise. "Louis, I thought I'd never see you again." She flicked through her memories to the last time she had seen him. It was the show. He had never returned.

"I thought so, too. You were such a popular girl the last time we met. How can a simple Frenchman compete?" He smiled apologetically.

"Ow," she winced. "I'm so sorry. I had too much to drink, and unfortunately, I couldn't get away from the guests." It wasn't the best excuse for the scene, but it was the only truth she knew. "I'm sorry if I was rude. I never meant to be. I did enjoy our conversation before the interruptions." She smiled and waved a hand at the open seat beside her. "Let me buy you a drink to make it up?"

"No, please. I am good." He tilted his glass, showing her his drink. "I meant no disrespect by not returning. I just didn't think you needed another admirer in the mix." Tipping his glass at her in a silent toast, he took a drink and joined her. "So, are you and the cowboy renewed?" His crossed legs came off elegantly, like Cary Grant in an old black and white movie. He wasn't the usual type of man she was used to running into in Texas. Smooth, intelligent, he exuded class and worldliness beyond his years. His amber eyes met hers and danced for a moment before she averted her gaze to the fire.

"No. I mean, we were never really in a relationship. I was married most of my life to a loser. N—no, I really shouldn't say that. Justin, my ex, he's a troubled soul. I haven't really dated much since my divorce, and then, well…" She paused, not knowing what to call her fling with Travis. "It was really nothing. Call it a milestone. Something that needed to pass." She smiled at her own cryptic answer.

"Good, then you are available now?" His dimple deepened as he smiled.

Ally clinked her champagne glass to his snifter. Butterflies fluttered in her stomach, but she kept it casual. "Maybe."

"I thought you would be back in Texas by now. When the show ended, I didn't think I would see you again, and I knew I shouldn't pursue something so far away. Besides the fact, you seemed taken at the time."

Ally blushed at his open interest. He was cutting to the chase.

"My sister is sick. I've stayed longer to help, but I need to return soon. I swear she is more stubborn than anyone I know. She loves the city, and I can never wait to get out of it."

"Sorry to hear about your sister's health. I've been longing for home as well, but my aunt has asked me to stay on a while longer. My mother insisted I stay since I am the only one of my five brothers who isn't married and tied down with kids." His French accent was so alluring. She assumed he was jesting when he spoke of his mother's direct order.

"Is that how you see married with kids?" Ally laughed. She had a similar viewpoint.

Louis turned serious, and his eyes glowed in the firelight. "Not with the right woman."

"Oh, c'mon. That's the worst line I have ever heard," Ally chortled and lay back in her chair, one leg lifting in her fit of giggles. "Louis, that is exactly why American women avoid European men. You think that is what women want to hear, but most of us just want to hear you speak period. You don't have to charm us with declarations of love or being *The Only One*." She tried to curtail her laughter when she noticed Louis's frown.

His brow knitted. "I am sorry if you think I was trying to mislead you. I did not mean to amuse you with my naiveté. Matters of the heart are not my forte." He paused, and his dimple tugged at his smile. "Sorry, my aunt says that I wear my heart on my sleeve and that some girl will pluck it off one day and smash it with her high heel." He chuckled, but his eyes couldn't hide that he was still a little wounded.

Ally tried to backpedal, "I'm sorry. Truly. I didn't know you were serious. I...um...I'm not good with matters of the heart either," she confessed as she shifted against the leather, hating the squeaky noise it made.

Louis nodded. His tone turned casual. "It's okay. I'm too serious tonight. Let's change the subject. Why are you at the hotel? Are you staying here?" Louis relaxed his head against the back of his chair, setting his drink on the rolled arm.

"No, I was during the show, but now I'm staying with Jessica, my sister. I'm just here for a much-needed massage. I've booked a ninety-minute hot stone," she shared with a gleeful smile.

His eyebrows rose with mock surprise, then his eyes twinkled. "Lucky you. I'm jealous."

"I know. I've been sleeping on her crazy-hard futon. I admit I am quite a bed snob. Thousand-thread count sheets, Westin Heavenly bedding, six pillows all made of down, etcetera, etcetera." Her smile was whimsical, as a dreamy look of what was to come crossed her face.

"I'm not sure what I am more envious of, the massage or the masseur who will touch every inch of your form." He sipped from the snifter, his gaze smoldering over the rim.

Ally choked a little on her own champagne, not missing his smile as she dabbed at her chest with a napkin. "I know that was a line. Are you practicing on me now?"

He shrugged his shoulders, leaning closer. "Maybe you can help me with my English, so I can express my desire without sounding foolish."

She felt heat ignite in the pit of her stomach, swirling well below the champagne. His fingers brushed hers. He was intriguing, sexy, masculine, and more handsome than any man she'd ever known. *What does he see in me?* He was younger than her. *Who cares?* He was sending her an obvious invitation, and if she didn't accept, she was likely to miss out on this perfect moment of pleasure. *I am here to relax.*

Would being with Louis so soon after Travis make her a loose woman? She hadn't made any promises to Travis, and as far as she knew, he might be seeing other people. He could change his mind once she returned home and decide he wasn't ready for a relationship after all. Louis lived in Paris. He wasn't offering more than tonight, and she didn't want more. If Jess's sickness had taught her anything, it was that life was unpredictable. Just because she was young didn't mean she had years to check off items on her bucket list. She could take a wrong turn on her motorcycle tomorrow, walk in front of an unseen cab, tumble into a sinkhole, who knew? Putting herself out there would be her new MO. She sighed and placed her drink on the small table before standing.

"It's time to go up for my massage. Will you be here later?" Her smile was light, but her eyes were direct.

"Give me a time, and I will meet you back here. I would love to take you to dinner." Louis sounded pleased.

"Give me three hours. I like to sit in the steam room after, and I'll need to shower. I didn't bring any extra clothes, so make it casual."

There were some earthly luxuries that Soledad truly missed. Massage was one of them. She had lingered in the beautiful lounge of the hotel, watching Ally's cheeks flush with excitement and pleasure. The Frenchman possessed an aura that was pure. He lent Soledad a sense of ease, and she was glad that Ally was going to meet him later, even if it was for one night of pleasure. Ally deserved happiness, and if it helped ease the pain of life, so be it.

Soledad had not been an alcoholic in her prior life as Katia, but she remembered the pleasure of fine wine and warm cognac on a cold night. The sensations that she had taken for granted in the physical world were now missed as she looked through the dense fog of the steam room. Ally lay atop a bed of towels over slick tiles as the steam washed away the stress in her beautiful limbs. Soledad didn't remember looking as gorgeous or as fit as Ally when embodied. She had worn more cosmetics and used enhancing beauty aids to turn heads. She tried to imagine the heat of the steam and the calm surrounding of the spa being pleasurable, but there was nothing different here to her than standing in Ally's living room. No one knew she existed, not even Ally, except for that time—and maybe that was merely fanciful intuition.

Soledad felt alone on this plane. The billowing steam reminded her of the clouds surrounding her when she awoke to Alekeen. She knew she existed for a purpose, and she clung to that one truth. As Katia Grey she had given up. In her current spirit state, she didn't own the luxury. It wasn't how the in-between world or soul-watching worked. The knowledge that there was no quitting honed her focus back to her ward. Ally needed to find something, whether it be her soulmate, peace with Jess, inner strength, or something else. Soledad needed to guide her. Right now, she would wake the sleeping goddess to fill her evening with pleasure. Louis was waiting.

Soledad sent a vibration of encouraging energy in Ally's direction to invigorate and stir her. Ally's eyes fluttered as she stretched and yawned. The growing smile on her ward's face told Soledad that her energy channeling and the evening prospects had put Ally in a favorable mood. Ally stood and wrapped the towel around her, securing the plush cotton at her breast.

Soledad watched her ward take time to ready herself, blow-drying her hair into a straight, silken sheet of ebony. Ally applied a sheen of moisturizer over her face and body, dabbing lip gloss over her supple lips. She swiped a hint of perfume behind each knee, at the base of her neck, and the soft skin of her wrist. Her clothes were the same ones she had worn to the spa, with the exception of the undergarments she had packed to feel fresh when she left. The matching black lace and silk lingerie complemented her tawny skin and clung to her womanly curves. Louis wouldn't be disappointed.

Ally closed the empty locker, deposited the robe and slippers in the labeled bins and then took a second glance at her reflection before leaving the spa. She made her way to the first-floor lounge, where she spied Louis waiting at the bar. A bottle of Pellegrino rested on the bar next to his glass. She was glad that he was alert and ready for their evening. He smiled warmly, offering her a stool next to him, then a cocktail. Ally declined the drink, so he made short work of finishing his and led her from the bar to the hotel restaurant. The Grand was known for its amazing steaks and extensive wine list. Louis ordered a bottle of Chateau Margaux, and they began their evening with pleasant conversation and easy laughter.

"I swear 'twas an accident." Louis laughed as he reached for the port wine the chef paired with a charcuterie board. "Dumb luck. I could have been a bag boy the rest of my life." His eyes sparkled with mischief.

"Oh, I doubt that." Ally laughed before tossing a raspberry into her mouth. The meal had been amazing. Louis was educated in art, history, and well versed in current events. The conversation was never dull or elitist. He was warm, strong, yet laid back and casual. It was like they had known each other for years.

Though drawn to Louis, she found herself comparing him to Travis. Both were amazing men in different ways. Travis had a warm heart and simple Southern mannerisms with a talent for music and an inner character sworn to protect his family. Plus, he loved motorcycles. His Southern charm endeared him to her.

On the other hand, Louis loved traveling and found adventure in the most interesting places. An entrepreneur, he credited his success to a business guru that breezed into his father's grocery store one day to buy cigarettes. The man took a liking to the grocer's son, and because of that one moment, Louis now owned several businesses in Europe and was buying another in New York. He asked her about Texas and what things might be of a business interest to him there. Since the show, he was interested in purchasing a gallery of his own. This would have impressed a younger Ally, but she had earned her way in the art world, and she knew now that money wasn't everything. She couldn't deny the incredible physical attraction she felt when she was with Louis, but she couldn't see it going any further than tonight. Neither one of them were residents of New York, and their lives ran in totally different circles, though it didn't have to remain that way.

She lost track of what he said as she sorted through her own list of pros and cons in taking him to bed. There were definitely more pros, she admitted. Studying the curve of his bottom lip, she hadn't noticed he had quit talking. He stared languidly at her with a knowing smile. "Oh, sorry. I think I've had too much Bordeaux." Ally laughed then blushed.

"Shame on you. There is no such thing as too much Bordeaux. I am a Frenchman, so trust me, I know," he teased. Standing up, he reached for the bottle, tipping it over Ally's glass. The second bottle was indeed empty. "Oh my, we have a problem." Louis looked around to signal the bartender, but Ally protested.

"No, please, Louis. I don't think too much of a good thing will be good in this instance."

Louis didn't miss a beat. He moved around the intimate table and sat close to her on the seat before the fire and gazed into her eyes. "You deserve all I have to offer and more. So much more."

On anyone else, it would have sounded hollow, but she felt the passion in his words and believed what he said. The undercurrent of electricity between them was more than sexual interest. Louis had been a complete gentleman at every turn. It was Ally who leaned forward and touched *her* lips to his. It was *she* who nibbled his bottom lip and stroked her hand through his hair. It was *her* fingers that lingered at the nape of his neck until she slowly pulled back to look into his eyes.

He kissed her back with passion and expertise. He was slow and methodical and never pushy. He didn't advance but accepted what she offered. Ally was impressed and disappointed at the same time. She didn't want to be the aggressor. She wanted to be pursued. Ally needed him to devour her the way she wanted to consume every inch of him.

"Maybe we should have our next drink in my room?" He picked up her hand and kissed the sensitive skin at her wrist while searching her eyes for an answer.

Ally licked her lips and tried to suppress a moan that half escaped her when his teeth grazed her skin. She wasn't about to back down now. This is what she came for—wasn't it? She liked Louis a lot. A night between the sheets didn't equate to forever. She only wanted fun for now.

Her mind involuntarily moved to Jess, but before she could ruin the mood with worry, she reminded herself that life was short. The moment should be seized, and she needed to enjoy what she had while she had it. Ally had been a good girl for way too long, and having sex with a second man, after being divorced three years, didn't make her a slut. She needed to take herself off the shelf and dust off the feminine goods while she still had them. Her older friends spent too much time elaborating over their body and relationship changes that occurred after forty. Menopause, the shrinking man-pool, aging men who couldn't perform, and the available older men, who only wanted twenty-something-year-old women or *men*, were the meat of their conversations these days.

"Yes, I would love to see your room." A faint blush stained her cheeks. She didn't mean to sound so eager. Louis grinned wickedly and motioned for the tab. They took the elevator to the twelfth floor. It occurred to her that Louis had been staying with his aunt all this time.

As if sensing her question, he filled her in on how he had procured the room after they spoke earlier. Ally's eyebrows rose, and he quickly explained himself. "It's not that I had any plans. I didn't want to go back to my aunt's house late after drinking." His smile implied that he had indeed hoped for a tantalizing evening. Opening the door, he pulled her into his arms. He held her close, making her forget to be offended at his assumption. His lips were almost brushing hers as he said, "How could a man see you and not hope to spend an entire evening in your company?"

She didn't protest or back away when he moved her through the archway, kissing while guiding her into the plush sand-and-cream-colored room. Her heels sank into thick carpet, and she felt the smooth wall at her back as they moved into the small alcove. His tongue danced with hers, swirling its warmth as he stroked her desire. Her hand touched the edge of an entry table. She felt the cool waxy leaves of a real ivy plant, as she searched for something to grab onto. Ally steadied herself as he dipped his head from her lips to the deep V of her bodice, trailing hot kisses over the throbbing pulse in her neck. She arched against him as he lowered the thin fabric of her dress over one shoulder, freeing her breast from its lacy constraint. He was aggressive now, showing her the passion she longed for. He didn't say please or thank you or ask how she would like to be kissed. He was pushing her against the wall and taking what he wanted. It pleasured her to the point of weakness.

Her legs shook from the currents of ecstasy she felt at his touch. His teeth raked slightly over one erect nipple as she struggled to withstand the tantalizing pleasure. His strong hands ran over her slender form, caressing and kneading her rounded buttocks. His fingers streamed along her hips, pulling at her dress, and lifting the silk higher onto her thighs. Grazing the lace trim of her satin underwear, he paused before sliding a finger beneath the silk and through her sensuous folds. She moaned with pleasure, trying to hold off the wave of passion overwhelming her senses. He pulled one of her thighs up against him, holding her steady as she leaned against the table. He kneeled low before her and nipped at the soft flesh at the inside of her thigh.

It was too quick. They needed to slow down. She wasn't ready to be so intimate so fast, but as he discarded her moist panties on the floor, she knew the word *stop* would never fall from her lips. His tongue sent a shock of pleasure over her as he laved at the bud of her flesh. Sucking greedily at the soft folds of her woman's mound. He swirled his tongue around her nub, groaning in pleasure, "You taste exquisite."

Ally could take no more, pulling at his shoulders to rise. Louis obeyed reluctantly but smiled as he led them to a plush bed covered in a sea of freshly laundered white linen and a mountain of pillows. The sheets were cool on her naked skin, a deep contrast to Louis's warm hardened form as he shrugged from his dress shirt and lay on top of her. Her hands slid down his chest and found their way into his already unzipped pants. His soft briefs allowed her quick access to his hardened member, and she greedily wound her fingers around the erect shaft. Thinking about protection, she frowned at the fact she hadn't brought any.

"What's the matter?" His brows furrowed in concern as he stared down at her.

"Nothing, it's just that I didn't bring anything, and I'm not on the pill, but even if I were, I don't think we should without—" Ally babbled as Louis nodded understanding and leaned down to kiss away her consternation. Ally lifted onto her elbows, pushing up until she heard the familiar sound of the foil packet. Sighing with relief, she relaxed into the soft mattress. Thank God for small favors.

Soledad could see when she wasn't needed, so she made her exit when the happy couple left the lounge. Ally was tipsy but had made her decision when she was sober, so Soledad wasn't worried about her ward. Anything that added wealth to her life and allowed escape from her sister's medical routine was good for Ally. It was now time to break the love spell surrounding her in slumber. Jess was sick again and needed Ally. The home-health nurse found Jess throwing up this morning, and an ambulance was called to take Jess back to the hospital. Ally needed to wake up and attend to her sister.

Soledad stood by the bed. Louis was wrapped around her like a sleek cat, one hand at her breast and his head buried in her hair. She looked small against his athletic form. His short, rich ebony hair against her long, dark tresses blended into one seamless waterfall. His features were softened by sleep and the full evening they had shared. Soledad wondered about the state of Louis's spirit. She could feel nothing but goodness in his energy. He didn't seem afflicted or traumatized by life. He was simply happy. Soledad smiled. It was just what Ally needed.

Begrudgingly, her thoughts went back to the stressful energy Jess emitted, and Soledad started the channeling that would fill Ally's head with concern. Her soul-watching efforts pushed her ward to check her phone. The hospital would have called by now, and Ally needed to see the message.

Soledad watched her ward stir. Louis wrapped his arms tight around her naked form in retaliation. He buried his face in her neck and whispered for her to sleep. Languishing in the aftermath of the evening's fulfillment, he brushed his hips against her, trying to entice Ally into more lovemaking. She untangled herself from his ardent grasp and the soft, warm sheets. Soledad pushed more urgent pulses to her ward as she paused to admire

Louis's magnificent body. *If I had only been half as lucky when I was alive, things might have gone differently.*

Ally reacted to the energy bursts and finally broke free of her lover. She hurried to the lavatory while Louis admired her beautiful naked backside. Ally's figure looked like a work of art. Soledad observed the handsome Frenchman as he lay staring out the corner room window. Light poured over his half-naked physique as he stirred beneath the sheets and smiled. She could only guess what he was thinking, but she didn't have time to ponder embodied men's thoughts of sex. She anxiously awaited Ally to attend to her toilette and find her phone. Sending energy in the direction of the bathroom to hasten her ward, Soledad was satisfied when the door finally opened, and Ally emerged in a hotel robe.

"No fair! I liked you better the other way," Louis groaned from the bed, tossing a pillow in Ally's direction. She giggled.

"I need my phone. Have you seen my bag? I don't recall where I left it. Jess has a nurse coming in this morning, and her friends were supposed to stay the night, but I still want to check in." Ally looked on the couch and behind it, though they never got close to it the evening before. They had left the entryway and went straight to the bed. Soledad felt waves of sexual energy pour off Ally as her body reacted to the memory, sending visible goosebumps down her extremities. As if putting the pieces of a puzzle together, she exclaimed, "Entry table!"

There it was, half-buried under the ivy plant where Ally dropped it in her attempt to brace herself before slithering into a pool of lust.

Louis propped himself up as he watched Ally skim through her messages and call her voice mail. "Everything okay?"

Ally faltered. She made a mad dash for her clothes, pulling them on in a rush. She hopped about as she tried to buckle her shoes, making Louis sit up in concern.

"It's Jess. The nurse called an ambulance to take her to the ER. She was vomiting uncontrollably, but the nurse says she's stable now. I need to go, sorry." Ally paused for a millisecond, looking fascinated at the picture he made. Black tousled hair, honey-colored skin with flashing white teeth. He had devilish good looks, but with Ally, he was an angel. Soledad contemplated whether he might be that rare, good man. Observing the way her ward scurried around with her eyes darting back to Louis, Soledad knew that Ally was wondering how she would paint his portrait. Hurrying for the door, she called back, "I'll text when I get to the hospital. Later."

Soledad frowned as the door closed hard, and Louis's worried expression made her wonder if he was clairvoyant. She felt it too, an ominous presence far off in the distance but moving closer. Outside the window, storm clouds moved in the heavy sky, casting a gray, flat light across the bed. The two walls of windows gave a perfect view of the city, a gorgeous panorama that went dull in the aftermath of the moment. The sun, eclipsed by clouds, shed little indication of the time of day, and the wind batted an empty plastic bag down the sidewalk. She felt herself fading, like the light, and in a flash, she was gone.

CHAPTER 13

Ally made her way to the ER where Jessica was still waiting to be assigned to a regular room. She was updated on her sister's health status outside of the small, curtained area where her sister lay. Jess's phosphorus was dangerously high, and the dietician was due to stop by to go over the foods Jess should avoid eating. Ally mentally rolled her eyes since she knew the previous evening's pizza binge probably had something to do with this incident. Cheese was high in phosphorus. Nothing a dietician would suggest to Jess would last more than a week in her head.

Ally nodded to the nurse, taking in the note of concern and condemnation in her voice. Ally frowned. *How does this lady know what Jess is going through?* Sure, she may see dialysis patients every day, but she didn't walk in their shoes. Ally didn't bother telling the nurse that preaching about a diet was useless. Her sister's grip on the relationship between her health and the reality of her bad habits was zero. Jess was the queen of denial, and truth be told, she might have ended up in her current medical crisis even if she had been a veggie-eating yogi. Who was Ally kidding? Jess had never been that. Her voracious appetite for Mickey D's and Hostess Ho-Hos was going to land her in the morgue way too many years before her time, but the nurse could still show a little more compassion.

After the nurse left to do her rounds, Ally stood staring at the ceiling. She blinked back a tear of frustration for the unfairness. She was angry that Jess wouldn't try harder and mad that her sister had to go through the illness to begin with. She remembered when Jess was diagnosed with diabetes after her tenth birthday party. She was sick from the pound of sugar she had consumed in birthday cake and ice cream, and her parents took her to the family physician for a checkup.

Their mother fussed, lectured, and cajoled Jess to make better food choices, but she ignored them and played the poor, sick-little-girl routine to anyone who would cave. She milked it for all it was worth, getting out of school functions, bad lunchroom food, and groundings. Jess never took her disease seriously. Now would hardly be any different, but it *was* different, dammit! She couldn't live with her phosphorous this high, and type-one diabetics on dialysis had a short life span already. Ally would do just about anything for Jess, but she couldn't trade places with her, and right now, that was about the only thing that would save her sister's life.

"Ally?" Jess's hoarse voice was soft. Probably an effect of her earlier sickness. They had given Jess an anti-nausea medication in her drip to calm her stomach, letting her rest for a while. A lady in blue scrubs arrived with a mobile dialysis unit as Ally entered through the slit in the curtain.

Jess looked small and frail in the large hospital bed. A white blanket lay draped over her chest, and another lay around her head, giving her an ethereal appearance. Her weak form looked drab in the fluorescent lights. Her paleness blended with the bright, bleached linens.

"Has anyone told you, you look like a less exotic version of King Tut?" Ally half-chuckled, trying not to reveal her feelings of distress.

Jess rolled her eyes and snorted. Both sisters started a chorus of unlady-like peals of laughter. Ally took a cell phone pic of the Egyptian deity her sister portrayed, and Jess immediately uploaded it to her social media site then began texting to catch up with her professor friends. Ally wondered where the pizza gang had disappeared to.

"I'm so glad you brought your phone. I've been bored to tears, and the food around this place is nonexistent. Can you bring me something from the vending machine? I'm starved!"

"Jess, didn't you hear the nurse? I can't sneak stuff to you right now. They need to get your body back on track. I don't think it's time for cookies and a Diet Coke."

Jess rolled her eyes, let out a low growl, and then shouted. "Then what are you here for?"

"I'm getting sick and tired of you asking me that question." Ally's voice was clipped as she tried not to lose it. "I'm here for you, Jess. And in case you seem to have forgotten, I have a life. One that I have abandoned for weeks to help you. I don't deserve all the flack you are giving me for your

irresponsibility. You need to grow up and take this seriously before you…"
Ally's voice trailed off as the words almost rolled off her tongue.

"Die." Jess's words were cold and flat as she finished Ally's sentence. It made
Soledad's heart break listening to the two bicker. The sisters had a rough
path between them. They could never quite give in to the love they both felt
because of the brick wall they had spent months building between them.
The room was silent as Ally moved to a chair and picked up the remote.
There weren't any more words. Hours passed with gameshow hosts blaring
through the bed speakers, followed by comedies, news, and late-night TV.

Jess was dialyzed then admitted to a room around two in the morning. Ally slept in the hard side chair that didn't recline. An array of nurses
paraded in and out around six in the morning, sending her in search of
hot tea and something to feed her growling stomach. Soledad hadn't seen
Ally eat since dining with Louis the day before. The reflection in the ladies'
room mirror told them both that Ally needed to make her way back to Jess's
apartment to refresh her wardrobe. Ally's hair was a mess, and all traces of
makeup were gone. She was in dire need of a toothbrush, and it wasn't like
the riveting conversation was keeping her at the hospital. Jess had barely
spoken three words to her sister since their spat. Ally's phone was out of
juice, thanks to Jess's non-stop use the previous day. Soledad had seen Ally's
text to Louis that she would be staying at the hospital, but that was the last
communication.

Worry wracked Ally as she made her way to the hospital exit. She wondered
how Ella and Harley were doing, and if she might ever get home. Her heart
pulled her mind toward her new involvement, and she hoped she might
see Louis again soon. If she could leave New York now, would she? It was

useless to explore that avenue since she doubted Jess could manage on her own, but this couldn't go on forever. She had a life and a career. On some distant plane in her consciousness, she wondered about Travis and if he was thinking about her. Odd that she could think about two men in two different cities when she had spent the last three years alone.

Soledad spent the next week following Ally to the hospital, Jess's apartment, and the hotel where Louis and Ally continued their rendezvous. They were becoming a regular thing, and it was a great escape for Ally, who spent hours trying to cheer up her sister. Jess was getting out of the hospital in a few days, and Ally finally made her flight plans to go home. A home-health nurse would be there for the first few days, but their mother and Aunt Rose were flying in to take over. Jess was almost herself again. Ally had called her mother and alerted her of Jess's hospital visit but hadn't shared the gravity of the situation. Their mother's frail mental state after losing Aunt Katia made Ally wary of disclosing too much. Originally, she had played down Jess's health condition and told her mother to stay with Alyssa. Together they could care for both sisters. Jess would be okay for a while if she stuck to the diet and made her regular appointments to dialyze. Soledad pushed comforting waves of energy to her ward, who was realizing that she couldn't protect her mother from knowing the truth forever. Maybe their mother could ease into the knowledge by helping Jess get back on track. Her ward needed to get home to Ella, Harley, Alyssa, and her life.

Soledad floated above the lake outside the hospital. She didn't know why she appeared here, but she had. It was more of a retention pond for the ducks and geese to enjoy. A paved walkway surrounded the water with an elaborate fountain pouring from the middle. She admired the serene setting, watching people walk along the path. Visitors and hospital staff took breaks to smoke or stretch their legs and think. Soledad was lost in her own thoughts as she examined Ally's decisions to date. What direction would her ward go next? Soledad's very presence here meant that she wasn't achieving her ward's goal. Without progress, she would not be sent back to the land of the living—the only place, she could reunite with her soulmate and live a golden life known to so few. As if on cue, Soledad spotted a man in blue scrubs taking a long drag from a cigarette. She didn't need to see the sharp features of his beautiful face or the glint of his ice-blue eyes to know it was Onegan, her soulmate. His physical shape in this life was much like that of the past.

Reincarnation could grant life in any form of embodiment. A soul had little influence in choosing its sex or race, but the light within each embodied spirit was the same energy throughout time. The essence of the soul's existence was strangely always the same. Soledad's energy on this plane was always and would always be feminine, as Onegan was eternally masculine. Their two souls together would create the perfect symmetry, to unify their existence, in the embodied or soul watcher state.

Soledad hovered closer until she stood within a breath of his face, taking in his human form and all the things that encased his soulful energy. He stared at the fountain, his brow furrowed in concentration. It was as if he were solving a puzzle or an ambiguous equation. She knew the rules about engaging with other earthly beings or interfering in their life's path. She could watch him, even be near him, but she could not talk to him or interfere with the choices he would make. Soledad felt another unearthly presence nearby. She did not recognize the soul who watched over Onegan but knew he was on a path with his guide. Soledad reached out and ran her luminous hand over Onegan's face and kissed the corner of his mouth. His soul watcher pushed energy toward her, stinging her core with an electrifying jolt. Soledad knew there could be no communication between her and the entity, so she didn't bother to explain herself or ask about the journey of Onegan's life. Frustration welled inside her. His watcher should feel the pureness in her approach and know she was not a threat to Onegan. Soledad could not alter anything in his life just by being near him. The pleasure felt was a sense all her own.

She looked down at his fit torso, noticing the hair that raised on his muscular forearms. He shivered and shook his head, bringing a hand up to massage his neck. He then passed through her and walked back to the hospital. Soledad longed for her other half. It was a gift to have seen him, but she knew it was not by coincidence that he was there so close to Ally and Jess. It was a trial of sorts. She followed him through the corridors of the hospital to the surgery ward.

He scrubbed his hands clean of the traces of cigarette, toweled himself from the elbows down, and grabbed a white lab coat from the rack. She watched him as he went through his rounds. He was a nephrologist, and, as it happened, he was Jess's doctor. He was checking on Jess as Ally returned with a few staples Jess had requested. Ally set a bag on the chair next to the bed and moved closer to hear what the doctor was saying.

"So, I don't see any reason we should keep you. Your phosphorus levels are normal now. The echocardiogram and other tests on your heart are stable. I'll send the paperwork out to the nurse, and she can start the process for your release. I'll need to see you in two weeks, but you're scheduled at the dialysis clinic where I do rounds, so I'll check on you there. Morning shift okay?" He looked up briefly to see Jess nod without enthusiasm. "I know it's early, but look at it this way—you can sleep through the procedure and have the rest of the day to do whatever you want."

He smiled, clacking his pen against the clipboard. His eyes shone with interest as he noticed Ally's presence.

"Hi, I'm Ally," she said, putting out her hand to shake. The doctor's radiant energy made her smile. "I'm Jessica's sister. I guess everything is good?"

"Yes. Dr. Nick Carpelli. Pleased to meet you. Jessica says you're a famous artist."

Ally smiled self-consciously. "Uh, I don't know about that, but there is a gallery here that displays my work from time to time."

"I would love to see your paintings. I don't know a lot about painting techniques, but I can appreciate looking at nice things. I mean, I like art. I just don't know much about it." Dr. Carpelli flashed a winning smile that beamed confidence. It was a stark contrast to his serious expression by the walking path. He was so handsome and even had a cleft in his chin. Soledad couldn't believe he was tripping over himself in Ally's presence.

"I would love to show you sometime, but unfortunately, I'm flying out in two days. The show is over, and I have to return to my life in Texas. Our mom is coming out with our aunt to help Jess for a while. Maybe if I ever get my website up and going, I can email you a link."

"That would be great! Here's my card. Call me if you have any questions at all about your sister's health, and if you don't mind, I'll be in Austin next month. Maybe I could come by your studio—if you're selling paintings there, of course. I mean, I have this spot above my mantel, and my decorator says I need to find something that speaks to me." Again, he ended awkwardly.

Onegan fidgeted. Soledad could tell he wasn't sure if the proposal was too pushy.

Ally smiled then reached into her bag to procure one of her cards. "That would be great. I do sell paintings, and I have a lot in my studio. I would love to show you my work. If nothing else, maybe I can help you find what you're looking for. There is a gallery downtown off Sixth Street that has some amazing art." She smiled politely and watched as he backed out of the room, nodding, smiling, and holding up her card. She winced as he almost backed into the door jam.

Jess squealed after he left, "Oh my God, Ally, is there anyone that you aren't interested in these days? Aren't you seeing that French guy still? Henri? And what about the guy from Texas who followed you to the show?"

"It's Louis, not Henri. And yes, I see him regularly, but we aren't an item. And for the record, I was not coming on to your doctor. He was interested in me." Ally smiled, swinging her hips side to side as she held his business card to her chest. "He's pretty hot."

Jess threw a magazine at her sister in frustration.

This was complicated to Soledad, who hovered at the door of Jess's room. She felt Onegan pass through her without taking note of the soul that would complete him. Knowing she was Onegan's soulmate, Soledad knew Ally could only be a soul complement at best, but maybe they could have a good life. It would be complicated to channel energy to her ward now.

She hadn't known she could experience jealousy in her soul-watching state, but what she felt now was something twisted and cold. She didn't want to see Onegan with her former niece, yet it was her duty to guide Ally to all good possibilities in her life.

It was the only way Soledad could advance. If she let her emotions overshadow her duty, Soledad would be banished from contact with Ally for a long duration, making it even more difficult for her to accomplish her mission. If Soledad did not succeed with Ally, she would not be granted an embodied state to share a lifetime with Onegan.

Ally rubbed her arms over the cardigan she wore as if a chill passed through the room unexpectedly. Soledad sighed. She had been sending out vibes of her own distress unintentionally, and now her ward was confused. Maybe the solitary plastic bag she saw roll down the empty sidewalk was a premonition of her own solitude on this plane and the next if she didn't do her job. It could also be why Louis looked so forlorn. Maybe he could sense the change to come. If Ally really liked Louis enough to commit to a real relationship, she wouldn't have given Onegan that look of interest. Soledad felt the room fading and wondered where she might appear next.

She floated once more in a sea of fog and began to panic. Soledad was never aware of the time not spent in Ally's presence but knew there were gaps in her soul watcher's consciousness. Alekeen sat before a canvas, swiping teal paint in broad strokes across a beautiful landscape of a rocky coast. Sun streaked across the sky and glimmered onto the real water as the portrait came to life within its frame. It reminded her of a television picture. Katia Grey would have asked where he studied and if he intended on the soft imagery, or was he just lucky enough to have the expertise to know how to paint the perfect scene.

"Are you surprised?" His voice sounded soft and far away, yet he was only a few feet in front of her.

She floated closer, enchanted by the lapping water of his surreal painting and her own presence. "Do you mean surprised you paint or surprised that I am here?"

"Both, I suppose." He waved his hand before the canvas and it disappeared. He stood and faced her with smooth grace.

"Then, yes, I am surprised by both. You were a painter when you were alive?" Soledad studied his luminous features, wondering if he had ever been human.

"I was a man once, very long ago. The painting was for you, Soledad. Something to appease your soul. You have created beauty in all your lives, as you will continue to do so with each life you live."

"Why is that? Isn't the point of this reincarnation gig to learn as we live? To reach each new lesson and turn the page to the next?"

"You are not to question what is to come, but how you will fulfill your time on this watch."

"Then why am I here?"

Alekeen looked disappointed. "You have asked this before."

"I don't mean why my soul exists. I mean, why am I here now? I have never been aware of my own existence outside of my watching hours or meditation. Have I failed, or has she moved on? What happened to Ally? I must know." Soledad was surprised by the desperate sound of her own voice. She still felt love for Katia Grey's niece and needed to know what happened.

"You haven't failed—yet." Alekeen paused. His image softened and faded.

Soledad reappeared in a busy intersection somewhere in the city. For a moment, she was lost but then saw the hotel that Louis and Ally frequented. She recognized the bakery across the street where the plastic bag had rolled across the sidewalk on that empty, gloomy day. She heard brakes screeching as a cab plowed into an oncoming car. The small red Mercedes had run through the light, trying to make it through the intersection. It got broadsided by the yellow taxi. Traffic halted, and people stopped to stare. Anxiety seeped through Soledad at the prospect of who might be in the cars. She neared the steaming, crumpled hood to peer into the taxi. The driver lay still across the exploded airbag, his body limp. Soledad watched as his soul separated and stared down at his body inside the twisted metal. Sirens blared across the city, casting an eerie sensation around the accident for a brief moment.

"Oh, my God! I think he's dead," a man called out as he pulled his hand away from the non-existent pulse in the cabby's neck. "Ma'am, don't move. An ambulance is coming. Are you in pain? What's your name?" The man knelt beside the open cab door holding Ally's hand. "It's going to be okay. You're going to be okay. Stay with me now. What's your name?" he repeated the question as he patted her hand to keep her alert. "You got anyone we should call?"

Soledad peered over the concerned man who attended her ward. There was blood pouring from Ally's head wound, and her other arm hung at an odd angle. The man was trying to keep her alert until help arrived. Soledad sent soothing waves of energy to Ally, bidding her to hang on. She was not sure of the medical severity, but she didn't think her mission ended here.

Ten minutes felt like a lifetime waiting for the ambulance to arrive. The twenty-minute ride to the hospital that was only ten miles away felt like an eternity because of the rush-hour traffic. Soledad gripped Ally in a protective hug, murmuring in her ear. She could hear the EMT guy sounding off medical terms to his partner. "I think she has a clavicle fracture, maybe a dislocated shoulder, concussion, and a possible broken rib."

Ally moaned, clutching her one good arm around her middle. Her fair skin took on a bluish hue. "Her blood pressure is dropping! Dan, I think her trachea has deviated. We might have a tension pneumo here!" The EMT lifted her shirt, feeling around the outer part of her ribs. Ally wheezed like she was trying to suck in air through a straw before passing out. The EMT stabbed her with a syringe above her third rib. A hissing noise poured forth. He then put a pillow against Ally's stomach, wrapping her good arm around it for support. Ally came to with a great breath of air.

"Out of the woods?" Dan asked.

"Yeah, I think we're good here. She'll make it."

Soledad sighed with relief, wishing she could cry. Tears had been a soothing way to release sorrow or tension when she was human. She remembered something she had read about mermaids long ago, by Hans Christian Andersen. They suffered more because they couldn't weep.

CHAPTER 14

I didn't think I would be seeing you so soon." Dr. Nick Carpelli looked over his chart, peering down at Ally. She wasn't shocked to wake up in the hospital. She'd seen countless doctors and nurses already, but she was surprised to see Jess's kidney doctor at the end of her bed.

"Why are you here?" she said with slight alarm.

"Good to see you too." His sarcasm was followed by a lopsided grin and a raised eyebrow. "Other than your contusion, your CT looks fine. I want you under observation for another twenty-four hours. Nothing to be alarmed about. We'll keep tabs on your creatinine levels until you're released. I want you to take it easy for the next few weeks and try to rest while you're here." He reassured her, patting her lower leg through the hospital blankets. Ally thought she must look a fright but was afraid to ask for a mirror.

"Will I get to go home soon? What day is it, anyway?" Ally looked around as if she could find a calendar hovering nearby. "I'm not sure how long I have been here?"

"A couple of days. Your sister was released to your mother and aunt two days ago."

Her mind leaped to Aunt Katia, then she shook her head. Aunt Kat was gone. It must be Aunt Rose, her mother's younger sister.

"Dr. Anzel says you can be released in the morning. I know you said you have a flight to catch, but maybe give it a few days before taking off. Stay with your family, and if you feel well enough, you can travel by the weekend. I want to see you in my office before you leave New York." His tone was no-nonsense. "Then maybe I can take you to lunch."

Ally was shocked at the impromptu date proposal. "Onegan—I mean, Dr. Carpelli." She shook her head, not knowing where that word came from. Why had she said Onegan? Was that even a name?

"Yes, we are on again!" He winked. "Don't worry. You hit your head hard. You're lucky the concussion was slight. Things might seem scrambled for a while, but you will straighten it all out." He patted her leg once more and turned for the door. "I've got your number now, so is it okay if I call you? I make house calls." His smile was mischievous.

Ally wondered if he was allowed to ask patients out. Wasn't there a rule about that sort of behavior? Of course, it wasn't like she would report him. "Sure, I'd like that, the call, I mean." Ally's thoughts were jumbled, but she was still smiling when Jess, her mother, and aunt arrived.

"Ally!" Her aunt cried out, bouncing against the bed as she leaned over to embrace her.

Her mother's soft voice could be heard from somewhere beyond.

"Rose, let her breathe. You are going to hurt her arm."

Jess begrudgingly chimed in. "I guess the shoe is on the other foot." She was trying to sound sarcastic, but Ally could hear the faint worry in her voice.

"Hah. I'm all right. Just bruised up a bit. No serious breaks, a few hairline fractures to be careful of." Her voice was raspy, and she groaned with pain. "The dislocated shoulder was the most painful, but now that it's back in place, it's the least of my worries." Ally hadn't been able to see herself, so she wondered how bad she looked. "Got a mirror?"

"Besides a few stitches on your forehead, you look great!" Rose chimed in, sitting back to get a good look at her niece. Rose was only a few years younger than Ally's mom. They were close when Ally was small until her mother and father divorced, and they moved away to Texas. After that, they didn't see each other except for scattered holidays or special occasions. Ally loved Aunt Rose dearly, but it was difficult to find time to visit.

"Anyone got a mirror?" Her mother shot a worried glance at Rose, but it was Jess who was more than happy to accommodate Ally, pulling an oversized compact from her purse.

"Better hope Louis likes the vamp look."

Jess's smugness made Ally glare back. "I see what you mean." She looked like the bride of Frankenstein with zipper stitches curling up her forehead. A line of tightly woven thread meandered from eyebrow to hairline along her temple. At least it wasn't in the center of her forehead. "I guess it could be worse." She clipped the compact shut and handed it back to Jess. "I could always get eyeliner tattooed." Ally swept her finger up her eye, pursing her lips, then winced at the pain in her shoulder and back.

"You are very lucky, Ally Katia Castell. You could have been killed," her mother admonished. "When the hospital called and told us about the accident, I thought I would faint right there." Her voice choked, and she began to weep.

"I'm okay, Mom, really." Ally tried to reassure her and leaned forward to pat her hand. The attempt at movement made her breath catch. She blew it out slowly and tried to relax. "I'm just a little beat up. The doctors say I'll be fine in a few weeks. I think I'm getting out of here soon. I would fuss at you for being here if you hadn't already been coming to New York for Jess."

She looked at her sister, who still looked a little pale. "Why don't you guys go get some coffee or tea in the cafeteria, then take Jess home. I'll be fine. She did her time, and I think she could use some rest." Jess rolled her eyes but headed to the door.

After saying their good-byes, they promised to return later to keep her company. She nodded politely but was relieved to slip back into the darkness of healing sleep.

Ally had said Onegan. It was impossible for her to know Nick Carpelli's soul name. Soledad must have been channeling it subconsciously. It wasn't a mistake. Her desperation to intervene in his interest in Ally was overriding her duty to help. She was supposed to assist Ally in grasping what was right for her happiness.

Soledad was not a total idiot. She knew this was a test, and she knew she was failing. Onegan could never be hers while she was in the soul-watching state, and he was embodied. She loved him with every fiber of her being, but she could not be with him. She wanted to lead him to happiness, but was Ally his happiness? Would he be happy in a world with no soulmate? Maybe Ally's soulmate did not exist in this life, and the best she could do was to be comfortable with Onegan—or Travis, or Louis. Maybe Ally would break Onegan's heart for one of the other men she favored. Soledad could lead Ally away because she knew for sure that Onegan was not Ally's soulmate. He was hers. Though she didn't possess a literal heart, it felt like hers was breaking.

Watching Ally sleep, Soledad sat at the edge of her bed. She loved this soul for reasons she could not define. Ally was her niece in the previous life, and long-ago she'd been Soledad's child, but that was so many lives past, it was hard to remember. There was a link between them, a bond that wouldn't let Soledad fail Ally in her progression to the next life. She channeled positive energy through Ally's spirit, hoping to ignite the healing part of her mind to incite the rejuvenation of her cells.

"I think you are doing a crap job, and you might want to rethink your career." Ally's voice croaked softly. There was no one in the room, and her eyes were still closed. *She must be dreaming.* "Who is Onegan?" Ally rasped.

Uh-oh, whether Ally was dreaming or not, she felt Soledad's thoughts. Her dilemma had been too great, and her energy leaked images through her channeling to Ally's perceptive mind. Soledad tried to retract the thoughts of Onegan to clear a pathway.

"Mum, Mum! Where are you? I'm cold, oh, so cold. Is it time to go in yet?" This time Ally's eyes were open. She was staring at Soledad as if she could see her, but her voice had spoken in fluent German, the voice of a child. What was happening? Ally couldn't remember that life. Soledad could barely remember it herself. There had been a war. It was deathly cold, and they had left their home with only their lives in hand. The village was burned, and Soledad took Ally, who was then known as Elka, into the forest to hide. Their time was short. Elka was lucky to have frozen to death before dawn. Soledad was found by soldiers, raped, then slaughtered. She hadn't remembered any of that life until hearing Elka's small voice.

"Hush, child, all will be warmer in the morning. The sun will come out and heat our way home." Soledad repeated the words she had promised her child so many lives ago. This was why Ally had been one of her options, she was sure of it. Her core spirit felt a fire ignite within, and she swore to find the right path for her spirit daughter. She owed her that much. This time she would protect the child within.

"I'm scared…" Ally's words trailed off as she melted deeper into her dreams.

"Rest child. I'll stay by your side." But even as she channeled the thought, Soledad felt herself fading. Willing herself to stay, she focused on pouring all of her energy toward Ally. As the monitors beeped in a steady rhythm, and the buzz of nurses changing shift filtered in through the open door, Soledad sensed his presence. She looked away from Ally and found her energy lost in the eyes of her soulmate. Nick Carpelli was the last thing she saw before fading from consciousness.

It had been rough recovering the first few days at Jessica's with her mom and aunt flittering about, offering something every few minutes. All Ally wanted to do was sleep, and the abominable television shows were distressing. She was never much of a couch potato, and reality TV was not her thing. Louis had come by Jess's apartment unannounced, and she was sure he felt awkward during the short visit with her whole family lurking. Ally asked him to give her some space until she recovered. She was sure he was relieved, and she wasn't in the mood for visitors while feeling, and looking, like a battered soldier. There would be a few battle scars from the accident, but she felt lucky to be alive. Ally was at a loss as to what condolence action was appropriate when the man who tried to drive you home was dead. She finally decided to send flowers and a donation to the cab driver's family. The bruises would fade, and a few weeks of physical therapy should put her back to work, but the poor driver was gone forever, and she knew his family would suffer from his loss.

Marcel and Rebecca were already asking about dates for the next show. Ally was bursting with ideas for her canvas. The golden-winged angel from the last show would become a series. Recurring dreams of the entity's cryptic messages had Ally's creativity screaming for release. Scenes from the car wreck were splashed across her mind. She envisioned cayenne red, marigold yellow, and deepest black sprays of acrylic or maybe oil. She hadn't yet decided. While the angel watched over her life, Ally had a feeling this entity was somehow serving penance for the misdeeds of its past.

Her mind wandered back to *David Reborn*. Should there be one of Louis and Nick too? She giggled at the shocking thought. Who was this new femme fatale she had become? Maybe she was the black widow spider. Men did serve a purpose, after all.

Somehow she knew these thoughts could not be her own. Always neutral in the war between the sexes, she had never been a women's libber or a man-hater. Ally loved to see women take charge or head up a company. She wasn't the type to disrespect others, and she wasn't willing to step on the shoulders of colleagues to get ahead. There wasn't a canyon between sexes in her mind, simply human beings with different agendas. No black, white, or *other* checked boxes, just individuals trying to make their way in the world.

Her thoughts of art and the things she wanted to create made her pick up the phone and dial the airline. She had enjoyed seeing her family but missed Ella and Harley more than anyone could imagine. It was well past time to go home.

CHAPTER 15

As the 737 touched the runway with the thump of wheels and a squeal of brakes, Ally breathed a sigh of relief. Her return flight home was smoother than the trip to New York, though so much later than she had planned. She caught a taxi from the airport, noting how lucky she was not to have valeted her car. The fees would have been astronomical by now. The cabby tapped his brakes and veered around another car, causing Ally to wince. She tried to stay calm, reminding herself she had been in a million taxis before the accident. It wasn't likely to happen again. She tipped the cab driver extra to help her with the bags up the porch steps to the door.

Ella and Harley bounded out to greet them, making a slobbering mess of kisses on them both. The pups thanked the cabby thoroughly for bringing their loved one home. Ally apologized, but the driver was good-natured, laughing and stroking them both behind the ears. He told her about his two Yorkies who waited for him in the window every night.

"They go nuts when I get home. You'd think I had left for a century," he said with a smile.

Ally thought he must look funny when he walked the two tiny furballs. He was built like a linebacker and had a South African accent. She grabbed the ball from the front porch swing and threw it long and hard. Ella and Harley didn't miss a beat. The trick worked, and the cabby was able to get the bags up to the door unmolested.

It was almost dusk, and Ally was exhausted. She looked forward to lighting a small fire, brewing a cup of tea, and lying in the fuzzy beanbag chair with the two most important fur-buddies of her life. Her phone chirped, indicating she had received a text as she rolled her luggage through the kitchen to the kettle. The contact labeled "Hot French guy" lit up in bold letters across the screen.

You didn't even say goodbye? he texted.

Ugh, Ally thought as she laid the phone on the counter. Things might have ended differently if it hadn't been for the accident, but Louis was never meant to be a long-term boyfriend. He lived in a different country, and he would return home to France at some point. The longer they shared a bed, the more vulnerable her heart would be. After the awkward visit at Jess's, she had just let him go. She didn't want to get any closer, and it seemed like a natural time to end things. Ally was leaving New York when the accident had happened, so she shouldn't feel guilty. Her phone chirped again.

This time, the text read, *Are you avoiding me?*

Ally sighed but then noticed the text was not from Louis. It was Dr. Carpelli. She smiled. That was another not-so-serious but tempting liaison. He lived in New York, which was closer, but she wasn't into long-distance relationships. Or was she? After the long stint between her divorce and Travis, she had been fine on her own. The past few months had been a boost to her ego, and maybe she didn't want or need serious entanglements. No commitments might be best. The space between her and Louis felt nice now that she was away, and in her heart, she knew she would see him again someday. Dr. Nick would be in town soon, and then he'd be gone. It could be a pleasant diversion.

Ally texted back. *I'm not avoiding you. I just needed to go home. Doctor's orders ;-)*

She copied and pasted the last two sentences into Louis's message, killing two birds with one stone. She had never made any promises to Louis and didn't owe him any other explanation. She never asked him to be faithful to her or for anything more than a casual affair. He hadn't asked her for anything either.

The next text was also from Nick. *You missed your appointment. Glad you are home safe. I will fly in tomorrow. Is Wednesday too soon to look at paintings?*

Ally giggled to herself like a schoolgirl, remembering his thick lashes and the sexy cleft in his chin. If he ever lost his medical license, he could definitely get some commercial or print work with that face. Filling the teapot with a soothing blend of jasmine, she put her cup on a tray and moved to the living room.

Ella and Harley were fast on her heels. Their noses were all over her as she sat and removed the lid from the treat jar next to the couch.

She revived the screen on her phone as she settled into the soft beanbag and clicked away at the keys. Since text communication had become a "thing," she rarely spoke with anyone on the phone. It was funny because a lot of written communication lost meaning without voice inflection. She thought about it as she typed. *I should be free Wednesday around noon. I have therapy in the morning.*

Louis texted back. *I think you meant that for someone else.*

"Oh, shit!" Ally covered her mouth with her hand, then thought about her response. It didn't say anything about Dr. Carpelli being hot or her taking him to bed. No real harm done. *Sorry, Louis. I'm just catching up on appointments. I was arranging a meeting with a prospective client.*

There! That should do it. She re-sent the first message to Nick accepting Wednesday.

Great! he wrote back. *Should I come to your studio, or would you like to meet somewhere else? I wouldn't want you to think I was stalking you.*

Louis sent back, *As long as it's not a hot male client that has ulterior motives.*

Lunch sounds great! Ally told Nick. *I'll meet you at the Driskill, and then we can come back to my place. I wouldn't be offended by the stalking…lol*

She pressed send then squealed as she realized she sent it *again* to Louis. She was starting to appreciate pre-text technology. How did she screw up twice? She re-sent it to Nick, cringing with embarrassment.

Louis: *?*

Nick: *It's a date then.*

Wednesday came around quick, and Ally found herself a bundle of nerves as she dressed to meet the handsome doctor. She barely knew the guy, so why was she so anxious?

Physical therapy had been grueling. She didn't know she was so immobilized until Rashid worked her over and gave her a folder of exercises to do every day. She hated therapy already, and it was only her second visit. At least her therapist was nice. He chatted away about his pending nuptials with zeal.

Rashid showed her a picture of a slip of a girl he had only met once. She was beautiful and so petite. Ally couldn't imagine committing the rest of her life to someone she just met. *Different strokes for different folks.* The handsome therapist was still so young and had no idea about relationships. He told

Ally he had only experienced one girlfriend before. She was an all-American blonde. His parents back in Iran didn't approve, so they picked out a proper Iranian wife for him as soon as he was dumped by the blonde. He flew in once to meet his parent's choice of mate, and the arrangement was made.

He smiled when he showed Ally the picture of the pretty Iranian girl, though she was mostly covered up by a burka in the picture. The young woman had beautiful eyes and skin. He seemed happy about his luck, so who was Ally to judge? She had dated her ex-husband through four years of college, and he was a total mistake. One meeting or four years, no one could say what would last. She was the first to admit that you could know someone all their life and not really know them.

CHAPTER 16

Ella and Harley yapped at her heels, playing muzzle tussle from under the bed. Harley found a way to drive Ella crazy by rolling tennis balls just out of reach. Every time the portly yellow lab stuck her head under the French chiffon dust ruffle, Harley would playfully nip at her nose. This sent Ella into a frenzy. Chuckling, Ally dabbed at the lipstick she had just reapplied and hoped it wasn't too bold. She had bought a vibrant red in New York, and she liked the way it set off her smooth complexion, enhancing the black color of her thick lashes. Blotting once more to be sure, she reached for her tasseled leather bag and a light jean jacket. Winter in her part of Texas was usually never more than a brisk fall anywhere else in the country, but spring was cooler than usual this year. Grabbing the keys to her Jeep, she bid the pups goodbye with a farewell treat and promised them a burger when she got home.

Traffic downtown was the usual mess, but she valeted and made her way to the front of the hotel. The aroma of warm roasted coffee beans and fresh-baked bread greeted her as she walked into the café. Nick sat waiting for her at the front of the restaurant. She smiled at the way he popped up to greet her. His eagerness was evident in his assessing gaze and the way he smiled.

"Hi, glad you could make it. How was therapy?"

"Grr," Ally growled playfully in response.

He laughed. "That bad, huh?"

They were shown to a corner table where afternoon sunlight streamed in.

"Rashid is a nice, handsome young man, but his arranged wedding distresses me for some reason. The exercise didn't make me feel any better, either." She sighed with a grimace.

"Yeah, I don't think I could have married Lizzy Buttoolie," he said solemnly.

Ally shook her head in confusion, sure that she had missed a beat. "What?"

"Lizzy was my neighbor and lab partner in seventh-grade biology. She's a biotech engineer who makes the big bucks now. Invented some important pharmaceutical for treating cancer patients. My mom tells me every time I visit what a lovely couple we would make, and how Lizzy is amazingly still single after all these years." Nick relaxed into the booth, chuckling as he shook his head.

"So, what's wrong with Lizzy? She sounds like a good catch."

"I'm pretty sure Lizzy is a lesbian or maybe just asexual, but as far as I know, she's never been spotted with another individual on a date. And she had a butt of a face. Pun intended." He grimaced at his terrible slip but laughed.

"Wait, are you saying she's a lesbian because she is homely?" Ally didn't know whether to laugh or be offended for all homely women, lesbians, or both.

"No, um, sorry, that didn't come out right. I was making a joke. In poor taste, I suppose. This is exactly how I get into trouble at work." He sighed. "The HR police are on me night and day. Luckily, I'm really good at what I do. Please forgive me. The world has become too politically correct, and I'm still emotionally thirteen." Nick looked at her with soft puppy dog eyes.

No way could Ally resist. "Sure. Everyone has gotten too uptight lately. The important part is that you aren't hurting anyone or stopping them from living their lives. You're a doctor, and you help people, so I think I can let that one slide." She paused, thinking how to word her next question. "Incidentally, do you often ask your patients out?"

"Technically, I asked you out before you were my patient, so HR can't get me for that." His mischievous grin made Ally laugh. He was too handsome for her not to be flattered by his playful charm.

He ordered wine with lunch, and Ally didn't object. She didn't plan on driving anytime soon, and hopefully, they would have time to walk off their dessert. She had promised to show Nick around town, and her studio could wait. He was here for a few days, and they could make another afternoon of it if things went well.

Nick was a voracious reader, loved old movies, and fine port. He told her about his extensive travels abroad and how he volunteered every year to help at children's hospitals around the world. They toured the gallery on Sixth and browsed some of the swank furniture and antique shops.

Time flew by as their conversation fizzled into the evening air. There was a long pause as they found themselves back where they started, in front of the hotel café.

"I'm sorry, Nick, but I need to get back. Can I show you my artwork tomorrow? I'm afraid Ella and Harley will be upset if I don't get their dinner to them soon." Ally smiled up at him, holding the two plain burgers she purchased at the food truck. It had been a wonderful and full afternoon, and she was glad she had agreed to meet him downtown. It wasn't often that she crawled out of her lake retreat to go into the city—especially after all the time she spent in New York, but today she was reminded why she loved Austin. It truly was a multicultural city, that offered so much to its inhabitants, without feeling like it had grown too big to accommodate individuals with small-town aspirations.

Nick smiled down at her. "Are you sure you're not attached to some big bodybuilder boyfriend?"

"What? Why do you ask that?" She slapped his arm playfully, smiling up at him and shaking her head. "Do I look like the bodybuilder type? I am just...unlucky in love. I've sworn off serious interests and decided to take life day by day." She nodded sagely as she let go of his arm and stared down the street at the oncoming traffic. She couldn't look Nick in the eye. He was too handsome, too intelligent, too...she couldn't name it, but he gave her goosebumps. She thought Travis was the one she would fall for, but after he let her down, she felt too vulnerable to open her heart again. Louis was amazing, but too young and lived too far away. He had been a great stepping-stone, but to what, she wasn't sure.

While Ally was pondering the day and her emotions, Nick leaned down and kissed her, catching her by surprise. It was a nice kiss. His full lips brushed against her mouth, grazing her bottom lip, and nipping at the pout she had shared moments before. She caught herself leaning into him and tried to suppress the small whimper in the back of her throat. Damn, he was good. She didn't want to invite any discussion about their kiss for fear she'd ask him back to her cottage for a wild romp in her bed, or that she might just skip all propriety and tell him to take her upstairs to his room. Lucky for Ally, the valet recognized her and brought her Jeep without request. She smiled at Nick, then fished in her purse for a tip. Nick put his hands over hers and handed the valet a crisp twenty from his pocket.

"Tomorrow," was all he said as he squeezed her wrist then let go.

It was only their second date, and Ally felt like her heart was in her throat. Why was she vibrating with anticipation? Hadn't she just left a lover in New York? Yes, but that was over, and she had known it was just a fling even then. Nick was different. He was a few years older than her, smart, funny, and oh so charming. From the moment she met him in the hospital, she had felt a pull of energy between them. Was it possible they were soul mates? *Don't be ridiculous, Ally. Soulmates are a thing of fiction.*

Ella barked twice and turned in a circle before making a beeline toward the front door. Harley was fast on her heels. The canine duo's paws clattered across the hardwood, making sliding noises as they tried to reach the visitor first. Alley brushed her hair one last time and quickly misted herself with perfume. Her date had arrived, and she somehow felt like this night could be special.

Grabbing her purse, she went to the front door to meet Nick. Ally gave Ella a stern order to sit and behave, but as soon as the door opened, all bets were off. Ella circled Nick, while Harley danced on his two back legs, pawing at the air to be picked up.

"Sorry, I need to send them both to obedience school, but I think I am the one that needs training." Ally laughed as Nick picked up Harley, tucking the small dust mop of a dog underneath one arm while scratching Ella behind the ears. Harley took advantage of the situation to give Nick several wet kisses.

"No worries. I love dogs. I used to have one, but after my golden retriever passed away, I didn't have the time to get a puppy. Doctor's hours and all." He waved his hand in a casual manner, expressing how crazy his schedule could be. Ella protested by putting a paw on his leg to remind him he had been scratching her and needed to continue. They both laughed.

When the humor subsided, Nick looked at Alley with warm appreciation. "You look beautiful."

Ally preened from the compliment and pushed her shoulders back, giving him a coy smile. "Thanks. You look good too. Do you want a drink? I can show you the studio," she suggested.

"I can wait for the drink, but I would love to see your art."

Ally showed him through the back door and into the small cottage she used for painting. She was between shows and hadn't had time to work on the next series. A few landscape scenes and portraits from a past show on aging graced the easels. An angel portrait, similar to the one she sold at the last show, stood in the center of the room. Ally couldn't shake her fascination with the apparition she thought she had seen on several occasions.

"Wow, she's lovely." Nick was immediately drawn to the portrait. Ally beamed. The angel was one of her favorite works, and she had sold many variations of the portrait. "I know this may sound odd, but she looks so familiar. Did you use a local model? I visited my aunt here a few times, but it was years ago."

Ally smiled, tilting her head in thought. "No, just something I imagined." She didn't want to linger on the subject of her guardian angel too long. How would she explain that she wasn't crazy? Who knew, maybe she was. It was best to move on to dinner. A glass of champagne sounded great right now, and the thought of what might happen for dessert had her walking toward the door.

Dinner was amazing. She'd never been to the new restaurant on the up-and-coming east side. The menu was different, the style was simple yet elegant, and they didn't rush the entrees or the wine. Ally was entranced by the easy conversation, quick wit, and handsome smile that emanated from her dinner companion. She liked that he'd hired a driver so they could both relax. They walked Sixth Street back to his hotel, giving them more time for their food to settle and take in the fresh evening air. They entered the lounge to share a glass of port, which turned into a bottle and easier conversation. Nick leaned in when he talked to her, and Ally watched the muscles in his neck as he threw back his head in laughter. He was too good to be true, a gorgeous doctor, who was slightly older than her, and it was a plus that he appreciated art. So what if he didn't have a French accent or ride a Harley.

Alley tried to rein in her thoughts, as her mind raced to retrieve hidden memories of her past two lovers for comparison. As she waited for him to come back from the men's room, she thought about the first night she was with Louis in the hotel in New York. Would Nick ask her up to his room, or would she invite herself up?

Nick had an easy grin on his face when he returned, and instead of sitting down next to her, he held out his hand for her to stand. "I know it's only our second date, but I've been dreaming of that first kiss ever since it happened. I hope you won't think I'm a letch if I ask you to come upstairs to see my etchings."

Ally couldn't help but giggle. Nick made everything so easy to say yes to. In fact, they hadn't had one disagreement. She knew she wanted this as much as he did, but Ally worried it might make a difference in their future if she went to his room. Afterward, would he retreat like Travis, or was he open-minded like Louis? Ally shook the questions and doubt from her meandering thoughts. This wasn't Travis or Louis, this was Nick, and she would be a fool if she didn't follow her heart.

Soledad didn't know how much time had passed since her last visit with Ally. Her hair was shorter, falling just below her shoulders, and she was holding a baby in her arms. "What had happened?" Soledad wondered in panic mode.

It was like the lights flicking on and off, and the images that appeared were out of sync. She was with Ally so much before, then time scattered in New York, and she disappeared, but she was back with Ally now. Like waking up from a drug-induced sleep, it had been some time since Soledad had existed on this plane or anywhere. Realization settled over her that soul-sleep had entranced her for a long stint. The jealousy from Ally's interest in Onegan must have banished Soledad from her ward.

Her heart was heavy as she contemplated her fate. Was she doomed to follow Ally until she soul-watched and then lived again? Soledad was so close to her soulmate, yet lifetimes away. She watched as Ally handed the baby to the other lady at the table. Relief flowed over her in waves of realization. It wasn't Ally's baby.

Guilt washed over Soledad. She knew the flaws she needed to overcome as a soul watcher in order to succeed. She didn't need to make a mental tally of all her failures. How many lives would pass before she understood how to alleviate these petty flaws? For now, Soledad admitted to being the one responsible for her own absence. She couldn't fool Alekeen, and she wasn't fooling herself. Soledad envied Ally, and she wanted more than anything for an opportunity to have a life with Onegan.

Searching around, she tried to gauge time by glimpsing at the cars on the street outside the restaurant window, the crinkles around Ally's eyes, the tapered bottom of the jeans the waitress wore. Nothing seemed out of the ordinary. Soledad spied a paper lying in a bus tub on a nearby table. It was July. Nearly six months had passed, longer than the few months she had soul-watched over Ally. She tried to remember if this long of a slumber had ever occurred before. There was another entire plane of existence that she couldn't remember at all, and that's where she spent her hours sleeping away months of time. Soledad tried to remember where she had been last, but her efforts were fruitless.

Her focus drew back to Ally and the young woman she sat with. Soledad remembered Rebecca from the New York gallery. From the conversation, Soledad gathered Rebecca was here to view Ally's new paintings and had brought her new baby for Ally to see. Rebecca's recent relationship was a swift romance that produced a quickie marriage, followed by young Andy, four months later. The chubby baby was an adorable bundle of joy.

As Soledad admired his soft cheeks, she became paralyzed by the vision of a knight on horseback. His chainmail gleamed in the morning sun as the red plume of his helmet shook in the wind. She shivered at the dream-like scene of him galloping to his death. Impaled on a splintering lance, Andy had died a grueling death over five-hundred years before this life. His bright blue eyes blinked in rounded curiosity as he stared at Soledad in the empty chair. He reached his hands toward her, and she knew the wee mite had a gift of sight. He wailed as Rebecca turned him toward her and away from the curious being he had spotted.

"Oh dear, I guess it's that time." Rebecca stood, carrying young Andy to the ladies' room to breastfeed.

Soledad felt sorry for the uptight generation that still thought a mother should do natural feedings in private. Denying their maternal existence and rushing into the distinct advancement of a technologically driven society, this generation held the blueprints for a floundering population of bottle-fed babies. Severed from their natural world forever, humanity would suffer for the denial of their animal nature.

Ally excused Rebecca, smiling. Soledad spotted the whimsical look on her niece's face. She recognized the longing of a woman without a baby. The look of pleasure that filled Ally's eyes when she was alone with Ella and Harley said she longed to be a mother. The dogs had served as her pseudo children for too long. Her biological clock was ticking, and Ally didn't have much time to make her dream happen if that was what she wanted. As Soledad watched Nick approach the table and Ally stand to greet him, she felt something break free inside herself. She could see that the couple's relationship had intensified. In the months she had existed elsewhere, Ally and Nick had begun to build a life. Listening in on their greeting, she tried to gauge how much the relationship had advanced.

"So how about I pick you up? We can fly together, and I'll hold your hand from takeoff to landing," Nick's smile was brilliant as he waited for Ally's acceptance.

"First, you give up your job in New York, then you fly back to help my ailing sister and my Aunt Rose move here, then you dog sit every gallery showing, and you even mow my lawn." Ally held his hand and tilted her head, imploring him silently to stop. "I can't let you give up your life for me, Nick."

"I didn't give up my job. I transferred to Austin, and FYI, I love it here. Lawn mowing is a man's job, and besides, I need to earn my keep somehow, since you won't let me pay rent."

"I own the cottage, and I have enough money, Nick, so I don't need you paying rent to me." Ally smiled. "If you're really concerned, how about we work it out in sexual favors?"

"With or without Ella and Harley watching?"

Ally laughed playfully, nudging his chest. "Are they too much for you?"

"Are you kidding? They look out for me. They know I can't survive without you, so they make sure I don't sulk in the Lovesac chair without eating for too long." Nick was teasing her now, and Soledad could see how much Ally loved him. It was a life Soledad should have—a life she had lived only a few times.

She felt herself fading. She contemplated how she could stop and stay there with him, with them. A light shone down on her from her own plane. She understood she had to accept Nick in Ally's life if she wanted to stay and help her ward. Her job was to facilitate happiness for the soul she watched. The knowledge weighed on Soledad, and she consciously grounded herself to this world with the force of her immense love for her soulmate and her ward. She vowed that she did have enough love for them both, and she would help them succeed in a world that challenged even the strongest bonds. After all, when you love a soulmate, you give them everything they want, and Nick wanted Ally. Accepting that would make it easier for Soledad to achieve her goal.

She engaged a steady hum of approval, sending reassuring vibrations to Ally. As if feeling the awe-filled power of one soulmate's love for another, Ally wrapped her arms around Nick's neck and proclaimed, "Let's have a baby!" She leaned back in his arms to assess his look of absolute shock. "Don't you want a child?"

"Yeah, sure, but that's sort of out of the blue and definitely out of order. Shouldn't we get married first?"

That changed the expression on Ally's face. Soledad felt her hesitant, wary vibes. Her ward had been bitten before, and it had left her hurt and lonely.

Nick stared at her contemplative expression with a furrowed brow. "What are you saying? You want to have my child, but not me?"

"Oh, no, I definitely want you," Ally exclaimed without delay. "It's just that we have both done the marriage thing before, and it didn't work so well." She pressed her lips together in thought, then suggested, "Maybe we could just live in sin, and I'll be your baby-momma."

Nick's broad smile lightened the moment, but he refused to let her go from his embrace. "Will you marry me?"

His voice had turned serious, and his eyes searched hers as Ally's laughter faded. Tables around them came to a hushed silence, watching with sudden interest at what had been such a light greeting. Nick relaxed his arms, bending down on one knee. He reached into his coat pocket and pulled out a small ring box.

Ally covered her mouth, gasping in surprise. "Are you serious?"

"Yes, I've been carrying this ring around for two weeks trying to find the right moment, but as with every wonderful idea I have, you beat me to the punch." He beamed up at her, flashing his white teeth. The dimple at his chin was a perfect complement to his full lips. She kneeled in front of him, not breaking eye contact, running her fingers over his beautiful jawline.

"You really think you want to spend the rest of your life with me? A crazy painter with numerous family obligations, two very needy dogs, and half of the time afraid of my own shadow?"

"You are only afraid of airplanes. Ally, you're a strong, beautiful woman, and I want to spend eternity with you, but if I can only have the rest of this life, I'll gladly take it and fill all of Texas with our beautiful brats."

A burst of "ahhs" came from the diners, and then a lady shouted, "Are you nuts? Hurry up and say yes before I take him!"

The crowd laughed at the prompt. Ally threw her arms around Nick and kissed him. Rebecca walked over as they both turned to greet her and Andy. "I wish John had been that romantic. I swear if I wasn't lactating milk and holding a baby in my arms, I just might fall in love with Nick myself."

Ally and Nick laughed at Rebecca's proclamation, and other tables resumed their normal conversations. It wasn't lost on Soledad that Ally had never actually said yes, but the ring glinted on her finger as they ordered dessert and champagne for the table.

Later that night, as Soledad stared down at Nick's handsome form holding Ally, she felt a pang of emotion she couldn't identify. It was like the day she had watched the empty bag roll across the deserted street in New York. Impending doom was something that others would scoff at. Knowing the future or predicting a path was for charlatans. Soledad was burned at the stake for predictions in a previous life, but she knew the skill was a gift. Some scientific studies theorized that premonitions were a part of the brain that wasn't understood yet and that all humans possessed the capability to foresee the future.

Soledad knew her ability with intuition. Whether living or dead, she always sensed possibilities to come but scoffed at ever knowing the future. Lives were like intricate golden threads woven together on a complex loom, being mashed and pulled into oblivion. The future was like a river rushing over rocks, turning around the bend, and lingering in deep eddies. It was unpredictable, ever-changing, with multiple outcomes that could sometimes beat all odds—for better or worse. Soledad only knew the bad possibilities because people didn't need to know about the good things to come. Knowing in advance could be beneficial in changing the outcome, or it could seal someone's fate. She fidgeted as she watched Ella roll over onto her back in the dark, exposing her stomach to the ceiling. Harley lay snug against Ally's side. A symphony of light snores played throughout the room as the small family slept. Soledad sensed Ally's conception this night as she sensed most things about Ally's life. She truly wished them many years of happiness.

CHAPTER 17

Six weeks had passed since their surprise engagement, and Ally was flying again to New York. She boarded the plane and settled into her first-class seat. She had never been a snob, but having a little money had perks for a white-knuckle flier. The upgraded seat gave her room to extend her tired legs and hide her crushing fear as they ascended and descended in the massive metal plane.

Business was better than ever, and the paintings from the last show sold in record time. Ally would soon be flying to meet an important buyer at a gallery in Paris. She would be required to paint more for a show to debut in six months, and she imagined she would still be able to fly by then. Ally hadn't told Nick about the baby yet because she wanted to make sure there wasn't a glitch in the five pregnancy tests she took last week. She was early along and didn't want him rushing her down the aisle to make things right. A lot could happen in the first three months.

It wasn't that she didn't want to spend the rest of her life with Nick, but things seemed to work so well for them in their current partnership. She had no idea he was such a traditionalist until he started looking for wedding venues and cakes. *Really, wasn't that the bride's job?* She would be happy to let him take over the planning of their lives. The only thing she had time for was painting. Lately, even poor Ella and Harley got shorted for time on their walks. Most days, it was a ten-minute session of playing fetch in the yard and then back to work.

The knowledge there would be another member of their family stirred inside her like a beacon of light. She had never wanted a child in her last marriage and hadn't known she wanted one in this relationship until seeing Rebecca at the café. She loved Nick as she had never loved anyone and hoped beyond hope that this time she would have a happy ending. She couldn't chase away the fear of divorce that taunted her. Splitting weekends, separate houses, separate lives, and possibly having her child call someone else Mommy was enough to cause a panic attack. Ally shook her head. She was being ridiculous, and she figured it was hormones driving her to madness as the plane soared thirty-thousand feet in the air.

Ally peered out the oval window as she sipped her water and crunched on warmed cashews. She would have to form new habits now that she was pregnant. The diet soda she lived on would have to be curtailed. The wine they loved to share with a nice dinner would be replaced by sparkling water or juice. Her caffeine addiction was already giving her a massive headache. When the flight attendant passed by, she ordered hot chamomile. At least that would be a familiar selection.

The plane jolted and swayed. Ally sucked in a breath and tried to suppress the small squeal of terror that threatened to escape. She wasn't sure she could endure the long trip to Paris in six months, even if her doctor approved. She grappled with the seat rest and frantically searched for a bag to throw up in. *Please, please, Lord, don't let me be the one who barfs all over the plane, and two-hundred and thirty people remember me for smelling up the whole flight.*

Ally unlatched her seat belt and hurried toward the galley in desperation. She reached for the lavatory door, but it was occupied. An attendant in the galley way told her to be seated in a clipped voice, pointing to the illuminated seatbelt sign, as the plane lurched. Ally ignored her, grabbing at the garbage can attached to the beverage cart. As she heaved the contents of her Danish and orange juice into the can, she gave silent thanks for the curtain being drawn, separating her from other first-class guests. Only the two flight attendants saw her embarrassing action. The one who had scolded her now looked at her with sympathy and offered a napkin from the cart, holding the door to the lavatory open as the other passenger exited. Ally gratefully disappeared within.

As she left the small bathroom, the plane dipped and swayed as it hit another air pocket, sending Ally stumbling down the aisle to her seat. She had never been a religious person, except in the air. She placed her head against the cool double-paned, plastic window and silently made all the usual promises to her creator. If she could just land safely, she would give up swearing, eating sugar, complaining about her ex—but this time, it wasn't just for herself. She wanted this baby more than she had ever wanted anything before. The new life inside her filled a warm place in her heart that she never knew was empty. Ally wanted to hold this baby in her arms, protect it, and live with it in this world long enough to see grandchildren and possibly great-grandchildren.

Once the plane landed in New York, Ally reminded herself to stop by Jess's old apartment and settle the lease. It was broken when Jess had a mild stroke and needed more care. Ally paid for her sister's move to their mother's home, who now lived across the street from her cottage, and Ally hired a full-time worker to help attend Jess's needs. As the cardiologist predicted, the transplant hadn't been possible because of Jess's weak heart, and they relied upon the dialysis prolonging her dear sister's existence. Jess's life was stable for now, but Ally needed to plan more time to spend with her mother, aunt, and sisters before flying to Paris.

Jess could live another four to five years on dialysis if her heart endured, possibly more if science turned up new innovations. Ally hoped Jess would live to hold her new and only niece. *Niece, where did that come from?* Smiling broadly, Ally wondered if it was a mother's intuition. Suddenly she couldn't wait to see Nick again and tell him of their gift. She imagined them both in bed, pouring over baby names, and petting Ella and Harley's heads, tails thumping wildly. The dogs would love this baby.

A horn blared, shocking Ally back to reality. She was lost in her thoughts and had almost stepped in front of a public transit bus. Chills ran down her spine. How could she be so casual after what happened in New York last time? Nick visiting her in the hospital was the only good that came from the accident. Did she have pregnancy brain already? Rebecca had complained of it often, losing keys or her cell phone, staring at the fridge for ten minutes, wondering why in the world she was in the kitchen. She had also misplaced important gallery sheets, having no idea what shipments had arrived or what they were still waiting for half of the time she carried Andy. Oh, dear, Ally didn't have time to be lost in the convoluted maze of her mind. She had to get to the gallery, or she was going to be late for her meeting.

Hailing a cab, she made her way to Nineteenth Street and hurried up the stairs to the second floor. She was happy for once that she didn't have to take a crowded elevator to the top of some high-rise. Ally had been to the top of the John Hancock Tower once when she was in Chicago, shortly before the terror attacks of nine-eleven. As she had sat there, sipping champagne, she imagined a plane flying into the building. When she went home, Ally painted a whole series of art she thought would be great for a show. It was eerie when she put them into storage after the event happened just a few months later. There was no way that she would show them in the aftermath of such a tragedy. Who would believe she had painted it before the event?

As the door opened to Rebecca's office, Ally raced in, almost knocking over the man coming out. She noticed his tailored Armani suit and leather attaché case as she inhaled his amazing cologne. She identified the scent before she recognized the attractive man.

"Louis?" She heard her own breathless voice and then blushed suddenly under his intense stare.

"I didn't know you were here. I was just here to see Rebecca about…" His voice trailed off as he seemed to forget what he was saying. He looked back toward Rebecca's office.

"I, uh, am late for a meeting. She didn't mention I was coming?" Ally shook her head, trying to cover up her silly question. "I'm sorry, how could you know? I mean, why would she tell you?" She raised a hand to her new shoulder-length hair, self-consciously stroking the ends.

"You cut your hair." Louis's gaze held hers, and the energy that emanated between them became palpable. Ally tried to break the trance. She was engaged to Nick. She loved Nick. She was going to have Nick's baby.

"Yes, it's hot in Texas. Too much upkeep with all the demands for new paintings." She smiled, trying to keep things light. Her gaze lingered on his face then looked over his shoulder toward Rebecca, who was approaching. "I, uh, gotta go. Are you staying in the city?" She didn't know why she had asked, except for politeness.

"Yes, at my aunt's. She—" He paused. "She passed away a few days ago. I'm here with matters dealing with her estate." His eyes were dark, and it was then that Ally could see the circles of grief that smudged the sensitive hollows beneath his eyes.

"I am so sorry, Louis. I had no idea." She didn't know what else to say. Ally really did care about this special young man who had breezed into her life and opened her imagination. He'd given her the ability to explore love again. She knew she had hurt him when she returned to Texas and started seeing Nick. Ally didn't regret the more-mature relationship and the growing commitment she had, but she did regret hurting someone decent that she cared about. Her current situation fit her life, her age, and now her future. She couldn't apologize for her choices, but she felt the need to apologize for hurting him. "Do you have time for a drink later? Maybe we could catch up," she asked.

"That would be great." His eyes lit up, and for a moment, they shone with interest, despite his grief. Ally didn't know how to downplay the invitation without further rubbing salt into the wound. She decided to let it go for now and arranged to meet with him later. She would tell him of her engagement then. Or maybe she wouldn't have to mention anything but just resume as old friends to say goodbye. He did live a continent away.

After her meeting with Rebecca, Marcel, and the Paris agent, Ally went back to the hotel where she had agreed to meet Louis, drawing a hot bath in her suite. The trip was a short one, and she would be back on a flight tomorrow afternoon. Toweling dry, she reached for the luxurious Bulgari lotion provided by the hotel. She loved their designer soap and kept it in her own bath at home. A pang of guilt flitted over her as she sprayed the expensive perfume on her neck and wrist and swiped sheer lip gloss over her full bottom lip. She reasoned that she would wear lipstick even if she were meeting Marcel at the bar, and Marcel was gay. It was purely personal pride in one's toilette that made her brush her hair to a high gloss and rub oil over her calves. It wasn't like she was going to bed with anyone. She was pregnant for heaven's sake.

Her phone vibrated on the hotel nightstand, and she reached to observe the text. It was a pic of Harley, Ella, and Nick.

Great selfie! Ally texted back.

It was Ella's idea. She misses you.

Be home soon, Ally responded. *Going down to the bar for a bite to eat with an old friend. Don't worry, I'll be in bed soon. I want to be at the airport early for my flight tomorrow. Don't want to miss it.*

Okay. Luv U. Nick sent back.

U2. Ally smiled with warmth as she pressed the send button and tossed her cell in her purse.

She knew it was odd that she hadn't actually spelled out love, but he knew that she did love him. Ally had to shake off the moment of guilt. She wasn't doing anything wrong. She was making amends to a relationship that needed closure, and she didn't need to tell Nick every detail of her life. She said she was meeting someone, and so she was. No big deal. She would tell him about the drink with Louis when she got home.

She grabbed the small leather handbag off the entry table and took the elevator to the lounge. Louis was sitting at the bar. His Armani suit and shiny shoes made him look like a classic male model for a designer catalog. It was surprising a man that good looking and fashionably in tune was straight, but he exuded the classic male elegance only seen in old movies. She smiled as he stood to greet her.

"I'm so glad you are here," Louis said, beaming.

"Me too. I mean, I'm really sorry about your aunt. I hope you aren't alone dealing with all the details." Ally's voice shimmered with sincerity.

"I'm not alone. You are here. What will you have?" He looked back at the bar, picking over options for her, then finally settled on one. "I know, let's have champagne! The best for the best," he proclaimed as he took her hand and kissed it.

"Thank you, Louis, but I'll just have cranberry and sprite." He ignored her, insisting to the bartender they would have the best bottle of champagne. She took the seat offered and sipped on sparkling water while they waited for the glasses and bucket of ice to be set up. She should have told him already, but his face was lit with such happiness that she didn't want to ruin the evening ahead. One glass of champagne would not hurt the baby if she just sipped it.

Time passed by so easily that she lost track of it in their shared stories and laughter. Louis was charming, engaging, and she had forgotten how much she enjoyed his company. The bar was nearing its closing hour as patrons wandered away. Ally smiled at Louis and stood to say good night. She faltered when she stood, feeling lightheaded. Louis caught her and steadied her against him.

"I think maybe the bubbles have affected you, no?" His French accent was adorable.

She smiled up at him. "I'm okay." She hated to tell him she hadn't drunk more than a few sips. Through the laughter and conversation, he never seemed to notice her ever-full glass.

"I'll walk you to your room. There are a lot of unsavory characters in the corridors. I need to know you are safe."

His eyes belied his intentions, and Ally tried to tamp down her reaction to his light charm. Louis had been her lover, and she adored him. She couldn't tell her body not to react, but she could tell her mind. Ally loved Nick, so nothing would happen tonight. She was going to tell Louis right then, but the bartender interrupted, thanking them for the generous tip. The place was too public. She decided to let him walk her to her room and tell him there. She let his arm slide firmly around her waist, steadying her to the elevator just outside the lounge. She did feel a little unsteady walking across the polished floors in high heels. The ride to the twenty-first floor was quiet, and Louis's hand slid down, reaching for her bottom. Ally smiled at him as she evaded his effort, stepping forward as the elevator doors slid open. She would tell him in the room.

Ally opened the suite that was similar to the one they had first made love in, and she invited him into the sitting area. "Look, I don't want you to get the wrong idea—" Her words were cut off as he spun her around and took her lips with his. Her arms grasped him in a reaction to steady herself. His lips moved hungrily over hers, and she was overwhelmed for a moment with the surprise of his sudden ardor. She tasted the champagne on his lips and remembered that the bottle was empty when they left the bar. Louis was probably a little tipsy.

She clasped his arm harder and pushed away. "Louis, I can't. I'm pregnant."

His face crumpled in confusion, then his eyes widened, reawakening.

"You're having a baby?" His voice trembled with excitement. "Is it...?" His words trailed off. "But why, why wouldn't you tell me?"

It had been six months or more since they had made love, surely he didn't think it was his, with her still flat stomach. Ally watched as other possibilities crossed his features.

She quickly sought to clear things up. "It's Nick's. We planned it—sort of. We're getting married." In a wan display, she lifted her hand, showing her engagement ring. Ally never wanted to hurt Louis, and now she had done it twice. She had to smooth things over. It wasn't fair to tug at his emotions when he was putting his aunt to rest.

"I thought it was a cocktail ring. Women always wear sparkly things. I've given up wondering what status they're trying to portray. And, you married. There hasn't been enough time for someone to steal your heart."

His words dripped with hope, but his eyes shone with regret. "I shouldn't have let you slip away.

"I'm sorry, Louis. I didn't mean to hurt you or to tell you this way. I just didn't want you to be alone in the city without a friend tonight. We are friends, aren't we?" Ally moaned at her own fumbled attempts at reassurance. Who was she kidding? It wasn't like she could see Louis visiting her and Nick in Austin, all of them in her living room, watching the baby play. "I'm so sorry. This was selfish of me. I wanted to enjoy this night. I love the time that we spent together, and I didn't want to let you go without an evening to remember you by. I truly am sorry for your loss. I should have told you earlier." Ally pressed both of her hands to her cheeks like she was watching her own personal horror movie.

Louis stood staring at her, dazed by the excitement moments ago and confused by too much champagne. She saw a multitude of emotions cross his features before he found the words he wanted to say to her. "I love you, Ally. I want to be angry with you right now, and I *am* hurt deeply that you love another. I would have moved here for you. I would have married you. I would love to be the father of your child—" He paused in thought with his hands shoved in his trouser pockets. "—but alas, I am not." He moved to her and tilted her chin. One hand reached for her and rested on her waist in a light, endearing clasp. "I am happy we had this night. I needed to see you, and if you are happy, then I am happy for you and your new life. If you ever need me, I will be here." He leaned forward and kissed her gently, a soft press of his lips to hers, then he walked to the door, pulled the latch, and walked out of her life.

Ally gripped the credenza as she had so long ago. A tear slid down her cheek. That night had turned out differently. Life had changed irreversibly, and she would be a mother soon.

CHAPTER 18

Soledad sat on the windowsill, watching Ally swim through the wake of Louis's last words. She had wondered how far this night would go and felt a little guilty about not channeling to Ally as the night plunged deeper into possibilities of betrayal. It wasn't her job to guide Ally away from love or mistakes in love. What if Louis was Ally's soulmate or Travis? Soledad's job was to protect Ally from harm and to help her pass through the obstacles that inhibited her soul. Louis's words were heartfelt, leaving Soledad wondering if Ally wasn't settling for a good life with Nick when she could have a soulmate life with Louis.

As Ally slinked to the bathroom to brush her teeth and then settle into bed, Soledad contemplated her own existence throughout time and the multitude of lives she could remember shades of living. Only Onegan had made her complete. She looked forward to her next existence with him and prayed it wouldn't be too many lives between their reunion. It occurred to her during this contemplation that just because she knew of only one soulmate for her, it didn't mean that the occurrence was absolute for others. Maybe Onegan was Ally's soulmate too. Maybe Louis and Travis were, as well. Soledad knew very little of the energy sphere she belonged to. The cyclical birth to life and afterlife was an ongoing circle that provided knowledge from experience. Maybe she would know another soulmate over time. It was a mind-boggling and undesirable thought. She pushed it away and tried to focus on her charge. Her *two* charges. She could hear the baby's heartbeat and envisioned it growing steadily within Ally's womb.

Soledad remembered a song of another time and place. She sang it to Ally and the baby in Italian the way she remembered singing it to her own child so long ago. Her connection to her ward grew stronger each day. As Ally drifted to sleep in the soft white bedding. Soledad felt Ally's energy relax as she dozed in and out of slumber. The lines that had creased her brow smoothed, and she looked like a younger woman in the large hotel bed. Soledad channeled positive energy for the baby to grow. Only the best for the ones she loved.

A week had passed since Nick had picked her up from the airport and taken her to lunch. When she told him their exciting news, he had laughed with joy, picking her up and squeezing her in a bear-hug. He was so happy they were going to have a baby that she left out the details of her trip and Louis back in New York. She and Nick had plans to have dinner in Houston tonight and visit a friend's art show. The fourth-largest city in the US had amazing food and a late-night atmosphere that was filled with the young, trendy vibes of a multicultural city. She loved visiting the museums and seeing operas there, but tonight was more of a special getaway for her and Nick.

Enjoying Mediterranean food on an elevated terrace, that overflowed with botanical greenery, made Ally feel carefree. Nick's first instinct was to order a bottle of champagne for the occasion, but when she cleared her throat, he smiled and ordered a single beer and sparkling water for the table. The waiter had an accent, and though it wasn't French, his dark hair and good looks made her think of Louis. She didn't want to ruin their perfect evening, but she didn't want to have any secrets between them. Ally let him enjoy his lager as she filled him in on details of the Paris show, Rebecca, and Marcel. They laughed over episodes between Ella and Harley's bone-hiding game. Apparently, Nick found toys in the pantry and an old steak bone under his pillow. It was sweet how much they loved Nick and even more amazing how much he loved them.

"I met Louis in New York—" She paused, surprising herself at her sudden declaration. She sat on her hands, waiting for his reaction.

"Oh?" His eyebrows rose, but he waited patiently for her to continue.

"Yes, he was at the gallery talking to Rebecca about shipping some things of his aunt's. She passed away."

"I'm sorry to hear that. He must be upset." Nick's words were sincere, but the light in his eye told her he was waiting for more.

"I asked him to have a drink." Ally hated the sound of her own voice. She sounded like she was in a confessional booth. She sounded guilty.

Nick shifted in his chair, showing his discomfort with the course of their conversation.

"It was nothing. I mean, nothing happened or anything. It's just that I wanted to tell you is all." Ally felt parched. Reaching for her glass, she filled it and squeezed a lime into the fizzy water. Damn, she needed a drink. It would be a long nine months.

"You seem uncomfortable," was all he said. It was all he needed to say.

"Yes, I guess I feel a little guilty, because he was my lover, and I enjoyed seeing him, and he kissed me before I could stop him." Ally looked self-conscious as she scanned the other tables. Nick looked angry.

"Did you kiss him back? Did you sleep with him, Ally?" Nick's voice was strained but calm.

"Yes, no! I mean, when Louis kissed me, it caught me by surprise, but I stopped him and told him about us. I told him we were having a baby, that we were in love and getting married." She smiled at him. At that moment, she could feel that her heart was in her eyes. There was no confusion. She knew what she wanted.

"Where did he kiss you?" Nick's voice was still firm.

"He walked me to my room. I didn't feel like it was the right thing to say in the hotel bar. It seems silly now, I know, but I didn't intend for anything to happen. *Nothing happened!*" she corrected with haste. "I love you, Nick. I sent him away. I was just saying goodbye." Ally reached across the table and squeezed his hand, pleading for his understanding.

"It's okay, Ally. I understand. You told me about Louis, and I know sometimes it is important to say goodbye. The fact that you're telling me says you're honest, and I appreciate it." He waved to the waiter, who brought another drink for them both. "Just remember this episode when I have a similar situation with Gloria Vandere." His smile was wicked. The adorable cleft in his chin made her want to kiss him over the table.

"Gloria Vandere may have every man in America by the crux of his pants, and every super-model worried she will steal the spotlight, but she can't have you, Nick Carpelli. I won't let her." Ally stood slightly, bending over the table to claim him with her lips. They both laughed. The mood was officially lightened, and they finished their dinner with a massive crème-filled sweet cake and hot tea.

"If I continue eating like this, the baby will be huge, and I will be obese," Ally complained, leaning back and patting her belly.

"If I continue to help you eat like this, we will all be fat and sassy."

Nick stared into the darkened sky. The reflection of the wavering candle in his eyes made Ally wonder if he had any doubts or ghosts of his own to say goodbye to. She had never asked him about past loves or relationships. She had never wanted to talk about her own failed marriage. She would ask him someday, but not now. She wanted to meet Jody Love. Her friend was having his first showing, and she had promised to be there for support.

Jody Love's exhibit was not going as Ally had hoped for her dear friend. His art was new, and she thought he had amazing potential, but the canvases were arranged all wrong, making it hard to form a progression through the artist's thoughts. The turnout was less than favorable, and there weren't many buyers in the crowd. Free champagne seemed to be the main draw, and the show was scheduled too late. The location was close to a trendy night club down the road. She and Nick stood in front of a lifelike bleeding heart in thoughtful silence.

"Is it supposed to be dripping like that?" Nick asked, motioning with his glass to the dripping wall. Fishing line with globs of red paint coating its surface protruded toward the tiled floor. A pan of wet red paint sat below.

Ally sipped her ginger ale. "Um, yes. I believe it is."

"So, the person who buys it—they get the sludge pan, too?"

Ally tried not to giggle at the preposterous, yet valid, question. "Shh!" She hushed her soon-to-be husband and father of her child. How was she to introduce him? The question was answered by Jody Love as he extended a hand to Nick.

"Hi, I'm Ally's baby-daddy." Nick shamelessly grinned at her.

Jody beamed with pleasure. "Oh, my goodness! She told me you had proposed, but not that you were already having a family," he tsked.

"This is my fiancé and soon-to-be father of my child, but it was somewhat planned. Due to my aging eggs, we decided to put our lives on rush order," she quipped. "How is the show?" She mentally kicked herself for asking.

"It's not good, I'm afraid." Jody winced. "To everyone else, it's *fabulous*! But you, Ally, you are a true friend and a professional. I'm sure it's obvious that it sucks." He blew out the last word with a deep sigh, one hand on his hip while the other waved in the air.

Ally smiled and pouted at the same time. Nothing ever got Jody down, not even when he came out of the closet in college, and his family disowned him. It had been more heartbreaking for her than him. He never shed a tear, and instead claimed he was adopted, and that his real family was from the moon. She always applauded his ability to make lemonade. This was one of those times, and she was determined to help with the show if she could.

"I can help, but you will have to let me talk to the gallery director. We need to move a few things. What kind of advertising has he done? Wait, forget that, it's too late to put ads out for something that's already open." Ally saw three twenty-something girls walk in with mini sequined dresses and stiletto heels that they hadn't learned to walk in yet. She abruptly left Jody with Nick. After a few minutes of conversing with the three beauties, the girls returned with her.

"Jody, this is Amber, Anna, and Kat. They are your new marketers. They will be handing out fliers near all the elite hotels and night clubs in town tonight and to the hospital reception desk, to spread the word amongst the staff. Nurses and doctors love free booze, and they have the paychecks to pay for good art. The girls will hit the business district tomorrow afternoon." Ally tapped at her phone a few minutes while Jody chatted with the girls. "Get the fliers from the office and load them up, Jody. Girls, if you do this job right, and we get enough street traffic, you'll get an extra one-hundred-dollar bonus. I've just texted you a list of the top ten hotels in the city and the addresses. Keep all transit receipts, and you'll be reimbursed by me." She tapped at the phone once more. "Jody, my sister just sent out a social media blast. She has ten thousand followers in her Twitter account alone, so I think things should turn around by tomorrow night." She beamed at Jody as he lit up with surprise and excitement.

"*Oh. My. God!*" He exclaimed then hugged her tight. Then his hands flew to his mouth as he gasped. "You are the best-est ever, but, Ally, what did you promise to pay them? I haven't sold a painting yet, and what if I don't sell any?"

"You just did, my friend." Nick handed him the yellow slip of paper showing the purchase of Bleeding Heart III for a whopping one thousand dollars. Jody danced around in a circle doing his infamous happy dance. Ally appraised her thoughtful and very generous soon-to-be husband. She hadn't asked him to do it, but she had planned to do the same. It was great that he was on board with helping a young, struggling artist and friend. When Jody moved on to find the gallery manager and greet other guests, Ally put her arms around Nick, hugging him tight.

"You are the best thing that has ever happened to me." She kissed him passionately, not caring about the older couple gaping at them nearby.

"So where will we hang this Bleeding Heart III? Do you think Ella and Harley might lap up the sludge tray?" An image of Ella chasing Harley with bloody fishing wires trailing out of her mouth made Ally giggle.

"I think it should be hung in your office." She smiled. Her eyes danced with mischief.

"At work?" Nick blanched.

Ally smiled, matter-of-fact, "At home. Every man needs an office or a mancave." She lingered, still caught in his arms.

"Where? My stuff is still in storage, and your place is out of room."

"I've been thinking about that. When the baby comes, we will need more space, and you can't live out of storage forever. Maybe we should buy a place together."

"You'd give up your cottage for me?" Nick's voice was soft. He knew how much she loved the property.

"I would give up everything for you." She knew it was sappy overload, but it was true. In that moment, standing there in his arms, she felt like she would move heaven and earth to be with him always.

"Why don't we build? I mean add on. My friend Jason is an architect, and I know how much you love your place. I love it too. Let's just expand." Nick's excitement was infectious. He seemed to always know the right thing to say. It was the perfect answer to their space issue, and by building, they could accommodate all their needs.

"You are a genius! That's exactly what we should do. Then we can have it all." She smiled, hugging him again.

Nick's breath was warm against her ear. "I already have everything I need, right here."

The birth was only a few months away, and their wedding had come and gone. They were married by a justice of the peace in a small park setting with just a few of their closest friends and family. Marcel and Rebecca had flown in. Jody had made a success of his first show and wanted to thank Ally and Nick for their help. He knew a friend who knew a friend who opened their opulent lake house for them, and he footed the bill for a catered dinner for two during their stay. The honeymoon in Tahoe was perfect. Now she had a second chance at happiness with Nick and their unborn child.

It warmed Ally to see Jess at the kitchen table, plucking away at the computer screen. Her prickly attitude had subsided after her physician prescribed a different anti-depressant. Ally didn't know how someone lived with the knowledge they could die any day—or best-case scenario, live just a few short years. As the saying went, *none of us are getting out of here alive*. Ally knew that life held no promises for anyone, and that made her emotional in her hormonal state. She never worried so much about her own expiration date until she became pregnant.

Jess's attitude had really turned around, and Ally was thankful for the helping hand. Her sister was in charge of the social media for Ally's artwork and a few others who had formed an aspiring artist group at the gallery. Jess was an internet guru, and Ally had to admit she was selling more paintings than ever. She was low on inventory and didn't have enough time to paint with all the doctors' appointments, traveling, contractors coming in and out, plus the menagerie of family. Mom and Aunt Rose were forever underfoot. They lived in the house across the street so that they could all help each other with Jess's dialysis appointments and see Alyssa more frequently. It was working well, but the distractions were too much.

"Ally, you have Gunther in room one, Nick on line three, and Mom wants to know what you are planning for lunch." Jess never looked up as she clicked away at her laptop and then her cell phone. She was apparently a great multitasker, unlike Ally.

"Room one?"

"The living room. I dubbed it room one because that's where all the contractors stand and wait until you take them to room two, the kitchen, and then room three, which is actually just a bunch of stakes out on the grass around the studio." Jess reached for a plate of cookies in the center of the table as she stared with interest at the computer screen.

Ally rolled her eyes and moved to the living room to tell the contractor to meet her outside. She usually invited them to the kitchen for a beverage to be polite, but she wasn't feeling polite today. They were taking too long, and nothing was getting done. The last guy asked her for more money before they even broke ground. She canceled the deposit before he could cash it and started more interviews. Nick's friend had been swamped, so finding a reputable contractor was difficult.

"I'm sorry, baby, it's not even noon, and I swear, I think I'm losing it!" she said, answering the old landline in the office. Not many people had home phones anymore, but it was necessary for Jess's alert button to work in case of an emergency. They had one put in both her and her mother's homes.

"Sorry to call you at the house. I know you are busy, but you weren't picking up your cell, and I got worried."

"Oh, sorry. Marcel is flying in to see the preliminary selections, and I'm not ready. Mom and Aunt Rose are driving me crazy wanting to go out to lunch, and I need a Calgon break!"

"Calgon break?" Nick asked, perplexed.

"You know, vintage commercial. 'Calgon, take me away.'" Silence met her on the other end of the line. "Sorry, honey, I haven't got time to explain. It's something my mom used to say all the time. Ask her at dinner."

"Well, that's what I was calling about. I have to work late tonight. You guys will have to enjoy dinner without me."

She hoped she heard the disappointment in his voice and that he wasn't relieved to miss the weekly family dinner. She felt guilty that so much of their alone time had been consumed by work and family obligations. She never hid that part of her life before they married, but she sometimes wondered if he felt put upon. He knew Jess's health issues better than most, so she hoped he understood.

"No worries. Ella, Harley, and I will catch you later in the bedroom." She made an effort to make her voice sound sexy, then realized she mentioned the dogs. *Oh hell.*

"Room six!" Jess called out, cackling.

"What was that?" Nick asked.

"Nothing, just Jess feeling very much at home with her new brother-in-law. Take care, sweetie. See you tonight." Ally made a kissing noise into the receiver and hung up the cordless phone. Besides the contractor, her mother, Rose, and Jess, she needed to go out for dog food and a few grocery items. She would settle everyone's issues and then drive to town.

CHAPTER 19

The farmers market was closed, so Ally had to rely on the local grocery chain. She was trying to go vegan, but it was rather hard when you were pregnant and eating for two, plus everyone in her house loved red meat, including Ella and Harley. She imagined how she might talk them out of their venison kibble or duck-fat hotdog treats. Smiling at the thought, she parked the car and headed into the upscale pet supply store. Her dogs were spoiled rotten, but she never forgot about the strays. While shopping, she picked up an extra bag of dog food and put it in the donation bin by the door before exiting. As she loaded the items from her cart into the Jeep, she got a sudden, wet nudge in the rear by an over-friendly dog nose. She turned around in surprise, laughing at the black lab.

"Hey, I know you, big boy," she gasped.

Travis smiled, surprised. "Oh, hey, sorry, Ally. I didn't know it was you!"

Her eyebrows rose in mock offense. "So, you let Jake run around groping women you don't know?"

"No, I mean, I couldn't catch his leash in time, and I had no idea it was you. Of course, this now gives me a great idea about how to meet women," He waggled his brows, and she laughed, wagging her finger at them both. "Um, it's good to see you. When did you—I mean, when are you due?"

"You're a brave man for asking that. Some men ask women who are not pregnant that very question and get punched," she teased.

"I think I'm safe on this one. You are as tiny as ever everywhere else. Who's the lucky guy?" She detected a little sullenness in his soft voice, and it made her think of another she had cared about but let go.

"Nick Carpelli. He was my sister's doctor in New York and then mine. Long story. I met him after you left New York," she finished with an awkward pause then rushed on. "Baby's due in three months."

"Well, congratulations." Travis's smile was genuine, and she was happy it hadn't been too weird. She had wanted to say good-bye to him in person, but she had delayed, and time passed, making it awkward to call him back.

"Hey, I'm sorry about after New York. I should have called you back. Things were just…complicated." She pressed her lips together in an uneasy smile. She never told him about Louis or the accident.

"It's okay, Ally. It wasn't in the stars. Maybe in another life. It was my mistake and my loss." He paused, looking at her like he was trying to imprint her features in his mind so he would never forget.

He suddenly winked. Pulling Jake's leash, they headed toward the store and out of Ally's life. Endings could be subtle and sad, but she felt okay about saying goodbye this time. She felt a lurch in her stomach from the girl she now knew she carried. Swirls of elation, she supposed. Clearing the conscience was good for them both. Now to get home with duck-fat hotdog treats and everyone would be happy.

Ally lay in bed that evening with Ella at her feet and Harley warming her stomach under the covers. Her little dust mop of a dog was a burrower. Ally thought of the day she rescued Harley. It was the day she met Travis. For all the heartache she'd suffered from her many years married to Justin, Travis had helped her to move on. She had to thank him for that. It was the titillation of what a good relationship might be like that moved her forward. His masculine energy was still there when she saw him today, and she wondered what might have happened between them if she hadn't met Nick. Harley's paws pushed against her thigh. His little claws were digging into her sensitive flesh as he wiggled in a dream. A small bark came from under the covers, and Ally smiled. *Chasing rabbits?* She looked at the digital clock on her phone display that told her it was almost midnight, and she wondered how late Nick would be.

"Yes, Harley, you're right. Life keeps moving forward, and there isn't much time to look back." She gently rolled the small pooch over so his claws faced her husband's side of the bed. She laughed to herself, remembering Nick's complaint of Harley puncturing his briefs during one of his night-time stretches. The little guy liked to stretch and flex his paws against his bed partner's rump on many occasions. Ally made a mental note to stop by the men's store downtown to pick up a few pairs of the boxers Nick liked to wear.

Jess, Mom, and Aunt Rose were going to see a movie tomorrow, so Ally would have time to paint. She felt butterflies in her stomach at the thought of time alone. Harley came out of the blankets, panting and flopped across the top of the duvet. The baby must have disturbed him. When Ally was happy or excited about something, the baby liked to kick. Ally wondered what Ella and Harley would think of their new family addition. She would have to watch that Ella didn't sit on the infant or that Harley didn't clean her face of cookies every available chance.

Ally didn't remember Nick coming to bed. She opened one eye slowly to the natural light pouring through the bedroom window, and the lamp on the nightstand was turned off. She stretched out her arm. Nick's side of the bed was cold and empty, and Ally could see the indent of where his head had lain. Harley sat patiently staring, waiting for her to open both eyes. His tail thumped wildly, and she decided to give in. He danced in a circle then crawled on top of her to do the morning kiss ritual. Ella patiently waited by the side of the bed with a ball in her mouth, anxious for Ally to walk them outside.

Jess was in her usual spot at the end of the kitchen table, and Ally could hear Aunt Rose talking on the phone in the office.

"Where's Nick?" Ally inquired as she reached to fill the tea kettle.

"Don't know," Jess said around a bite of cinnamon roll.

Ally rolled her eyes heavenward, knowing any diet lecture would fall on deaf ears and ruin both of their days. Jess would never change, and Ally just sounded like a nag when she tried to help. She was tired of cooking healthy meals that were discarded or humoring Jess by ordering pizza. She was between a rock and a hard place, but she didn't think it was fair that they all give up so much of their lives to help Jess when Jess wouldn't help herself. They had gone over and over it before, but in the end, Ally was the self-righteous, mean sister. She saw Jess as selfish and scared. Knowing she would be too, Ally took a deep breath, made her tea, and walked out to her studio.

The contractors had poured the concrete for the expansion the day before. Ally and Nick had originally wanted to double the existing building, but they purchased the lot that came up for sale next to them and were quadrupling their original blueprints. Ally nodded at the contractor as he directed the workers. It was now easy to see the project coming together. She paused for a moment, surveying the construction, and smiled at the life they would have. Nick was nowhere in sight, so she assumed he must have had an early morning.

The greater part of the day was spent sketching for a series she was doing on women with children. Life events always spun her into different creative modes, and her current pregnant state was no different. Rebecca posed with Andy for a few photos after a little cajoling. She was shy when it came to her portrait, but Ally explained it would be more about the feeling of motherhood than Rebecca's actual likeness. Ally had taken the photos on a separate trip to New York, not trusting anyone else to capture on film what she would reproduce on canvas. It had been another one-day visit that had her back home with Nick late the same evening. She hated all the time that their work separated them, but she tried to cut out any extra hours away.

This gallery exhibit would be her absolute favorite. She loved the curve of Rebecca's protective arm around her son. The soft roundness of the baby's cheek against his mother's breast. The picture looked Renaissance elegant yet could have been from any era. Others were a variation of modern and vintage. She wondered what her own child would look like and how it would feel in her arms. At present, she was beginning to feel uncomfortable and was anxious to bring the child into the world, out of her ever-growing belly. She was afraid, too, liking the sense of the child being safe, tucked away inside her. Once the baby was outside of her body, she couldn't protect it so easily. What about when she had to leave it with a sitter to fly to another country? Ally was momentarily lost in the many plots that could usurp the life of her child. The moment had her laying a fresh, broad canvas on the easel and sketching with coal in a flash of intensity.

Her hands were black, and her hair tangled in disarray as she finished the work that had heated her mind over the past few hours. Ella and Harley jumped from their beds, barking and turning in circles as Nick glided into the studio. She stopped, laying her charcoal pencils down, wanting to give him her entire attention. She felt like they were on a constant MIA list.

"Well, hello, stranger. Home for lunch, or has your shift ended early?" Ally flipped her hair back, so she could see better then rested one hand on her lower back to ease the tug of muscles pulling at her heavy abdomen.

"Lunch can wait. No one is home," he said, raising his eyebrows. "Where's the family?"

"Jess took Mom and Aunt Rose to see a chick-flick. I thought it was a great opportunity to catch up on some work." She smiled, showing him her newest addition to the mommy series. The canvas boasted a dark figure of a woman who was half lying on a table, hair strewn about her to hide her eyes, leaving the viewer to wonder if she was sleeping or dead. A cup of liquid sprayed over the table, seeping to the floor where a child lay on a blanket. It must have concerned Nick because he frowned.

"Is she dead or just exhausted?"

"I don't know. It's a mother's nightmare. I was thinking of all the things I would have to worry about once the child is born, and this is what came out." Ally stood, rubbing a hand at her brow, making a coal smudge where her fingers touched her smooth skin. "I think it's beautiful, and I feel better now."

"I guess this is your therapy." He smiled and pulled her into his arms, wiping away the smudge on her forehead. "My gorgeous, talented wife. I guess if I want to know what goes on behind those beautiful, sparkling eyes of yours, I have to study your paintings." He leaned down to kiss her softly and let his hands wander lower to caress her back. It had been a week since they made love, and it worried Ally that he didn't find her attractive in her fatted-calf state. He'd had more than a few late nights at the office, and she worried he would rather work than see her.

Many nights she wondered if maybe he picked up a cute nurse, and they were having a drink downtown after hours. Maybe he was telling the nurse all the woes of his newly married life. Ally knew the pregnancy hormones were making her crazy, but she was sane enough to keep her fears silent. Nick would surely think she was daft and dramatic.

His head dipped to the hollow of her neck, and he brushed his soft lips across the sensitive area below her ear as he steered her toward the Victorian couch. Washing all her fears away, he made slow, passionate love to her, showering her in caresses and assuring her of her motherly beauty. Sex continued to be amazing between them, but the assistance of the arms and back of the tall couch made it simpler in her condition. She felt awkward and clumsy most of the time, but she didn't feel that way in Nick's arms.

Ally eyed their reflection in the mirror on the adjacent wall. An erotic thrill darted through her at the scene of sexy art they created.

Her curved body was still toned and sleek. Her luminous skin shone in the streaks of sun that sprayed through the skylight. Her paint-specked hand laced through Nick's sandy, tousled hair as he kissed the back of her neck from his position behind her. Ally's head fell back against his shoulder, and she climaxed from the rhythmic movements of his hips and the quickening of his hand between her thighs. She held the arm and the back of the couch to assist her balance with her new weight. She begged him not to stop as she rolled through the crest of one orgasm and sped to the top of the next. Never so sexual before, Ally was pleased that Nick opened a new window in her life. He freed her from the chains of mistrust that previously bound her to reality.

Dazed in the aftermath of their lovemaking, Ally lay curled against her husband's chest, enjoying the smell of his skin and the beating of his heart. Nick loved her, and she loved him with all her heart. Maybe they always had loved. She wondered if he was her soulmate and if they had shared many lives together. A whimsical smile swept her face as she imagined him garbed in medieval armor astride a massive warhorse. She saw herself as a beautiful woman. A commoner with a little girl by her side. She was kissing him as he went off to war. The vision cleared, and her brow furrowed.

"What are you worrying yourself about, love?" Nick caressed her face, brushing the ebony locks away from her cheeks.

"I was imagining another life with you, me, and our child, but it was you with my Aunt Kat, and I was the child. Aunt Kat was the beautiful woman…" Her words trailed off as she tried to recall the flashing images.

He arched his eyebrows at her in mock surprise, tickling her side. "How kinky. I had no idea you had a daddy fetish."

She slapped at his hand and giggled at his lurid suggestion. "No, I'm serious. It was the strangest thing. My Aunt Kat was the artist who drowned herself when I was a child. She was beautiful and had so much to live for. When she lost her son, she went into a severe depression and took her life. Now that I'm carrying our child, I understand how tortured she must've been."

"I'm sure that must have been tough for her. And you. You were just a kid."

"I saw an angel once. It was before I met you when I was alone here and struggling to find a reason to get out of bed in the morning. I was going through a funk, I suppose, and I saw what could have been my Aunt Kat sitting on my bed like an ethereal angel. I felt her presence like I feel you next to me right now." She blinked up at him. Her eyes were filled with emotion. "Do you believe in angels, Nick? Do you believe in an afterlife, soulmates, working out our flaws until we get everything right?

"I don't know. I never thought about it, really. I was an altar boy, and I went to church every Sunday with my parents while I was growing up. I still go on Easter and Christmas so that my mom doesn't have a cow. Which brings up a subject we haven't discussed. Can we baptize the baby Catholic?"

He moved to a sitting position. She sensed a change in his demeanor. This was important to him.

"I don't know. I mean, I was Catholic until I was thirteen, and my mother told me I could choose. I'm not an atheist, but you know I don't think—" Ally had thought about it many times throughout her life, wondering what she believed. She still didn't know.

"But you were taught and allowed to make a choice. Our child should get to make that decision too. If you're honest with yourself, you will admit that the Bible has some great lessons to build character and moral sensitivity. You have to believe something greater than yourself to get by in this world. Why not Catholicism?"

Ally shuddered at the word. It sounded odd on Nick's tongue. He had never been an advocate of religion before. Dread crept over her. *Is this something we will actually fight about?* She had no idea he was so passionate about religion. It made her wonder what else she didn't know about her husband. "Are you serious about this? I'm not sure if I believe what I am hearing. You never touted Christianity before. The Bible tells women to take a back seat to men, and it tells a story of creation that is right out of a fairytale and look at all the things that are done in the name of organized religion." Standing up to dress, she shoved her arms through the painter's shirt and hastily pulled up the overalls she had been wearing.

"It also teaches about forgiveness, understanding, compassion toward others, loyalty, and a reason to be good in this life. I work at a hospital, Ally, and I have seen people die. I don't know what happens when we pass, but if I didn't think there was anything after, what would be the point in living?" His voice elevated as he reasoned with her.

"Us. Here. Now. That's the reason. You get what you get, and you make the best with what you have, and that's life!" Ally wasn't sure why she was so upset. She actually agreed with what he was saying, and she wasn't against baptizing their child. A small part of her still felt like it was their duty to give the child a choice. It needed some sort of protection in case she was wrong. She remembered a nice priest explaining all children went to limbo if they weren't baptized. Unless St. Augustine was right, and they went to hell. Her brows furrowed together as she dissected the ancient memories of her youthful days in catechism.

"Are you okay?" Nick was flustered, and she could tell he had no idea how to respond to her tirade. They didn't argue. They had never argued. It was the thing she loved about him most. If they disagreed, they negotiated or just agreed not to agree. It was simple.

"I'm sorry." Ally sighed and ran a hand through her hair, pulling it back from her forehead in a look she knew wasn't becoming. "I don't know what's come over me. I think it's not good to ponder the afterlife or death right now. I'm too hormonal." She ran her hands over her face in frustration. She twisted up the raven locks of her hair in a wide plastic clip, with the ends forming a paintbrush tail sticking out on top. She moved back to her canvas and started clearing the workspace for another sketch. Nick walked over, hugging her from behind. She placed his arms tighter around her middle, bringing him closer to her as she squeezed him back.

"I love you." He kissed the top of her head. "I'll see you later tonight."

Ally nodded as a tear slid down her cheek. The room seemed cold and empty when he left. She looked up at the skylight, and a cloud moved over the sun, casting the studio in moody gray. The hair lifted on her arms, and an emptiness drained her of their earlier passion. It was time for a walk. She grabbed the leashes off the hook and opened the door for Ella and Harley, who bolted across the yard and down to the front gate. She rounded them up and secured them to the metal clasps, so they could walk to the lake. She needed to blow the cobwebs from her mind, and the change of scenery would be good.

Soledad had disappeared when the couple took pleasure in the afternoon light. Sex was a spiritual thing when shared with the one you loved. It was sacred, and Soledad never trespassed on such a sharing of energy, but she reappeared when Ally mentioned Katia's name. Soledad didn't know how or why but presumed it was important that she hear about the vision.

Ally's senses were keen to the afterlife realm. She had lost her way with religion, but Soledad sensed her belief in God was strong. People were impassioned by their political and religious views, thinking theirs was the only way to believe. It was interesting that the embodied couldn't see a combined world that included all beliefs. Soledad didn't know any more than the embodied when it came to God, creation, and the afterlife, but who was to say the Christian God and Allah weren't one and the same? Maybe Jesus was a prophet, and maybe he was God himself. Reincarnation could coincide with Christianity. Maybe the multiple lives she embodied were to perfect her soul, to obtain the almighty heaven that so many religions believed in. She didn't know for sure. No one knew until they got to that moment and looked back on their experiences and finally understood. Soledad always envied the people who were grounded in their beliefs. At least they had the comfort of thinking they knew, even if they really didn't.

Soledad empathized with Ally, watching her march across the long blades of grass to the lake. Ally released the dogs. Ella's tail went round and round as Harley ran circles about her. The sky was moody, and the water reflected dull gray clouds over its luminous surface. Ally tossed the ball for Ella and Harley as they barked at the shore.

Soledad sensed the uneasiness of her ward in her pregnant state and wished to calm her and the baby. She sent warming currents of love and protection toward Ally and the unborn child. Drops of water began to poke holes in the flat surface of the lake, and Ally looked up at the sky. She smiled, and Soledad knew that her radiance had been felt. She followed them back through the sprinkling rain to the studio and watched as Ally sketched an amazing portrait of Onegan, Soledad, and Alitalia. Ally's soul name was close to her actual life name.

The canvas sketch was like a picture burned into Soledad's mind, but she hadn't known what she looked like in that life until seeing it through Ally's eyes. The only reflection she saw of herself in that life was her reflection in the water or a shiny piece of silver. She hadn't known she was so beautiful. Onegan was exactly as she remembered him, so handsome and young. It was the last time they were together as a family before she and Alitalia were killed. Soledad wondered if Onegan was killed in battle or if he returned to their starved, bruised corpses. She did not know.

Ally's sixth sense made her art flourish and her popularity grow. The passion that flowed from her mind to the canvas spoke volumes to the people who attended the galleries. She would be world-renowned at this rate, and what would that do to her life with Nick? Soledad fretted over her ward and wondered about the strains of marriage and parenting that might break Ally's fragile form. She had been unhappy for so long, and now that she was about to have everything she wanted, could she juggle the responsibilities? No one could have everything. It was not allowed. Soledad had never seen it or heard of it, except in fairytales.

CHAPTER 20

The house was empty when Ally returned from her studio. The air conditioning was too high, and a chill washed over her arms and face. She moved to adjust the temperature then went to the front window, glancing once more at the drive. Her mom's car was gone. Ally checked her watch and confirmed the time for them to return was past due. She meandered through the house, picking up coffee cups and a stray Kleenex off the table. She deposited the dishes into the sink and squirted soap into the hot running water. Staring at the foaming bubbles as she squeezed the sponge, Ally wondered where her family had gotten caught up.

Jess probably needed something from the pharmacy, or Aunt Rose wanted to tour the garden shop for the foxtail fern she had been hunting all over the city. Ella and Harley lay like floppy dust mops on the tile floor behind her, cooling off from their romp at the lake.

Ally hadn't heard from Nick since their earlier lovemaking and disagreement. She would apologize when he came home. She wanted everything for their baby, including christening. She would go through whatever steps it took to provide their child with all the protection it would need in the world. If she needed to hang a dream catcher over its crib and chant to the goddess naked at the lake every evening, she would. She needed to let Nick know she agreed to his request and just how much she loved him. Making the decision, she grabbed her keys. She wanted to see him now. If he worked overtime, she would be asleep when he got home. Ally had to tell him how much she loved him right then before the stress from earlier had time to seep into his brain, laying the first brick in the proverbial wall between them.

She valeted her car at the hospital, knowing it was too busy to find close parking. She didn't feel like waddling through the massive auto-filled garage when she just wanted to pop in to see Nick for a few minutes.

The sliding glass doors opened to the ER, and Ally waived at Maria, who was in charge of the front desk. The double doors buzzed as Ally was allowed through. She waded past the nurses and medical supply carts to the middle of the ward. She knew he was working in ER today but wasn't sure if he was with a patient or could be found in the small offices kept for the doctors. She stopped to ask a nurse, but then spied Nick wrapped in a woman's arms at the end of the hall. Shock and jealousy overwhelmed her as she forgot the nurse, who was explaining to her that Nick couldn't be bothered because an emergency code had just been called. Obviously, the code was being answered by someone else.

Angry and not knowing what to do, Ally started back toward the exit, but this time stopped in her tracks as she surveyed the lobby of the ER. "Mom, Aunt Rose?" Her voice cracked with silent questions.

Her mom stood up and began to sob. "She just went limp. I don't know what happened. I looked over, and she was out." Ally's mother shook her head.

"Was she having a reaction? Did you use the sugar pen?" Ally asked, referring to the emergency kit, the doctor had given Jess during the last nephrologist visit, in case she had a severe low blood sugar reaction. It was like an EpiPen, but you had to fill the syringe with liquid from one vial and inject it into the other vial before giving the shot. Ally knew her mother had gotten flustered before and injected Jess with plain water.

"I took her blood sugar, and it was fine. I don't know what was wrong, but we drove to the hospital, and they admitted her to the ER. They told us to wait here. We're waiting for a doctor to tell us she's okay." Her mother was visibly shaken as Aunt Rose patted her shoulder.

Ally turned back to the double doors marked ER as Nick walked through. Ally's anger was buried as fear bled through her veins, causing her to shake. It didn't take much to surmise the news. He looked haggard and sad. The unshed tears simmered behind the veil of a professional doctor coming to inform the patient's family of an unfortunate event—an event that couldn't be changed. "Ally, I'm sorry—I'm so, so sorry—" His voice cracked as he wrapped her in his arms, holding her up from falling to her knees.

"How? Why?" She sobbed, but she knew the multitude of answers.

Jess had been living on borrowed time. She had a plethora of ailments due to her diabetes, and a string of bad habits that she indulged in for twenty or more years. Forty was too young for anyone to die, but Ally knew that people died younger. Lives filled with nutritious eating, regular exercise, and a bill of clean health often passed into the night without warning. They had known something would take Jess before any of them were ready, most of all, Jess. She had been on an upswing. Her diet wasn't perfect, but she had been trying harder to exercise, and the new job, helping artists with their social media, had given her a new purpose. It wasn't teaching, but it had made Jess happy.

Rose and her mother clung to each other, and then all of them grouped together as Nick explained that Jess's heart had given out. They had managed to revive her for an hour and put her on a ventilator, but she never regained consciousness. Nick explained that he was coming out to get them when Jess went into another cardiac arrest and died. There was nothing they could do to save her.

He walked their small family into a private room, so they could collect their emotions and grieve before going to see Jess's body. Ally felt a wave of panic surge over her. Jess couldn't be gone. She wanted to see her sister now. Their mother was afraid to see Jess's body. Aunt Rose sat with her while Ally rose to go with Nick. In the hall, outside the door, she could see the staff pulling small round stickers from Jess's chest as she watched through the small window.

"Who was the woman you were hugging in the hall?" Ally asked, never taking her eyes from the hospital bed Jess lay in. She looked like she was sleeping.

"What woman? I haven't been in the hall with anyone but you, Ally."

She felt his eyes on her, but she refused to look at him. Maybe a nurse friend was comforting him. As she dissected what she had actually seen, she realized the woman had her arms around him as he stood motionless. "It's okay, I guess you needed strength, and I wasn't here. I didn't know. I was coming to see you, and then I saw her with you—that's when I saw Mom and Rose."

"Ally, you aren't making any sense. There was no one in the hall with me. I've only seen Jess, you, and your family." His voice was soft, pleading.

Ally looked into his eyes and saw his sincerity. Maybe she imagined it. Her hormones were pushing her sanity to its limits. She entered the room as a nurse exited and held the door for them to enter.

"Jess, oh God, Jess." Ally's hand flew to her mouth, suppressing a sob as she lay over her sister's still form. "I'm not ready for this. We're not ready for this. You were supposed to stay until the baby was born. You promised."

It sounded so selfish, but it was all Ally could think of. Jess had been happy she was going to be an aunt and had told Ally repeatedly not to worry.

Jess said she would be around until after the baby arrived. She even bought the baby a fur coat and matching booties for the non-existent Texas winter.

Nick patted her back. He was helpless to know how to soothe her, but she didn't want to be soothed right now. She needed to cry to relieve the tension inside. The sister she had known all of her life, fought with, laughed with, and who drove her nuts, was now gone. Ally would never be able to tell her about the crazy things that had happened in her day. She would never again watch old movie marathons with her and Alyssa. She would never have a normal Christmas with family or call her on the phone to find the comfort that siblings did with one another. This day would mark her life forever, and Ally knew she would never see the sun shine quite so brightly again.

Tears rolled across her cheeks and onto Jess's hand as Ally sobbed herself into exhaustion. Nick nudged her softly and led her away. After pulling herself together, she joined her mother and Aunt Rose, who then took turns viewing Jess's body to say goodbye. Afterward, they made their way to the car that pulled up to the hospital ER. It was Alyssa's caregiver and friend of the family, Jane, who quietly drove the trio home. She served them hot tea and sandwiches before leaving to get Alyssa. It would be the hardest task of all to tell her younger sister. It wasn't right that she wasn't there to see Jess one last time, but Ally didn't think Alyssa could understand or bear the pain. Ally and Jess had always protected Alyssa from the brunt of bad news. Now, it was a burden that Ally would have to shoulder alone. She poured a shot of cognac in her tea and mentally prepared herself for Jane to return with Alyssa. They would all stay together this sad night, and over time, they would help each other to heal.

Soledad watched from the large beanbag chair with Harley and Ella. Ally fluttered through the kitchen, organizing the pantry and helped Jane make more tea. Soledad felt somewhat responsible for the sad, heavy atmosphere. She had seen the ugly black shadow kneel on top of Jess's bed and breathe in the last remains of her life, but there was nothing Soledad could do. She railed at the ugly form, but it had no substance she could attack. She wasn't supposed to interfere with other living souls or their fate. The malevolent entity looked at her with jagged black teeth, reminding her of her place in the in-between world. The dark demonic form howled at her with a deafening scream that only she could hear. It was horrifying, even to a soul of the spirit world. It reminded her that maybe worse realities existed. A lifetime or eternity trapped in that monster's clutches was terrifying. She didn't know if Jess would wake up to an advisor like Alekeen, or if she would be lost in the inky blackness of eternity.

Soledad was the one who hugged Nick. He had not felt or known her presence, but Ally saw her as if she were a part of reality. She was real in spirit, but not to the embodied. Soledad sat in wonder, knowing she had never had this type of soul-watching relationship before. Even in her disembodied state, she was still learning.

Soledad was past longing for Onegan the way she had her entire existence, now focusing only on his presence as Nick, Ally's husband. Her hug was an instinct to comfort herself. She was sure she wasn't present to him in this world. It was a kneejerk reaction that she immediately stopped once she sensed Ally's presence. It wasn't a purposeful act, she told herself. Surely there was a pardon for moments of grief. It was only a hug. Maybe she did it to ground herself after seeing the black demon take Jess's life. *Will there be an ethereal intervention to save Jess?*

Soledad sent Ally soothing vibrations of love and reassurance when Nick came in that evening, promising her of his amazing potential as a father. The result had a calming effect over Ally. She slept curled in his arms, and *the woman* who hugged him was never mentioned again. Soledad was sad for their loss as a family, but she had felt foreboding energy for months. She couldn't know what the damning event would be, but she knew Jess was a possibility. Her concern over Ally and the baby had been palpable. Anything could happen during a pregnancy, and losing this baby would be the end of Ally's spirit. Losing a sibling was also terrible. Soledad would be there for Ally and walk beside her through the darkness that she would dwell in for many months.

Jess had wanted to be cremated and surrounded by friends. The day of the actual cremation had been sad but beautiful. It was sunny with fluffy white clouds dotting the sky. The casket had been driven to the crematory with just Nick and Ally driving behind the hearse. Mom and Rose stayed behind with Alyssa. Ally wondered why her mother couldn't bear to ride with them, but she reminded herself that everyone grieved differently.

Ally had felt a little guilty over not purchasing the top-of-the-line coffin, but she knew Jess didn't want a fancy wooden casket to be buried in. She wanted to be cremated, and her ashes spread over Stonehenge. Ally would have to contact the site's operator and ask if it was allowed. She had joked with Jess about putting her ashes in her coat pocket with a nice sized hole and walking circles around the rocks, shaking her coat if they didn't allow her to spread the ashes there. She was mostly kidding. Jess mentioned a beach in Florida that would be just as desirable.

The next two months passed like a slow-moving picture. They delayed spreading Jess's ashes until they could set a date for a memorial in her honor. It wasn't easy to arrange so many busy New York schedules with other out-of-town family members. Ally was forced to answer phone calls to set up appointments with the banquet hall and accommodate many of Jess's friends who flew in for the service. She had to put her emotions on the back burner as she dealt with a florist, caterers, and hotel reservations. Who would have thought being incinerated would be so involved? She was amazed by the professional staff at the Good Faith Funeral Home and wondered how they could endure the daily routine of asking sensitive questions of their clients and dealing with death and dying continually.

The day of the memorial, people closest to Jess flew in from New York, and all of the extended family from Florida and other states attended. The hall looked like a wedding reception, overflowing with white flowers and tablecloths. Jess had said she didn't want a funeral but a dinner party with champagne instead. Fond stories were told, and lots of tears shed, but laughter was the overflowing sound of the night. Jess was loved, missed, and well-remembered. It was just what she would have wanted.

As with most terrible occurrences in life, time heals all wounds. It wasn't that she didn't miss or think of Jess. Her endless conversations with her family about the life of her sister wouldn't let her forget that there was a permanent hole in her heart. The wound would never heal, but life must go on, and there were others to think about.

Ally had gone through the motions and checked all the boxes during the months of grieving, but today was a day for herself. She had a doctor's appointment, then a manicure and pedicure. It was terrible that she couldn't reach her toes this late in the pregnancy. She really had to lay off the ice cream until the baby was born. Ally hadn't been a big fan of ice cream until about three months into carrying the baby. She didn't want pickles, but somehow sushi and Blue Bell's rocky road sounded great together. The request made Nick gag.

He'd screwed up his face with disgust. "Ice cream is for baseball, and sushi is for hot date nights. I'll take mine with a cold Sapporo or warm Sake, thank you very much." He'd laughed as she rubbed her stomach and made an "mm" sound.

Aunt Rose and Ally's mother were still underfoot most of the time. Their close proximity had been to share the caretaking of Jess, but now their company had become old hat. Ally liked having them around, bumbling through her pantry, or starting coffee in her house before the crack of dawn. In truth, she had never spent this much time with her mother since she left home at eighteen, and she was now glad they had time to reconnect. Once the baby came, Ally was sure she would need help.

Ally needed to address the fact that Nick needed a buffer. She couldn't expect him to want her family around every second. Ally bought a YMCA membership for them to use. Nick usually ran at the lake most days or liked to go out on a bike, but it was a good excuse to get her mom and aunt enrolled in some senior programs to keep them busy in their own lives and to make friends.

The gym membership worked like a charm. The house was free by nine in the morning for Ally to start her day. Aunt Rose had even met a man while playing bridge who she started dating. Ally could only hope that her mother could find the same luck.

The Paris trip was canceled as her due date was only a month away. Things with the gallery in France had not gone as smoothly as in New York. The director, Andre Loirie, pushed the opening date back too far for Ally to travel safely. She was secretly, or not so secretly, relieved. The shipments were still made on time, and Marcel was going to oversee the opening, so there wasn't much to worry about. She knew it was critical for the artist to be present at most showings, but she didn't need the money, and Marcel and Rebecca were financially set from all of the previous work. Ally would make it up to Mr. Loirie by giving him a larger cut of the profit and doing a special event in six months' time. Right now, she needed to focus on her health and the baby.

Ally put her cup of tea on the counter and walked to her studio. She ran her hand over the bamboo holders of soft brushes and jars of unopened paint. The canvas she had been working on as a gift to her husband was a self-portrait of her in full pregnancy. She stood nude in the painting except for the sky-blue sheet draped over her shoulder that slithered around her belly like a silk snake. She stood before an antique gilded mirror painted into the portrait. Nick's reflection was portrayed lying naked on a bed looking at her adoringly with tousled hair. It was a common view that she was fortunate to have emblazoned in her memory. How many wives could say the same? To her, it was her crowning masterpiece. She would give it to him at the baby's birth, which happened to be scheduled on his birthday. Ally was elated. She was a Libra, and two Leos would be a world of excitement. She knew it might be an issue when their daughter became a teen. Two lions roaring through her house might not be fun, but she was sure Nick could handle it. They would all love and laugh together. Life would be wonderful.

CHAPTER 21

It happened on a Wednesday, August the eighth. Ally grew worried because she was one week past her due date, and she had given Nick the birthday portrait on the first. It was a good sign. Eight was the symbol for new beginnings. Her doctor had assured her she was fine and said it was common for first-time mothers to be late delivering. Ally wanted to do a natural birth, but as the contractions became closer and the pain more intense, she threw holistic medicine to the wind and cried out for drugs. It was twelve hours of intense labor and more crying than Ally liked to admit, but the fruit of her labor was a seven-pound, eight-ounce baby girl that they named Jessica Soledad Carpelli. They would call her Sole—pronounced Soul-Lay—for the light she would bring to their lives.

"What made you think of Soledad? I love it, but where did it come from?" Nick asked her as she announced what she wanted to name their child a week before the birth. They agreed on Jessica months ago, but the middle name had bounced through many options with nothing that seemed to stick.

"It was the title of a Spanish book I saw at an estate sale last week. It called to me from the bottom of a pile in a cluttered office. I had to ask an old woman to get it for me because I couldn't bend down to pick it up." She patted her bloated tummy. "O Sole Mio," she sang the title of the book. "I also knew a girl that reminded me of my Aunt Katia back in college. Her name was Soledad, and we called her Sole. I always thought it sounded so warm and exotic. The name also comes from Our Lady of Solitude. I looked it up."

She didn't want to tell him the name came from a presence that had haunted her for the past couple of years. He would think she was crazy. With all the hormone-filled moments of the last nine months, she didn't need to spook him more. She didn't need to explain her chasing this feeling, thought, spirit, or whatever it was around corners, through rooms, on walks, or when she woke up. It was too hard to explain, but she knew this soul existed to protect her and the child. Ally wanted to name their child something warm and pay tribute to her guardian angel.

She was tired and longed for sleep. She smiled up at Nick, blinking her eyes and yawning. "I love you."

"I love you more," she heard as she drifted into slumber.

Soledad began to weep the moment she heard the child's name. She had walked with Ally for the past two years channeling protection and encouragement. The last two months since Jess's passing had been emotionally difficult for Ally, being given death and birth all at once. It would be hard to fully enjoy the gift of motherhood while mourning the loss of her sister. Ally's life was not tragic by any means. People could lose much more than one loved one, and many endured the loss of a marriage. Serious relationships often fizzled into an angry abyss, but once love was found again, the wounds healed.

Soledad had been committed to Ally loving Onegan with all her heart. She wanted Ally to be happy, and it was the only way Soledad could assist her soulmate in his life as well. Somewhere in the channeling, she must have released her own name. It was felt by Ally, and it thrilled Soledad to know she was heard, that she wasn't alone, that she hadn't failed in this life and possibly could live again. It seemed that she had helped Ally achieve this one goal of happiness, and now Soledad's soul-watching time was ending.

As Soledad pushed through the darkness, it felt like she was smothering. She had to get out of the tight space contracting around her. Bursting forth with a loud wail, she startled herself.

This new, embodied state wasn't comfortable. Swaddled in blankets, something gripped her head and pinched her navel cord. She squalled and felt blood surging to her face, threatening to steal breath from her now small, embodied form. She heard a familiar hush as she was bobbed up and down. Someone walked her around the room, and her discomfort ceased as she looked up into a face as old as time. It was not old in the wrinkled state of skin, but in the azure blue eyes that looked back at her. Onegan was with her, holding her and loving her more than Soledad could ever remember. He was elated by her birth and swore to protect her, proclaiming over and over again how pretty she was.

"Oh my, I carry her around for nine months, go through all the hours of labor, and she falls in love with you," Ally complained, laughing. "It is so not fair."

"She is our princess, but you are my queen," Nick proclaimed as he laid Soledad in Ally's arms and snuggled next to them on the narrow hospital bed. "I have enough love for you both, but I confess I will probably love one of you just a tad bit more," he teased.

Ally looked at him with pretend irritation then softened as tears shimmered in her turquoise eyes. "Just promise you will never leave us."

The dam opened, and Soledad's new family huddled together until her emotionally charged mother fell asleep. This would be a dream life for her. Her father and mother were souls she loved and were connected to eternally. A moment of fear passed over her small new form, and she shivered. She was so tiny, young, and already, she had so much to lose.

She felt her consciousness fading. It was inevitable in every embodied life, otherwise, a person couldn't live renewed. How could you love if you remembered all the love you shared and lost? How could you risk if you recalled the chances you took and failed? The embodied would walk around in perpetual fear if they could remember all the tragedies that befell them in all their previous existences. It was the reason the mental health centers and asylums were full, and the homeless walked the streets. It wasn't that they couldn't endure this life, it was that sometimes part of their subconscious remembered something horrible from the past. She was aware of her soul at this moment, as she would be after this life ended. She gripped the substance of her memories and tried to hold on, though she knew it was a losing battle. Before her first birthday, she would only have her name to remind her of the soul-watching time she shared with Ally. It would be okay. Onegan was hers for a lifetime, at least as a doting father. She would be loved.

Ally was growing bored at home with feedings, changings, and talking to herself. Soledad was the love of her life besides Nick, but she needed more. She hadn't felt like painting since the baby had come, and her mom and Aunt Rose were always rustling through the house. They were a blessing when she needed time to go to the grocery, but she was never alone, something that was essential to the moody artist. She felt ill-kempt with straggly hair that Soledad wound around her hands, and she still hadn't taken off the excess baby weight. Ally hadn't had time alone with friends or been out as an adult in ages. The truth was, she felt like a frump. She wanted to be out, but not in her pudgy state. She hadn't had a motorcycle ride in who knew how long, and Ella and Harley needed a hike on the trails.

Fall was near, but that didn't mean a lot in Texas. Ally prayed for a cold snap to move in and allow her to go out covered from head to toe. If her friends couldn't see the squish of her tummy, she could at least go to lunch without feeling self-conscious.

She knew she shouldn't be so shallow. Her friends didn't care that she was fifteen pounds overweight or that her breasts seeped milk into her granny-sized bra at inopportune moments. She turned down a few invitations, but it bugged her that her friends had fallen off the grid with the passing of the last few months. Maybe it was the loss of Jess and not knowing what to say or having a baby when most of her friends were single and gay. They weren't the baby type. Ally wasn't either until she fell in love with Nick and Sole.

Ally scrolled through her phone until she found the number of the sports therapist she visited after her accident. They were social media friends now, but she hadn't really had time to connect with him personally. She texted his business number to ask if he could take on a private paying client for fitness training. His response was immediate. He was available later that afternoon, so Ally agreed to meet him at his gym. He said she was welcome to attend his training sessions as his guest, but he encouraged her to get a membership for her own future health. Ally didn't bother explaining she had a YMCA membership. She could afford both.

Mom and Aunt Rose were only too happy to watch Sole and shooed her out of the house to start her new fitness regime. There were a few teasing comments about getting her figure back for Nick. The statements were all true, but she needed to do it for herself first. Nick would reap the rewards of her renewed womanly confidence. Ally took the top off her Jeep and drove through the sunlit curves by the lake into town. The popular, warehouse-sized gym had every piece of fitness equipment one could imagine. Rashid met her at the door, and a staff member walked them through a short tour.

"I won't always be around to hold your hand, Mrs. Carpelli," Rashid teased as he mounted the stationary bike next to her. "But today I will work with you, so you don't feel alone. I find it is important to have motivation. Does your husband like to work out?"

"He's a runner, and they have a small gym at the hospital that he sometimes does a little weight training in. We also have a family membership at the Y." She smiled at the way Rashid said Mrs. Carpelli. She would never get tired of hearing her name linked to Nick's. "But don't worry, I can get another membership here if this is where you want to train. How are things with—" Ally couldn't remember the name of the girl Rashid was arranged to marry.

"Azar, yes, she is a good wife," he smiled, but it didn't quite reach his eyes.

"Sorry, I am so bad with names. Azar is such a pretty name." Ally puffed. She was so out of shape. There wasn't any real resistance to the pedals, and she was already half spent.

"It means flame," he informed her as he stared ahead, peddling fiercely. "and she is quite hot if you know what I mean."

Ally would usually assume a man meant hot, as in sexy, but the small amount of time she had spent with the sports therapist and his distant emotion about his new bride meant something else. "She is passionate?"

"She threw a spoon at my head."

He pointed at his ear. There was a small scratch there. Ally tried not to laugh, reminding herself that hitting someone was never acceptable. There were abused men out there, and they deserved empathy as well.

"She has a temper." Ally treaded carefully but didn't want to drop the conversation since he had shared something so intimate. Maybe she could help. Her first husband was verbally abusive and had threatened her physically, even pushed her down a few times during heated arguments. Maybe she could direct him to her counselor friend, Amy. Amy had helped her through some tough years after the divorce.

"Ah, sorry. I shouldn't have said that. I should be embarrassed that my own wife hates me." He looked like a sad little boy. He was much younger than Nick or herself.

"Do you want her to like you? I mean, do you like her? Do you still want to be married?"

"Oh, yes! She is a very beautiful woman, and I like her very much. My parents chose well. It's just that she doesn't want to be here. I think she is disappointed in the match. Disappointed in me." He frowned.

Ally felt a pang of sympathy for the young man, remembering that age was so tender for feelings and that emotions were driven by young hormones. She didn't doubt that Azar was quite beautiful and had Rashid smitten.

"Have you tried counseling?" Ally knew the answer by Rashid's offended look.

"We do not need counseling. My mother says these things just take time." Rashid was silent as he got off the bike and led her to the exercise mats. They began stretching, and Ally stayed silent. She hated that they had gone astray, and she had obviously offended Rashid by mentioning a therapist. After a few minutes, he couldn't resist going into a long tirade about Azar's list of complaints and how he had tried to correct the issues. He went into detail about his wife's days of sitting at home and how she could only cook rice and chicken. "I will grow feathers soon!" he said, flailing his arms in a huff.

Ally tried not to giggle, but the chicken dance was enough to make her laugh hysterically. Rashid looked aghast but then joined her laughter. He laughed heartily until he wiped a few tears from his eyes. "That felt good. I have not laughed like this since before I got married. This woman is stealing my happiness," he complained with sudden realization.

Ally froze. She hadn't meant to be the cause of anyone's break up. "Rashid, you like this girl very much, you said. What are the things you like about Azar?"

He was silent for a moment, contemplating his thoughts. "I like the way she brushes her hair each night before we go to bed. She sits in front of a vanity she brought with her from Iran and does one-hundred strokes before coming to sleep. It is a beautiful piece trimmed in gold, and when I look at her reflection as I lie on the bed, I fall in love with her beauty. She is good to my dog. He is old. He doesn't see well, and he sheds, but each day she brushes him and puts him next to the fan to stay cool, and she washes his water bowl every night. She loves him more than me. Because of this, I know she will be an excellent mother."

His face lit up when he talked of his new bride. Ally wanted to meet this woman. Maybe a few issues could be worked out if she engaged them socially with Amy. Obviously, Rashid's nature or culture would not allow him to seek out professional help. Maybe Ally could covertly help the young pair.

"I would love to meet your lovely wife. She sounds like someone I would love to paint. I have painted my husband just as you have spoken about yourself watching her in the mirror. I could do a series with you both if you would sit for me." Her voice was hopeful. "Would you come to our home for a barbecue next weekend? You could meet my husband, Nick, and my new baby, Soledad. My mom and Aunt Rose will be there and a few nice friends. It might be good for Azar to meet some people, too." She hoped the invite didn't sound too staged. He couldn't know that it wasn't previously planned.

Rashid liked the idea and accepted her offer. They agreed to meet three times a week to work out until she lost the baby fat, and he would bring his wife to meet her family.

The day had worked out beautifully. She was fixing her body to help her mental state, she was inspired to paint again, and hopefully, she would help a new friend. She somehow knew Rashid and Azar would be taken under her wing to grow with her family. Ally felt a kindred spirit in him, though he was probably a decade younger. She envisioned a future with Rashid and Azar's children playing with Sole.

Ally wondered if she had time to have more children. She knew they should wait one year before trying again. By then, she would be closer to forty. It wasn't physically too late, but she didn't want to be too old for the child to enjoy her as a parent.

Ally was struck by a daydream-like vision of Sole playing in the park with three younger boys: two Iranian-American brothers and a fair-haired child. The love Soledad felt for the boys was obvious in the way they held hands when they ran through the green grass. When the youngest child fell, Sole helped him up then hugged him tightly. In that moment, she decided to create pseudo siblings for Soledad. Her daughter would be the eldest, but the boys were not far behind in age. She smiled knowing that the problems Rashid and Azar had today would be long forgotten in the coming years, and they would probably tell the story of the wooden spoon for generations to come.

CHAPTER 22

Sole looked up at the stranger holding her and gurgled with affection. What beautiful princess gazed so lovingly upon her. The woman wore a pink fluff of silk over her hair, and the little stones sewn into the garment glittered in the afternoon sun. It was a beautiful fall afternoon and still very warm. The woman smiled at her, rocking her back and forth. Sole had no sense of knowing this stranger in this life, but the energy between them was good. She felt love and longing when the beautiful lady looked at her, singing softly so that others may not discover how wonderful her voice was.

The lady, who her mother called Azar, was a singer in another life. Soledad didn't know how she knew this, but it was a waking dream she had when the lady cradled her in her arms. The pretty woman was strangled to death in her dressing room after a lavish performance. Yellow, white, and red roses lay strewn over a wooden floor, and the exotic woman's face stared lifeless to the ceiling in Sole's dream. It was a different face than the one she saw now, but the eyes held the same energy.

"I think she likes you, Azar," her mother said over the woman's shoulder.

Azar looked up, smiling. "Your daughter is beautiful. I hope to have one of my own one day," she confessed, and Soledad felt Azar's heartbeat quicken.

"I am sure you and Rashid will have a house full of rug rats. I am envious you are young enough to do so. I'm afraid I have waited too long. Poor Sole will grow up an only child."

"Can you not..." Azar's words trailed off with worry. "I'm sorry. My mother tells me I have no manners."

"It's okay. I am not barren. It is just that I don't want to be an older parent. I know women at forty and later enjoy healthy children, but I don't want to be too old to enjoy an active life with my daughter, and I think, my sister being born with Cerebral Palsy, has made me forgo any risks." Soledad's mother gazed lovingly at her, but her brow was furrowed in deeper thought.

"Oh, I understand, but you look so young to me," Azar said with sincerity.

"I love your wife, Rashid." Her mother exclaimed over her shoulder to where the man, Rashid, stood next to her father over a flaming grill. They chatted over burgers and shrimp. "Can I keep her?" her mother teased.

"Only if you keep us both. Your place is truly amazing, Ally. I need to make more money, so I can buy a home out here. Our apartment is too small to raise a family in." Rashid gazed around at the new landscape and patio around the pool.

Her mother led Azar to a chair near the men to make conversation easier. "You should have seen it before we bought the lot next door. It was just a simple cottage with not much to it. I love it now, but a part of me misses that simple beauty." Her mother mooned over the old place as she grabbed the stick Ella proffered and threw it.

Harley yipped and danced at Ella's heals until she returned with the branch.

"Now she tells me." Her father planted the palm of his hand on his forehead and spun around like he would faint. Everyone laughed.

The man who was so in love with Azar stood over her, gazing curiously down at Sole in Azar's arms. "Do you want one of these?" he asked.

"Oh, yes! More than anything in the world," Azar beamed. "Do you want to hold her?" Rashid's brow arched with concern. "Me? I've never held a baby before."

"It's okay, she won't bite. She doesn't even have teeth yet," her mother joked, and Soledad gurgled with laughter.

Smiling, her mother lifted her from Azar's arms and presented her bundled to Rashid. He nervously clasped her at an awkward angle. Her mother smiled with encouragement. When Rashid's gaze found Soledad's small, baby-blue eyes, it was if a bolt of electricity went between them. Sole did know this man. He had been her son, father, grandfather, best friend, and even once her husband. The bond was not as strong as the one she had with Onegan, but she remembered her most recent love of him as Katia Gray's son. Though Rashid had no resemblance to the sun-touched surfer boy she remembered, she knew the energy in the soulful eyes that now gazed down upon her. Sole knew she was blessed with all the love of the world.

Amy had not been able to attend the barbecue that day, but Ally was sure Azar and Rashid would be fine with a little more time to work things out. As she swished the soft strokes of gold paint over the canvas, she envisioned the love of the two newlyweds. They had a spark and a pull between them that ignited when pushed too far. Azar was passionate and headstrong. She had not wanted this arranged marriage. The headstrong Iranian woman entered the contract with every intention of sabotaging it, so she could return to her siblings and parents in Iran. She was barely twenty.

Ally could see that Azar was slowly falling in love with the already besotted Rashid, and it would be just a matter of time before the stubborn vixen admitted her heart was with him. Ally was sure it was harder to fall in love with someone in this country when your family was half a world away.

It had been two months since Ally first met Azar, and she could see a change in her presence here. First, she had fallen in love with Sole and wanted to take her everywhere. Ally didn't mind the company and Azar was even teaching Ally how to make traditional Iranian meals. Mom and Rose were spending more time doing their own thing. Rashid and Azar were only too happy to help babysit so Nick and Ally could have a date night every now and then.

Ally was on the third portrait for the new series she was doing on the *Iranian Princess*. All the portraits were of Azar, and one included the vanity Rashid had mentioned. Its' golden-framed mirror, with colorful jewels, reflected him admiring his beautiful wife while she brushed her hair. She even included Rashid's aging dog by Azar's feet. Ally promised the portrait to them when the gallery show was over. Marcel was already salivating over the pictures of the art she texted him. What she really wanted was to take pictures of Azar's family and paint portraits of a traditional wedding, food, and culture. Ally was swimming with ideas, but she couldn't travel abroad with Sole so young. She talked to Nick, and he agreed it would benefit both families to fly Azar's sisters over for a visit. It might take time, and she wasn't sure what legal papers it would entail, but she was sure there must be a way.

When she brought up the idea to Azar during one of their painting sessions, the young woman began to weep. "It can't be done. I wish, but it seems impossible unless someone goes to Iran and marries my sisters," she sobbed.

Ally handed her a box of tissue and patted her on the back. "It's this crazy world we live in that challenges us, but I am sure there is a way."

Ally wasn't as sure as she sounded. She remembered her Brazilian friend who tried hard to get a Visa for her brother to visit the United States. They had declined him after a year of doing the preparatory work to make him look presentable. His only fault was being a poor, twenty-six-year-old male. He was declined for being considered an illegal immigration risk. Many foreign young men coming into the United States never intended on going home and tried to stay. The American Consulate wouldn't grant entrance. With the terrorism that currently threatened the U.S. and with Iran being a part of the Middle East, Ally imagined it would be a difficult feat to bring Azar's family over, but maybe Ally could eventually go there.

"If they cannot come here, then maybe Rashid wouldn't object to me treating you to a visit home if I can accompany you. I would take photographs and paint from those images. I would pay you since it benefits my business."

She knew Rashid made a decent income as a physical therapist and moonlighted as a personal trainer, but Azar didn't work. It was part of their marital problems because Azar was bored. She needed more in her life.

Azar's head bent, and her shoulders began to shake. "I'm pregnant," Azar wailed, confiding suddenly in her new friend.

"O—Oh—dear," Ally stammered. She was confused by the sudden sadness. "Azar, I thought you wanted children more than anything in the world," Ally reminded her.

"Yes, I do, but now it will be impossible to visit. Rashid will not let me go if I am carrying our child." Her voice was sad, then the tears stopped. She sat on the velvet-covered bench with her shoulders slumped and a tissue hanging limp from her fingers.

Ally nodded in understanding and apologized for upsetting Azar. She picked up the camera and took a photo. "May I be a terrible cad and exploit your sadness later in my paintings?" Ally smiled, hoping to lighten the mood. She was half-joking, but she knew this series would be her most famous. She snapped pictures while she continued speaking with Azar. "I believe in destiny, don't you?" Ally knew she might be opening a can of worms or alienating herself by sharing her thoughts with Azar, but she couldn't resist. Putting the camera down for a moment, she moved to Sole sleeping in her bassinet. She picked her up and took her to Azar. "Sometimes, there is a purpose greater than ourselves, and we do not understand why life is the way it is. We want something so badly, and it is given to us, then it is taken away, but something else replaces it." Ally paused for her words to sink in. "You wanted to have a baby, and now you are pregnant, yet I am offering you a trip home, and you cannot take it. Something will replace this sadness too, just wait and see."

Azar smiled up at Ally as she held the baby. "You are right. There will be a time and a place for all dreams." She gazed at Soledad once more. "Now, you will have a little brother to play with," she said softly to the baby.

Ally smiled, remembering she had seen Sole with two brothers, but how did Azar know it would be a boy?

"Isn't it too early to know the sex of the baby? Does Rashid know you are pregnant?"

"I have not shared with him yet, because I only found out this morning. I bought a test stick from the convenient store next to our apartment. I will tell him tonight," she smiled radiantly. "I just know in my heart it is a boy. I have been thinking of baby names all morning." She smiled. "It is good news, and I am really happy." Azar sighed. "I just miss my parents. What if they never see their grandchild?"

"It must be hard but focus on the positive side. You are blessed with a child. You will have your own family to look after soon."

Ally patted Azar on the shoulder and called for a break. They moved to the kitchen, where they sat and shared tea. Sole hugged her mother's breast and made slurping noises while Ella and Harley napped at Ally's feet. They never let the baby out of their sight, but when the feeding was over, and Azar agreed to watch the little one, they ran to the door where Ally jingled their leashes.

CHAPTER 23

It was a cold February morning, and the lady at the counter rechecked Ally's ID and her passport. She weighed the two pieces of luggage and complained about the extra pound in one bag. Ally leaned down with Soledad strapped to her chest and pulled out a diaper bag from one piece and pushed it into the second bag. The attendant frowned at the loss of revenue for the extra weight then continued pushing buttons on the computer. Sole began to cry, drooling down the front of Ally's new travel clothes. It was a two-week trip to Paris, but she refused to leave her daughter behind. Rebecca volunteered to watch Sole during the evening events at the gallery, opting to leave Andy with her mother back home. She had warned Ally of how hard it would be on such a long flight. Ally pondered her own sanity carrying a six-month-old to Europe.

Nick had dropped them off with a hug and a kiss, and they had waved goodbye from the curb outside Austin-Bergstrom International Airport. She could see the worried look in his eyes, and she reassured him they would be okay. Planes flew back and forth to Paris every day, and she would be mostly between the hotel and the gallery, which were right across the street from one another. It was the same conversation they had had when she initially brought up taking Soledad with her. Nick hadn't argued too much. It wasn't in his nature. He admitted he would be bogged down with work, and the baby would be safer with Ally than anywhere else they could leave her. Rose and her mother would be thrilled to watch Sole, but Ally wouldn't be at peace being so far away from her daughter while the baby was still so young.

The trip wasn't easy, and Ally couldn't indulge in the allotted flight Xanax to sleep. She needed to be alert for the baby. She was lucky Sole liked to doze most of the time, giving her loads of hours to sit white-knuckled in her first-class, cockpit-style seat. Once onboard, Ally browsed through movies, caught up on reading, and indulged in a hot-fudge sundae topped with nuts. There was enough formula packed in an insulated bag to make it to the hotel without breastfeeding. She hadn't considered being able to breastfeed her child on the plane, but the toilets were rather large in first class. The bathrooms even had a bench to relax on, so she decided to relieve her aching breast and feed Sole in private. Ally tried not to rush the baby when a few bumps disturbed them. There were two such bathrooms provided in first-class and only four other passengers, so she didn't need to hurry. Being strapped in her seat wouldn't help if the plane were going down, but she would try to be quick. She didn't want to be injured if they hit a pocket of turbulence.

When they arrived in Paris, Rebecca met them at the gate. She had taken a flight from New York that arrived an hour earlier. She was kind enough to wait for Ally and help her with the luggage. A driver was waiting for them outside of the baggage claim, and they rode in the comfort of the leather-upholstered Mercedes to the hotel. My, how her life had changed. She remembered getting through college, sharing a one-bedroom apartment within walking distance to campus, and living off of twenty dollars a week for groceries.

She was quickly becoming a household name in the art world. She missed Jess's worldly knowledge of computers and social media management. They had to hire a guy in New York that shadowed Marcel and constantly nagged her for pics of her daily life. People bought art because they liked what was on the canvas, not because she lived in Texas and liked to drive a Harley on occasion. She was asked to do a motorcycle series of the open road, but she wasn't feeling it right now. Maybe later, when she felt more secure in her life as a mother. One slip or fall, and she would be lost to the ones she loved. She never thought about that before Nick and Sole. In that way, they had changed her world forever.

The opening night was packed with energy. Cameras flashed, and champagne swirled around on laden silver trays beneath crystal chandeliers. Even the Starbucks in Paris was filled with plush velvet couches and beautiful light fixtures. She loved the romance of the city and dreamed of the end of the trip when Nick would join them for three days. It wouldn't be like a romantic holiday between newlyweds because they were parents now, but it would be beautiful as a family together in an old city steeped in history and culture. They needed this time together, and most of the show's work would be over by then. She just needed to do a few signings and help Marcel with shipment scheduling and orders.

She inspected herself in the ladies' room mirror, which was trimmed in rich gold. She had lost most of the pregnancy weight, thanks to Rashid and the calories she burned while breastfeeding. Azar was her new walking partner. The younger woman didn't engage in fitness like her husband, Rashid, but she loved to be outdoors walking the dogs with Sole in her stroller. Azar had volunteered to stay with Ella and Harley while Ally was in Paris. Rashid would join Azar at Ally's place in the evenings after Nick flew to meet her and Sole in Paris. Nick had invited their friends to camp out in the guest suite while Ally was gone since Azar was there all day, but they declined, giving Nick his privacy.

Ally knew everything would be in good hands while Azar watched over things. She promised them a new bassinet for all of her help, but Rashid declined, saying Ally and Nick had done too much for them already. Rashid had more work than he knew what to do with. All the referrals Nick sent his way really helped his business. Azar's happiness and Ally's family having amazing new friends was a blessing to them all. She couldn't imagine life without Azar's help.

The simple black evening dress with capped sleeves and a deep V-neck looked elegant and sexy with the bountiful cleavage she was sporting. Her stilettos were strappy black with a few glittering beads, and she carried a small iridescent clutch to hold a lipstick and her cell. She looked at the screen on her phone once more to make sure she wasn't missing a text from Nick or Rebecca before closing the purse and returning to Marcel, Mr. Loirie, and Grant, the social media assistant.

"It's an absolute smash. We have multiple bids on *Iranian Princess* and orders from six others who will accept prints, at a premium price, I might add." Marcel wore a very expensive custom designer suit, and Ally wondered if his head was growing too big from their success. She gave Marcel credit because she wouldn't be where she was today without his help and marketing skills. He was great for smoothing things over, like her last appearance cancellation in Paris. Mr. Loirie had been furious at the time, but here they were now, rubbing elbows with the fancy gallery owner and his finest collectors.

Ally was all the rave, and she felt Marcel was gouging their clients, but he insisted it was the true value of her work. She was still pushing herself to meet the demand. It wasn't what she'd signed up for, and she just wanted to paint, but who was she kidding? It provided a lavish lifestyle. Could she have survived her claustrophobia in coach with the baby? Ally would worry about her morality later. Right now, she had a date with her fans. She plastered on a smile and squared her shoulders before departing her inner circle of business colleagues and friends.

About a third of the way through the night, Ally had had enough. She wasn't used to keeping late hours, her feet hurt, there was nowhere to recline, and her breasts were aching. She needed to go back to the hotel and feed Sole, so she would find Marcel and make her excuses. With that in mind, Ally headed into the order area, where he was sure to be found selling unfinished work to anxious buyers. She shuffled through a few quick introductions before finally making her exit. Pushing the door too hard on the way out of the gallery, she clipped a distinguished male in the arm as he finished his cigarette. He was probably one of the buyers.

Ally apologized.

"So sorry, excuse me, hope you have a pleasant evening," She touched his arm in a friendly gesture to let him know it was an accident.

"Ally? I thought I missed you." The man's alluring voice was familiar.

"Louis?" She didn't recognize him with his quarter-inch trimmed beard and mustache. It made him look older and even better looking than she remembered. His beautiful hand reached out and touched her elbow, then without asking, pulled her to him.

"Oh, Ally, it's so good to see you." He hugged her tight. She was both surprised and happy at the same time. She had never quite let go of the affection she felt for her former lover. She would never take their relationship past the friendship they had declared in New York, but something in his tight embrace told her he still felt strongly about her.

"It's so good to see you too, Louis. I had no idea you were coming. I suppose I should have called, but my life has been so hectic with the baby and all." Her voice transferred from happiness to devastation in an instant. "Did you know Jess passed?"

"Yes, social media is quick to relay bad news. I am so sorry for your loss. I sent you a friend request to your site, but—" He lingered, holding her elbow, then let go. "I'm sure you are way too busy to keep up with those things, but

I didn't know how your husband would feel about me calling, so I didn't. I didn't know if you had ever mentioned me."

"Nick, oh, yes. I have told him about you, us. He knows we're friends." Ally smiled to reassure him.

Louis smiled, but his eyes still held regret.

"As far as social media goes, I am sorry. Marcel hired Grant to keep up with it all, and he probably forgot to pass on anything personal. The industry seems cash-driven these days. It's something on my list to fix." She rolled her eyes, then shrugged her shoulders, not knowing what else to say. "I'm glad to see you, but Sole is waiting. I won't even begin to explain to you the biological effects of motherhood." Ally's laugh rang out into the night. Gallery guests were heading toward the glass doors, and Ally started to hurry away to avoid being further detained. She turned, halfway across the street, and called back, "My number is still the same. Text me tomorrow, and we'll set up lunch. You can meet the love of my life." She waved then continued across the cobbled street to her hotel.

The man was beautiful. Soledad liked his soft whiskered face and kind eyes. He looked at her with pleasant interest, and she felt his longing. It wasn't the sort of desire she saw in women who needed a baby and longed to run away with her. His was a longing to have her mother and a family to love. That wouldn't be possible, because her father would not allow it. Sole didn't feel threatened by the young man's ardor, because his love for her mother was pure. She didn't know how she knew this, she just did, like she knew many things in her waking dreams. It was shrouded on the edge of her memory, like a burning flame beyond a gauzy curtain. The knowledge she possessed was illuminated but not brightly enough to find an answer.

She glimpsed a vision of her mother laughing with this man in a posh room. The name Louis rolled off her tongue with something more than friendship. Was he family? Sole smiled at him now with adoration. She didn't worry about her mommy in his presence because she knew her mother longed for her father. She felt safe with this Louis as she suckled at her bottle and looked up from her stroller to the leafy trees above. She heard the way the handsome stranger spoke her name, and she gushed with bubbling laughter.

"Oh my, she really likes you," Ally said.

"I bet you say that to everyone who swoons over her." Louis was touching Sole's cheek now and coaxing another smile.

Soledad kicked her legs in excitement. *Oh, I remember you! I remember. You tried to save us. You were the young knight who fought for us when the men were after mommy and me. While you were cut down for your efforts, we managed to escape for a few more days. You were chivalrous.*

"No, really, she doesn't cry much, but she doesn't dance with excitement over strangers either. I read somewhere that babies respond well to facial symmetry, and the more pleasant you are to look at, the more they like you."

"Are you saying that I am handsome?" He smiled wickedly, and Sole made a cooing sound.

Ally laughed. "I think you just proved my point."

"Really, she is beautiful. Your husband is a lucky man to have two such lovely women to call his own." It was a sincere compliment, but her mother frowned.

"Louis, I hope you aren't pining away over me. We were never that serious." Ally toyed with her napkin before taking another sip of water.

"Only because you didn't take me seriously. You thought I was too young, but love knows no age." His eyes crinkled with wisdom. The flecks of fresh gray at his temple belied his wisdom from loss.

"You live in Paris! My life is a world away, and so different now." Ally stopped for lack of a better explanation. He was younger than her mommy. Maybe her mother had held herself back from giving her heart because of his age. Soledad could see the warmth in the way her mother looked at this man. The whimsical smile of *what could have been* floated around their conversation.

"You don't have to explain yourself, Ally. It's okay. Truly, I am glad you have found happiness, and I want nothing more than to know you are well-loved. If you ever need me, as I promised before, I will always be here for you."

The man's words were soft-spoken, and the smile he granted them both was sincere. Sole couldn't help herself and gurgled with pleasure, sending both adults into laughter and lightening their mood.

CHAPTER 24

Ally bit at her thumbnail as she waited by the escalator to baggage claim. The flight was on time, and according to her cell phone, had landed ten minutes ago. She nervously looked at the airport security guards with their large assault rifles and skittered down past the large crowd waiting for the travelers coming out of the baggage claim area. She was from Texas, so firearms didn't scare her, but it wasn't comfortable being in the line of fire if there were any mishaps. Sole was sleeping soundly in her stroller and Rebecca, and the driver had parked in an outer lot, waiting for her call. She was going to meet Nick alone and leave the baby with Rebecca but changed her mind last minute. Rebecca's flight left later in the afternoon for New York, and she wanted to go to lunch before catching her own flight. Once Nick got in the car, they would all drive to Montmartre and eat at one of the street cafés. Ally just hoped Sole would be in a good mood.

Ally's cell vibrated at her breast. Startled, she exclaimed to no one in particular, "Oh crap!" She knew it was bad to stash electronic devices in her bra, but it was a hard habit to break when she usually had Soledad, a paintbrush and pallet, or all three in her hands at once. She tried to discretely fish the phone out of her shirt without too much attention, then quickly accepted the call.

"Is he late? Did he miss the plane? I will kill him if he is still at work," Ally gushed into the receiver. It was Azar's number on the screen, but Rashid's voice came through cautious, yet firm.

"He's not coming, Ally. Are you there with someone?" Rashid asked gently.

"Not coming? Did he have an emergency? I swear, the hospital *does* have other doctors." Ally continued, whirling around, surveying the airport passengers walking steadfast toward the exit to transportation.

"Ally, is Rebecca there?" Rashid asked in a louder tone.

"Yes, she's with the car in the outer lot. I'm supposed to ring her when Nick gets here." Ally's voice began to warble as a sickening dread crept over her. She heard Rashid clasp a hand to the phone, and she could hear his muffled voice tell Azar to call Rebecca. Azar had the number for emergencies.

Ally panicked. "Oh my God, something's wrong. Rashid, what is it?" Her words earned a few curious stares from other nearby passengers. There was a long pause as Azar whispered something in the background.

"Ally, I want you to walk to where Rebecca can pick you up. She is leaving the outer lot now, then I'll explain."

"Okay," Ally tried to remain calm. She didn't know what Rashid was holding on to, but it was surely bad news. Her head went through a dozen scenarios of Ella and Harley dead in the road, her mother and Rose in a terrible car accident, or the house on fire. She would stay calm and deal with whatever it was. Soledad was with her, and she needed to be strong, come what may.

The driver and Rebecca pulled up to the curb. Her friend was holding a tissue to her running nose and tear-filled eyes. Ally knew then that she didn't want to know. She had to physically force herself to go through the motions of passing the baby to Rebecca and folding the stroller for the driver to put in the trunk of the sedan. She belted Sole into her car seat and fastened her own seat belt as they drove away from Charles de Gaulle Airport. Rebecca hiccupped and looked over the front seat at her, and Ally remembered Rashid on the line. She raised the phone to her ear.

"I don't know if I can handle this," she admitted. "Is my life over?" She began to weep.

"Ally, your life is not over. You have Soledad to think of, and your family and friends await you here at home. Would it be easier if you wait for the details? May I spare you a few hours more from the sad news? It is a long journey you face ahead." Rashid paused. It sounded like he was holding back his own tears as he whispered softly, "Ally, it is time to come home."

Everything seemed to be on the tip of her tongue. Things were getting fuzzier, and she didn't know why. At birth, she had such clarity, but now she couldn't recall the memory of how she knew things. They were in the place her mother called home. She felt warm here, and she loved the smell of the big warm dog that snuggled next to her while she lay on her pallet. Sometimes the little dog would sneak in when her mom wasn't looking and snuggle in the swing next to her. He was small like her and enjoyed rocking. Both dogs cleaned her face with their tongues. Her mother would fuss and then laugh at the animals she called Harley and Ella.

The surfer boy and the singer were there at the house, and it should be a wonderful gathering, but a heavy mood blanketed them all. The somber party was colorless, and all the guests wore black. Grandma and Aunt Rose took turns holding her. They tried to feed her goopy stuff in her new chair. She loved the chair and kicked her feet with glee. It felt good to be around the table with her adult family and friends. She wondered why there were no babies like her.

She had seen other small beings, so she knew they existed. She had seen them at the park when her mother took her out. When play group was mentioned, she knew things would be fun. Her favorite baby friend was named Lance. Sole hoped she knew him for a long time. Mostly they lay in a circle on their bellies and kicked. She hadn't mastered crawling yet, but Ella had given her instructions, getting down on her belly and swimming across the floor. It gave her a great giggle, and she was sure she would get it next time.

Her mother picked her up and carried her around for a while. Sole sensed a need to bond and protect. Her mother was the one in need, and Sole thought she might be protecting her from the multitude of well-wishers saying something about *condolences*. Though she was held tight, she couldn't stop the flow of her mother's tears when the guests were no longer there. She had not seen her father since their long journey and wondered when he might return. She was beginning to forget what he looked like.

The surfer and the singer were at her home for what seemed like forever, helping her mother cook, clean, even dress on some occasions. Her mommy was always sad, and Grandma took her to play group for several weeks after the days of dark brooding.

Time stood still for no one, and soon it seemed she could walk across the floor holding Ella's back, and a grand cake with a single candle was put in front of her highest chair, as her mommy liked to call it. The party was festive with color and balloons, but the sadness still lurked at the edges of conversations.

Azar showered Sole with kisses, and she rewarded her friend with a hand filled with cake, but then pulled back. The singer was getting too fat. Rashid, the surfer, liked to rub Azar's extended belly often, promising Sole a little brother, but how could it be?

She had heard her mother cry too many nights over the subject and whisper the sad news. "You will be an only child Sole. Daddy's never coming home."

Sole's memory was too foggy to recall why she felt such a loss, but her heart ached as she cried with her mother. She tried not to cry too often because she wanted her mother to be happy again.

CHAPTER 25

It was her fifth birthday when colorful peacocks wandered the property while a crew of workers set up a jumping tent. Sole eyed the vanilla cake with white frosting and her name scrolled across it in pink lettering.

Azar made a tsking noise from the sink and said without looking, "Don't even think about it, Sole Joon."

Sole cocked her head to the side as she'd seen Ella and Harley do on many occasions when she spoke to them. "Azar, do you have eyes in the back of your head?"

Azar held a dishtowel to her hip as she turned and sauntered to the cake. "I don't have to have eyes in the back of my head to know what you are about to do, Sole Joon."

"Why do you call me Joon?" Soledad was full of questions for everything, but this question she knew the answer to, and she liked to hear the answer often.

"Joon is an endearment we save for the ones we love and I. Love. You!" Azar exclaimed as she tapped Sole's nose three times, emphasizing the words.

"Will my mom really be home today? She's been gone forever." It was the first time her mother had left for so long. Sole knew her mother carried her all the way to France when she was a baby, and she traveled with her on trips to New York and California frequently. It was hard to understand why she couldn't go this time. People teased her mother about giving Sole a break, but she didn't want any breaks. Life wasn't as fun when her mother wasn't around. Next time she was going to Paris with her mother.

"Yes, Sole Joon. Your mâmân will be home today." Azar's smile was radiant, and Sole laughed. Someone tickled her sides from behind, and she screamed with delight before being twirled around. "Rashi, stop!" Sole cried out. He held her steady as she found her feet, then he walked to Azar and took her in his arms. "Ugh, not again," Sole complained, covering her eyes and peeking through her small fingers as they kissed. "Why does the surfer king always kiss the singer?"

"Why does the birthday girl always call me the singer?" Azar's brow wrinkled. "I haven't sung to you since you were a small babe, and why does he get to be a surfer king? He does not surf. He can barely manage a paddleboard." Azar gave Rashid a gleeful look. "Besides, would that not make me his queen?"

"Rashi rode on a great wave of the ocean. He was lost to the great sea. You are not the queen. She was evil, and you are nice, not evil."

"Okay then, Sole Joon, but I do not sing."

"You are a beautiful singer. You sang in a big place with lots of candles, and so many people came to see you. You should sing more often," Soledad pleaded.

Rashid looked amused. "The girl is right. You do have a lovely voice. I have heard you sing to the boys when they were babes, and you thought I was not listening." Rashid's eyes held flames when he looked at his wife this way.

Azar chased the subject away. "Why is he your knight in shining armor? You love him so much more than me," she teased Sole with her serious inquiry, but her glance was mischievous when she looked at Rashid in silent accusation.

"Rashi isn't a knight. The knight is in love with mommy. He tried to save us from the soldiers. They were not near the ocean."

Azar's eyes widened, and her mouth fell open in grand shock. "I do not know where you get these stories, Sole Joon, but I dare say your mother lets you watch too much TV."

She swatted a dishtowel playfully at Sole's backside as Ella and Harley burst through the dog door, snatching Sole's new teddy bear and leading her out of the house on a merry chase. The sun beat down over the gnarled live oaks and cedar trees that dotted the property. Her pony was grazing on the oats left in a bucket hanging on the fence. She visited him at the riding stables once a week, but today he was brought here for her party.

Ally descended the stairs from the plane and walked across the tarmac. Life had changed with her becoming a mother and losing a husband, but the accumulated wealth from her painting allowed her to travel in style. Her private jet took her wherever she needed to go. She, for the most part, had conquered her fear of flying. Hoping she had lost enough in life that God wouldn't continue punishing her was only a loose comfort, but it worked to put most of her fears at bay. Life was complicated, and she hadn't figured it all out yet, but she was moving forward after four-plus years since the loss of Jess and Nick.

She admitted her first divorce was like a death. She felt as if she were dying back then, but after becoming a widow, she knew the true feeling of loss. Ally had experienced losing someone both ways and wore battle scars from each. Both endings filled her with painful grieving and longing for the one who was gone. The only difference was that she couldn't bring Nick back, no matter how hard she tried.

She went a little crazy after Nick's death. Spending long days in bed, she acted like she forgot she was a mother. Other days she clung to Sole and wouldn't let her out of her sight. People said Sole was too adult for her age and needed other children to play with, that she sounded too much like Ally, who had become a little cynical over time. She couldn't help it. Life had been so perfect before Jess died, then losing Nick had shaken Ally's world. The upside was finding Rashid and Azar before the quake set in. They were the glue that kept her from falling apart. Azar helped Ally with Soledad and household management. Ally paid her well, and it was an ideal job for Azar, raising her two boys with Sole to play with. Amir and Hassan were now three and four. Azar had wanted to fill the house with children, but after complications with the birth of Hassan, she could no longer have any more.

Azar and Rashid protested the money that Ally deposited in their account each month, but she explained sharing her wealth was like them sharing theirs with each other. They were her family now, and she was theirs. Azar acquired the responsibility of carting Ally's mother around to bingo, her Silver Woman's group, and Friday night's potluck dances at the YMCA. Ally often referred to Azar as her Iranian sister or her right hand. She couldn't manage everyday chores without the invaluable help.

Over time, they worked through all the necessary documents to fly Azar's family over for visits, and Azar found happiness. The amazing series Ally painted from Azar's beautiful sisters was her most famous to date, but the one of Nick and Ally pregnant with Sole was still her favorite. It hung over the mantle in their home so Soledad wouldn't forget her father. She asked so many questions about him. Ally was surprised that she didn't know all the answers. When she looked at the short time span of her life with Nick, it was just under three years. There was a quick courtship and a pregnancy, though planned before they were married. Sole was barely six months when he died.

If it hadn't been for the birth of Amir a month before Sole's first birthday, followed by the chaos of Hassan's birth ten months later, she might have dwelled forever in her own sadness. She missed Nick every day of her existence, yet time passed, and the children filled her life with constant laughing and mischief. She felt full again and confident enough to start letting go.

As a black sedan rolled up to the plane, Ally got in. She pulled out her cell phone and called Azar. "I'm running just a little behind, but if there isn't any traffic, I'll still make it before the guests arrive. Sorry, I got delayed in New York with a refuel," Ally explained.

"Ally, your Sole Joon's something else. I think you will have your hands full with the stories she is telling today."

Ally laughed. "I know she is too much sometimes. I'm glad she has the boys to play with. It makes her more normal. Can you imagine a Sole with no one to teach her how to be a child?"

"I'm looking out the window right now, and she has both boys and the dogs sitting around the patio table for a tea party. I don't know how she does it, but only she can tame the wildness in my Hassan."

"She probably told him she was Elsa of Arendelle and would freeze him if he moved."

Both women laughed and said their goodbyes. Ally hoped they would receive her news with pleasure. It had been a sudden decision, but as she had learned the hard way, time waited for no one.

Guests arrived, and the birthday party was a huge success. The children were full of cake and ice cream, and the adults enjoyed relief from the occupied children playing. The wine flowed freely as the adults engaged in conversation and laughter. Ally bussed away a few of the half-filled glasses forgotten near her table. Amy's date had imbibed too much and needed to lose his glass for a while. She knew her therapist friend could call a ride, but Ally wanted to subtly remind the guy with Amy that it was first and foremost a children's afternoon party. As it was, she could see that others were settling in, and Rashid was starting a fire in the brazier as the sun began to set. Blankets were laid on the grass for the small ones to nap, and marshmallows were brought out for the older kids, who still retained many hours of energy before bedtime. Sometimes Ally threw too good of a party. She sighed, directing the servers to collect the remaining lunch plates and start the evening appetizers.

Azar had ordered the catering, so Ally had no clue what would be offered to her guests. Once again, she found her dear friend to thank her for her successful care in planning Sole's birthday. The presents were laid aside in the great room for another time. The room held too many gifts to unwrap each and thank everyone politely. Instead, there were three identical gifts for each child, so that no one was upset or left in envy of another child's prize. The guest list was long, so Ally suggested Azar use an online distributor to wrap and mail the gifts to the respective homes. Everyone was well satisfied, and as dinner was about to be served, Ally's surprise arrived.

She watched him take the steps that descended to the lower deck with quick strides. He looked like a million Euros, and his smile flashed a display of magazine-quality white teeth. He was as happy to see her as if they had been separated a lifetime, though she had just seen him only hours ago leaving Paris. She had planned to tell her family about him tonight. He was supposed to be waiting for her to return. Ally was to spend two weeks there once Sole started kindergarten in the fall.

"Louis," she said breathlessly, staring up at him.

"I couldn't wait, mon amour," he said as he hugged her and kissed her cheek.

He would not divulge their rekindled relationship by kissing her in public, but anyone who saw his grand entrance and the way he looked at her now would assume they were lovers. Ally told him in Paris she had just come to say hello. She looked him up on a whim and decided she wanted to get back in touch. Her life had been lonely for the past several years. She was too busy mourning Nick to notice before, but long evenings of sitting at an empty dinner table after midnight or lying in her bed alone made her realize that she needed to go on. She was too young to never have sex again, and since she had found peace in her world as of late, she'd began to live again.

Louis was ecstatic and overjoyed to accept her dinner invitation. They dined at her hotel and made love until the early morning hours. Ally awoke to guilt and awkward feelings eating at her. She had not felt anything for a man in a long time. Though she was in her early forties, she still looked good naked, but she didn't own the confidence she once possessed. She was put upon a shelf too long and wasn't sure how to interact intimately with a man, even if he wasn't a stranger.

Louis went overboard with his enthusiasm, but she had warned him she wasn't ready for anything but casual friendship and maybe a little hot sex. Of course, they had eaten most of their meals in bed and gone through a box and a half of condoms. Ally felt like she was a teenager again. She wasn't sure that she and Nick ever had the chemistry that she and Louis found in bed.

Louis wasn't twenty-nine anymore. Thirty-five and forty-two didn't sound so odd, did it? Women dated younger men all the time, and it wasn't like she was a cougar. Those were women her age who liked men in their early twenties, wasn't it? She just needed a diversion, adult companionship, and maybe a little romance.

Azar stood waiting for an introduction, as were several other friends nearby. Ally decided it was now or never. Marcel and Rebecca stood to her left, and Rebecca's husband held their newest family member to her right. Rashid held Sole just beyond their ring on the patio. She raised her glass and tapped the side with a silver knife from the nearest table. Guests stopped and gathered around. Most had not found their seats for dinner yet.

"Everyone, this is Louis. He is a dear friend of mine, who I have known for a long time. He lives in Paris, and he is my newest business partner. These last few weeks that I have been away, we have decided that it is time to expand." Ally beamed with happiness. "We are opening our own gallery in Paris!" She paused for a minute to let the news sink in. "I know this is a surprise for all of you since I haven't told a soul yet. I hope Marcel and Rebecca will join me with this expansion since they are the driving forces behind my huge success, but it is time we put down roots in a city that lives and breathes art the way I live and breathe painting." She paused, searching out Sole's eyes. "I know it means I might be away more, and I will be busier than ever, but with growth, there are always new positions that need to be filled, and as I start this new journey, my little girl will start her own this fall.

"Sole's birthday marks an age that young ones start attending school, and in this, I hope she will meet many new friends and form a life of her own. Not right away, of course," Ally laughed as she saw Azar's expression changing from one of happiness to confusion. "But school will be a building block for the future Soledad will carve out over her lifetime. She will one day be a woman grown, and I anxiously await the day when I see her old enough to make choices for her own family.

"That being said, I am purchasing a home in Paris to get the business off the ground, and sometime next year, this home we reside in now may be our *part-time* residence. We are moving to Paris."

There was an eruption of clapping and awe as Ally relayed the news. Marcel jumped for joy while Rebecca looked subtly alarmed. It would mean a lot of changes, and Ally understood it could be difficult to wrap their minds around, but she was ready to be in charge of her own life and her own profits. The company that connected Marcel, Rebecca, and Ally would probably find it difficult to let go, and she anticipated a backlash from the corporation. Her contract with them was over, and as an independent, she could pick and choose where she wanted to go. It would be better for them all, and now Ally could host upcoming artists and help aspiring students by teaching classes. It would be great for Soledad to learn French while she was still young and if she developed a love of painting, then what better city to be in?

Ally's gaze settled on Azar, whose eyes shimmered with tears now. "What about your family here?" she said softly.

"Sole and I will come back often for visits. Unless mom and Aunt Rose are moving permanently, I'll have to come back to sort out all the bingo drama and meet Rose's multitude of boyfriends," Ally teased, but she knew what Azar was asking.

She needed Azar, but it wasn't fair for Ally to ask her to uproot her life and start again in another country with two young boys. It was impossible to ask Rashid to leave his very successful career. His connections with the hospital had evolved into him owning his own rehab clinic, and he didn't have time for vacation, let alone dumping all his clients and moving to France. "I will always come back to see you. You both are my best friends, our family." Ally squeezed Azar and Rashid's hands simultaneously, assuring them both that all would be okay. Rashid grabbed her in a bearhug.

"It is wonderful news. Of course, Azar and I are most happy for you. All will be a great success, I am sure." Rashid put an arm around his wife's shoulder as Hassan pulled at his pant leg.

Hassan's face screwed up, threatening tears. "Baba, Sole go away?"

Rashid bent to pick his son up and comfort him.

"Not today, my son," he assured Hassan and stroked his black, silken hair before letting him down and shooing him on to play. Rashid held up a glass to the multitude of guests and made a toast. "To our greatest friend and eternal family member. No matter how far away she flies, her heart will always know where home is. To Ally's greatest success in Paris."

It was what she loved about Rashid the most. He had become the glue in Soledad's and her life after Nick passed, taking up the role of protector, confidant, and personal cheerleader. He would never show his sadness in public or shed any tears to cause Ally guilt and contemplate staying. It would be all right in the end. They'd managed to get Azar's sisters to visit, which was a great feat in itself. Anything was possible if you wanted it badly enough.

Ally loved her art and wanted to make a go of it as an independent. Who knew where moving to Paris would lead with her career or with Louis. She had a bankroll big enough to chase her dreams, and she couldn't let her friends and family anchor her to Texas. As much as she loved the hill country, there was so much of the world left to see.

Azar needed to find her own path with Rashid and the boys. She had helped Ally more than she knew, but it might help Azar if she worked for someone else who appreciated her organizational talents. Independence and self-motivation were the key to personal growth. Ally wanted Azar to feel she stood on equal ground with others and not a step below, organizing the details of her world, watching Sole, and cooking dinner for her mother and Rose. She would still need Azar to manage her Austin home when she was in Paris, but there wouldn't be as much to do after they moved.

Louis mingled as Ally searched out Amy, who knew a mutual friend in need of a household manager for a large estate. The lawyer was drowning in business and household details that needed attending since his partner ran off with his secretary and half of his clients a few months back. Ally knew he had trust issues, and the few assistants he hired had gone by the wayside. Talking to Amy and offering a reference for Azar would make the employment a done deal if Azar wanted the work.

The evening grew late, and the guests saw themselves to the gates, letting themselves out to find their cars or catch rides. The clean-up crew would return the next day and retrieve the blowup tent and leftover dishes that needed to go back to the caterer. Rashid and Azar took Sole home with the boys and promised to bring her home the next afternoon when they would all go to brunch.

Ally felt awkward standing in the kitchen with Louis. He had never been to her home in Texas. It occurred to her that all their liaisons had been in hotels in New York or Paris. It felt odd having him in a real part of her life, a room she used to share with Nick. She ran her hand over the island, thinking of how Nick made love to her before Sole's birth on the black and gray granite. She shook her head. It was time to let go of the past.

"How do you Americans say...penny for your thoughts?" Louis ran a finger down the island countertop until he came to her waist, then ran his fingers up her arm to touch her cheek.

"Nothing. It's not important. It's just that we have never been in a real place together."

His eyes widened. "Real place?"

"Outside of a hotel or a restaurant. We've only done it in hotel rooms." She paused, thinking of what she should or shouldn't share. "I built this house with..." Ally bit back her words, trying not to start a conversation she didn't want to have. Louis backed away, giving her space.

"I was planning to book a hotel downtown. I just came here first. If you want to ride with me, I have a rental car out front." His words were casual, but she saw the uncertainty in his eyes. She was being rude.

"No, that's crazy. You have flown all this way, and I have this huge house. You should stay. I want you to stay. I just have to put you in the guest house when Sole comes home tomorrow. I know it's old-fashioned, but I'm kind of a traditional mom. I don't want anything to be said about me that she can't understand. I'm not a prude, it's just logistics, understand?"

Louis smiled at her and moved forward, pushing his hips against hers and tilting her face up so he could lightly brush his lips against hers. "I would understand anything to be with you. You love your daughter, and I love you. Whatever you choose is fine with me." He said it. He said the L-word.

"I—I—" Ally stammered. "I don't know."

"It's not a big deal, Ally. I think I have caught you off guard. I'm sorry. I should have waited for you to come back, but I have this time off, and I thought it might be good to see your studio and how you work. If we are going to be business partners, I need to learn more about you in your world." His hands were wrapped in her hair, and his face was close to hers, inspecting her eyes with appreciative wonder. His allure knotted the lower part of her abdomen, quickening her blood flow in a steady pulse of longing. "I can stay anywhere, as long as I can see you." His lips touched hers. The pressure of his mouth opened hers for their tongues to intertwine in familiar titillation. He was becoming a habit. She loved his scent, his touch, his warming of her bed, and the way he made her climax several times before finding his own release.

Ally knew what she wanted. "Let's go to bed."

CHAPTER 26

Ally stretched and moaned, opening her eyes to the streaming light that poured across her champagne-colored sheets. She was a light sleeper and did everything necessary to make her time in bed luxurious. Her hand snaked across the cool cotton bedding to find Louis, but the big bed was as empty as usual. Ella's nose sat patiently on the edge of the mattress, while Harley lay still sleeping at her feet.

"The dog door is open, Ella. Won't you ever go out without an escort?" She teased the big drooling lab, noticing the mostly white hair that now replaced her once golden hue. "I know Sole is happy to play this game with you every morning, but don't I get relief when I finally have the house all to myself? Well, almost to myself. Have you seen a tall, dark, and handsome man this morning?"

Ella barked once and spun around in a circle, waking Harley, who shot out of the covers like a cannonball, barking as if a burglar was in the house.

Ally sighed and threw her legs over the side of the bed. Reaching for the robe she kept on the nearby chaise, she moved down the hall and to the kitchen. Seeing no sign of Louis, she walked out onto the open deck. Workmen had just arrived and were tearing down the jumper, and the catering crew was cleaning up the last of the trash. It was almost normal again, but her prince charming was nowhere in sight. She returned to the kitchen and found a piece of paper with a small sprig of clover on it.

You have no flowers. I have gone to correct this issue.
Consider it my first course of business for our partnership.

He signed it with a scrawling L.

Ally laughed, twirling the clover in her fingers. She supposed he had missed the knock-out roses on the side of the house, but she had never been one to keep plants alive, so they only bloomed if Azar was here to water them or if the sprinkler system was in reach.

Thinking of Azar and Rashid's arrival with her daughter, Ally went to shower and prepare herself for brunch. When she was ready, she wandered outside and looked at the August sun beating down from the sky. It was too hot to ride her motorcycle, and she felt neglectful as she thought of her iron garage queen. She didn't have time to ride it and she felt guilty when she did. The thought of leaving Sole an orphan had made her ponder selling it more than a few times. The only thing that made her reconsider was the idea of losing her own identity.

Ally knew that personalities changed as people grew older and went through the many stages of life, but the bike was part of her. She was a free spirit. It was the way she could let go and clear her head, even if the ride was only to Marble Falls and back. She wondered what Louis would think if he saw her on her Harley. Maybe she would surprise him.

Louis parked his rental car and met her in the center of the lawn. He was holding a great bouquet of red roses and a hanging basket of begonias. "I thought this might give your front window a pop of color," he smiled, pleased with his purchase.

"They are beautiful, thanks." She hugged him, and they walked into the shade that the porch provided. When he placed the flowers down on the small table by the door, he surprised her by pulling her into his arms and kissing her until her breath came in quick gasps of air.

"So are you." He gazed down at her as she shyly looked away. She spied Azar and Sole coming from beyond the driveway fence, through the small gate. Ella and Harley bounded toward them.

"Your friends have arrived."

"More than friends. They are my life. Our life," she corrected, thinking about Sole.

"Will it be so easy to leave them behind?" Louis asked in a serious tone.

She wasn't sure if he was asking from a business or a personal standpoint. "I'll never leave them behind. They are only a Facetime call away or a flight home for the holidays. It may not be forever." She walked toward her daughter, leaving his quizzical gaze behind her. She could predict the next line of questioning and wasn't ready to delve into those thoughts. She had given him a business proposal and a time to have no-strings-attached fun. She didn't know what she wanted after that.

Days streamed by with simple pleasures. Sole found a bunny in the bushes with a lame leg and wanted to keep him as a pet. Ally took it to the wildlife rescue, and the nice lady who took the bunny showed Sole all the injured wildlife being nursed back to health.

Ella was starting to show signs of aging, and Harley was getting up in years. It wasn't the time to take on a new pet since their relocation would happen soon. She distracted Sole by taking Azar and the children to a water park. Louis accompanied them on their day of fun. He was wonderful with the kids, and the boys especially loved him. They slid down slides of every construction and tubed the many manmade rivers that the water park created from a natural spring.

Summer was almost over, and soon the kids would start school. This marked the time that Ally would travel to Paris for two weeks to find their second home. She wouldn't officially move until the gallery opened, possibly the following summer, but her time at home and with Sole would be limited the first year they opened in Paris. She would depend on Azar to step in when she wasn't assisting the lawyer, and Ally hoped her mother and Rose wouldn't mind filling in until Sole could make the trips with her. Ally hired a private tutor who spent a couple of hours, several days a week, preparing Sole for school.

Today was the day that Louis took a flight home, and she had arranged to join him in a few weeks. He promised her a wonderful evening of opera and champagne the night after her arrival, and of course, he relayed in detail the wicked pleasures they would share. She was near-drowning in the lust she had developed for his athletic form, and not sure how she would manage for so long without his touch. Sex was therapeutic for the soul, but without love, it was just a physical release that she could manage on her own if needed.

She loved being with Louis, and he made her laugh almost all the time. She didn't know what was missing, because he seemed perfect. Even Sole was captured by his charisma. It was apparent that her young daughter had a great imagination. It seemed that all the men who entered her life were knights or gallant natured. She had told Rashid he was a surfer king, and now she insisted that Louis was a red-plumed knight on a black steed. The odd part was that she never referred to herself as a princess, like most little girls. She always pretended to be a peasant who helped her mother in the garden.

Sole said goodbye to Louis before Ally drove him to the airport. They returned his car after the first week of his stay, seeing it was silly to have two cars when they were always together. They rode most of the way in silence. Their energy was drained from such a wonderful few weeks of fun. Ally imagined her guest house without him and wondered how she would now fill the hours of her day. Work was the most reasonable answer. Her brain was already pairing airplane images with Parisian landscapes. A tingle at the back of her neck signaled the creative energy that was about to flow, but it would have to wait. She turned her mind to the present. Louis was leaving.

In his absence, Sole would start school, and Ally would have time to prepare a new series for the last show in New York. Her contract was over, but she had verbally agreed to do a show before Christmas with all-new paintings. She wanted to fulfill that promise and keep her karma clean. It was good to preserve relationships for future business. If the gallery didn't turn on her for opening her own studio in Paris, then they might maintain a long business relationship that would benefit both houses. She loved promoting new artists, and she would be happy to invite their work to her gallery.

Louis looked at her from the driver's side as they turned into the exit for the airport. "Ally, I'm going to miss you terribly. I don't feel safe in leaving you here alone. I worry you will change your mind."

"Don't be silly. I'll be there in a few weeks, and I'm not alone." She smiled, reassuring him that he would be missed as well. "Besides, you are bad for my painting career. I haven't so much as looked at a brush since you arrived. If I don't paint, what will we sell?"

"I know. I don't want to detain you from your work. It's part of what I love about you most. You are so passionate with your painting…and in bed." He clasped her fingers in his and raised her hand to his lips as he pulled up to the curb. "I wish you could fly with me."

"Trust me, you don't ever want to be stuck flying next to me. I'm a white-knuckle flier and no matter what class I sit in, I am a nervous wreck." She made light of the tension he was feeling. She felt it too. She wasn't sure why she would have reservations now. Their time together had been perfect.

She'd never had a bad moment with Louis, he was wonderful with Soledad, and they never argued. Soon, they would look back on their reservations as separation anxiety and nothing more. Louis parked her Jeep and drew his luggage out of the back. His sleek designer case and carry-on made her wonder how a man so beautiful and fashionable could be straight. He was so appealing to look at, and Marcel was forever in envy of her catch. She loved to look at Louis, to touch him, and she would miss his attention, but the question still lingered. Why wasn't she in love with him?

Mistaking the lane for drop-offs, Louis ended up in the baggage claim pickup area. She laughed and told him not to worry. Austin was a small airport, and all he had to do was take the escalator upstairs to ticketing. Their embrace was short, and their kiss almost chaste as Ally nervously looked around. She hated long goodbyes and displays of public affection. He at least knew this about her, but she could see the muscle in his neck convulse with the emotion he was trying to hide. She may not be able to define her feelings for him, but Louis was open in his heartfelt affection for her. He said many times that he loved her over the past two weeks, but he finally agreed not to say the words again until she was ready—if she was ever ready.

She watched him disappear behind sliding glass doors into the terminal, and she reluctantly got back into the Jeep. Louis liked to drive, and Ally liked to ride. It had been weeks since she was behind the wheel of her own car. She adjusted the seat and mirrors to support her shorter frame and pulled away from the curb. If she had looked away for a moment longer, she would have missed the image of a man with a little boy standing outside of a white SUV at the end of the terminal. A beautiful woman with gold-framed sunglasses hugged the man with adoration, squeezing him tight. When the man took off his hat, she recognized him. She wouldn't have stopped, but a pedestrian crossed in front of her on the crosswalk, and the man saw her before she could drive away. His expression was one of surprise and joy. He waved and started toward her.

"Ally?" His voice was tinged with pleasure.

Ally didn't know why her heart was in her throat. It wasn't like they were longtime lovers or friends. They had only slept together the two times, and it was years ago. She hadn't seen him since she was pregnant with Sole. It would be rude to drive away, so she rolled her window down and smiled at the handsome older man he had become. She calculated he must be in his early fifties now, but age had been kind to him. Still virile and strong, the new lines that creased his cheeks and eyes were more character-forming than age defining. He was still as handsome as ever, and his new silver hair blended nicely with the sandy blond tresses that grew longer around his neck. She would paint him as a rock star-cowboy. She had a mental image of him on his vintage motorcycle, and it instantly made her crave a ride.

She smiled. "Travis, you haven't changed a bit." A car behind her honked, and Travis waved for them to go around. The black Mercedes driver sped around Ally's Jeep. She laughed. "Probably not a great place to catch up," she mused but ignored the queue they were causing.

"Let them honk. I haven't seen you in ages. How's married life?"

It was a harmless question, but Ally gulped with silence. She wasn't sure what to say in the middle of traffic. Another car honked.

Travis tried to backtrack. "I'm sorry. I shouldn't have asked that. Stupid question."

"Um, I'm a widow, like you." Ally confessed, but then looked at the woman holding the young boy's hand looking back at them. "Or like you were. I see you are settled now?"

"That's my niece, Audrey. You never got a chance to meet her. That's my son, Noah. I'd love for you to meet them. You got time for a late lunch? I'm starving. Crap on the plane was inedible." His broad smile beckoned her to say yes. She had just eaten a rather large lunch before dropping Louis at the airport, and something felt odd about joining a past lover for lunch as her current lover hopped a plane to Paris. For reasons unknown to her, she nodded yes. He waved at his niece to get in the car and follow them, inviting himself into Ally's Jeep to give her directions to a nearby restaurant. "You like barbecue, right?" He pulled the door shut as she shifted into traffic.

"I live in Texas, don't I?" Ally's sarcasm came with a smile.

"You never know in Austin anymore. The whole city is filled with California, yogi-vegetarians. I swear they'll be the death of southern manners," he joked. It had only been a few moments, and she already felt the familiar chemistry they once shared. His magnetism was disarming, and she couldn't feel angry at him for standing her up so long ago. He had had a good excuse, and to his credit, he had flown to New York to try to make it up to her. In the end, she had been the one who didn't call him when she returned home. There was too much water under the bridge, and she was ready to let go of the past.

"Tell me about your son. My daughter is five now. Her birthday was just a few weeks ago."

"Noah is four. He's not my biological son, but I spent a lot of time doing big brother work with the fireman association, and Noah stole my heart. His parents died a few years back in a fire, and I volunteered to be a foster parent. Foster failure is more like it. I never had kids, and the prospects of marriage and kids at my age seemed unlikely, so I adopted him. I thought I was saving him from the system, but to tell you the truth, he saved me. Children are such a blessing, and they put what is important in your life into perspective."

His voice was a little scratchier than she remembered, but it was filled with emotion. He rambled on about play groups and daycare, and how Audrey and his brother's wife helped him as a single dad. Ally didn't know why she was so relieved that Travis was still single. Her heart tripped over the love that poured from him as he talked about the last two years with his son.

He directed her down South Congress, to one of her favorite outdoor eateries. It wasn't too hot in the shade, and the grove of trees overhead provided much comfort as they ate. Ally had a wine spritzer to keep her cool and picked at the small green salad she ordered. Audrey was amazing and reminded Ally of a younger version of Rebecca. She was just out of college and worked as a first-grade teacher. Having her at lunch was a wealth of information since Sole would attend school soon. Ally didn't mention Louis or moving to Paris. She skirted around her immediate life timeline and dabbled over the past few years raising Soledad as a single mom. Audrey beamed as Ally described her art tours to Paris, but eventually, the question surfaced that forced her to bring up Louis.

"So, who were you dropping off at the airport?" Audrey asked. Ally toyed with her salad a moment, taking her time, chewing before speaking. "My friend, Louis. He was visiting the past few weeks. We are thinking of opening a gallery together in Paris."

"Paris, how exciting. I have always wanted to go, but on a teacher's salary and what my uncle pays for babysitting, well, let's just say it doesn't afford trips abroad."

While Audrey gushed over possible future travel, Ally's eyes flicked to Travis. He smiled politely, but his eyes weren't as shiny as they had been before. She didn't know why it bothered her, but she continued nodding politely at Audrey's fervor, ignoring the tug at her conscience.

"I wish I shared your enthusiasm for travel. I like going places and seeing new things, but I admit I'm a baby when it comes to flying. I've gotten better about it, but I picture myself as a hermit when I get older. They say that everyone becomes more phobic with age, so if that's the case, I will be stuck within the confines of whatever continent I call home."

Ally made light of her fear of flying, but she knew she spoke the truth about her lack of enthusiasm for travel. If she was honest with herself, she didn't want to live in Paris when she was old, and all of what she knew was here. Trips to Texas to visit friends and family would taper off as she aged, and she suddenly didn't like the idea of dying on foreign soil. She was still young now and had many years to worry about logistics. Taking Soledad there to grow up could change her entire future. It hadn't occurred to her so plainly until now. Was she willing to risk changing everything?

"So, will you be moving then? To France?" Travis's tone had changed, and he seemed too concerned for a man she hadn't seen in years.

"Honestly, I thought I would, but…" Ally's words trailed off as she explored her own thoughts. "I know it sounds crazy, but right here and now, I'm no longer sure. You're making me think about my life, Audrey. All your enthusiasm for exploring new cultures and travel has wilted my own eagerness for a new life in France. If I move, I would be forever traveling back and forth, and though I try to trick myself, flying never seems to get easier. Every time I take off, I think to myself, 'If I crash, please let it be on American soil, and if that's the case, let it be home.' Texas *is* home, and I think I forgot that until just now." Ally paused for a moment, pondering a new thought. "Maybe I should open up a gallery here."

Audrey was silent for a beat. Her expression exposed her sudden regret for speaking. "Oh no, Ally. I didn't mean to change your plans."

"You didn't. I've had a lot on my mind and not a lot of time to think about the logistics. Two weeks ago, I thought it was what I really wanted, but I began to question the decision a few days ago. Your excitement about teaching, Travis's love of his son and how they came together, it reminds me of who I am and what gives me pleasure. If I want to see Paris, I can fly there, but the place I want to be most is here, where the people are still warm and have hope for the future. I have been to Paris, and it's amazing, but it's like New York, only they speak French. I want to raise Sole amongst people who are friendly to strangers, and you don't find that in any big city. Austin is rich in outdoor beauty and the people we love. I think maybe it's the life less-traveled that's more appealing to me right now." Ally sat back in her chair, relaxing. She took a long sip of the chilled spritzer and smiled at the two, who beamed back at her with wonder.

"Swing, Daddy." Noah blurted out, throwing up his arms as they all laughed.

Travis picked up the small boy and swung him around in the nearby open space and then returned to the table. "When we are happy, we swing," he explained to Ally. "I think we are all going to be very happy."

CHAPTER 27

Sole looked up at the blue sky with cotton-ball shaped clouds dotting its surface. She thought about her many-colored markers at home and wished she had them now so she could draw a picture for her mom and Azar. Her mother had informed her they were meeting new friends today. It was her favorite park, but all the swings were taken. She scanned the grass, looking for another form of amusement amongst the many see-saws and monkey bars.

She spotted Hassan and Amir rolling down a small hill leading into the park. Azar was trailing behind with a green wagon filled with a red cooler and many grocery bags. Sole loved Azar as much as her own mother and was relieved they would not move to Paris. She would miss their knight friend, but he would visit them again—hopefully. Azar's happiness had been renewed, and she spent many more hours at the house once more. The family was whole again, and life was good.

Sole spied a small boy with a red and white striped shirt hiding in the bushes just past the swings. He looked shy, like he may need a friend. When he spied her looking at him, she waved, and he waved back. He walked out of the bushes and beckoned her to him. He was younger than her and smaller, but he seemed familiar.

"Hi there." Sole greeted him with a big smile. "What's your name?"

"Noah. What's yours?"

"I'm Soledad, but my friends call me Sole, like the sun." As they played, she chirped about her mom, Azar, Rashid, and her brothers Hassan and Amir. "They are your age. You will love them." She informed him. "You can be my brother, too." She liked the way the sun bounced off his shiny brown hair like a halo, and his eyes were the lightest blue with a dark outer ring.

"Will you marry me?" His serious inquiry was that of a besotted child with his first crush.

Sole smiled with glee. "Of course, I'll marry you. We will be married many years from now, and this will be a good life for us. You wait and see, Onegan. This time it will be perfect."

The End

SNEAK PEEK
CHASE THE MOON
THE GUARDIAN SERIES—BOOK 1

Minette Lauren

CHAPTER 1

"Regan Hope Landry, you get back in this house and finish cleaning your room!"

Regan ignored her mother and revved the engine of the tangerine-colored Mustang. She didn't mean to peel out of the driveway, but she'd just gotten her license last week, and she was going stir crazy stuck in the house. It was April, and school was almost out. She would graduate in a few weeks. The car had been a gift from her dead-beat dad who showed up once every five years to worm his way back into her broke mom's heart. He didn't have money, but somehow always came up with something to offer. Regan had accepted the car and pretended everything was forgiven. That was two weeks ago, and he was already gone.

"Where are we goin'?"

Regan swerved, nearly careening off the narrow, curvy highway headed out of Bonne Fete, Louisiana. "Rain! What are you doing back there?" She swore with a hiss and brought the car to a skidding halt. "You almost gave me a heart attack. Get out!" Her little sister had this new habit of hiding in the back seat to tag along. Regan was a senior in high school and she didn't need her little sister following her everywhere. Making her walk home might teach her a lesson.

"You can't put me out here, Regan. Mom will kill you if something happens to me. Didn't you see that thing on the news? A girl was kidnapped last week in New Orleans and they found her body out at Butte La Rose." Her eyes teared up. "I don't want to be gator bait, Regan. Don't put me out here." Rain's strawberry blonde hair showed their mother's Irish heritage, a stark contrast to Regan's own long dark tresses. Regan looked like her father's side. Coon-asses, all of them. They both had inherited their mother's fair skin, but Regan and Rain shared their father's green eyes.

Regan blew out a breath, stirring a lock of hair that had fallen over one eye. She started driving again and turned on the radio.

"Where are we goin'?"

The older woman with coffee-colored skin and rumpled green clothes a size too big and two decades past the current fashion stared at Regan over the crystal ball. The color combination made her look like a Mardi Gras float.

"You're a new soul, ain't cha, chile?" She nodded to Regan as if she knew the answer, but Regan was sure she was full of shit. She'd left her sister sitting on the concrete bench in front of St. Louis Cathedral waiting for her so this old woman could tell her fortune. It was clear by the purple turban on the woman's head and the long toenails that stretched over her neon yellow flipflops that Regan had just wasted her week's worth of allowance.

The woman was still nodding, but now her eyes were closed, and she hummed as she rocked her shoulders back and forth like she was listening to some soulful music that must be playing in her crazy head. The only thing Regan could hear was the bubbling of water from an old fountain in the courtyard. Her hackles went up. This was a bad idea. She was alone and pretty far from the square. Why had she told Rain to wait there? No one would even know where to look for her if she went missing. Regan remembered the story of Hansel and Gretel, lured into the ovens by the old witch….She gasped as the fortune teller's head reared back, the whites of her eyes bright against the black of her skin.

"I see a dark sky with a bright shining moon. You've been here before. This isn't your first life, but this time and place is new to you. You're not an old soul, but you did exist long ago. I see lights, lots of candlelight, and hear music. A lot of people gathered." The woman smiled as she nodded, gripping Regan's hand. She rubbed her thumb back and forth over the lined palm, though she didn't look at the lines. There was a pause and the older woman looked like she was holding her breath. "Water, so much water. The news. It's everywhere. I see your name and picture in the paper…." The woman's head flung forward, and her shoulders sagged. Her breath came in ragged gasps. Regan worried that the lady's insanity might cause her to have a heart attack, though she wanted to believe what the old crone said was true. The band she played in was surely destined for fame, and she was the lead singer and songwriter for the group. It was 1985 and Regan knew she would come on the heels of Joan Jett and Pat Benatar before the decade was over. She just needed the right break. It was one week from her eighteenth birthday and after that, no one could stop her from hopping a bus or moving to the city to get real gigs. The fortune teller had just described her fame. It would happen. Regan knew she would make it somehow. Despite her earlier doubts of the seer's gift, Regan was now convinced of the old woman's skill. How would the seer know of the band's new song, "Walk on Water"? Why would she mention the paper, people speaking her name, candlelight? The woman must have had a vision of Regan singing on stage, the crowd holding lighters and shouting her name.

Regan fished out a twenty-dollar bill from her jeans pocket and placed it on the table next to the crystal ball. The woman's head slowly rose to peer at her with bloodshot eyes. The twenty would probably buy her another bottle of wine, beer, or whatever the source of that fermented odor was.

"Thanks, lady." Regan turned to leave.

As she reached the door to the courtyard, the woman called out, "Live each day as if it were your last, sweetheart. The dream you seek won't come the way you think it will, but you'll get there. We all get there in time."

Regan paused, studying the neon-green bellbottom pants and sage print wrap-around blouse the woman brushed at as if she were wiping away cat hair or a spider's web. Clearly, she had issues and apparently spoke in riddles so no one could accuse her of not getting their fortunes right. Without replying, Regan stalked to the door and retraced her path back to Rain. It was eighty-four degrees, but the humidity made it feel like summer already. For Regan, summer couldn't come soon enough. She was a senior and her four years of high school were finally coming to an end. Freedom was in reach and she was itching to start her future.

Rain lay on a bench, staring at a flock of pigeons roosting in a tree. Regan bumped her foot. "Get up, we need to get back before Momma has a coronary."

"What took you so long? I was about to walk to the police station."

Regan looked at her sister's sleep-lined face. "Yeah, you look really worried."

The silver bangles on her wrist jangled as she reached in her pocket for her key. Regan didn't look behind her as she started toward the parked

Mustang. Rain would never leave her shadow. They stopped at an open bar on the way. Music and cool air conditioning poured out onto the street. A saxophone blew out a soulful solo to solicit potential patrons. Regan leaned into the cool wood frame of the old door with its doorknob as low as her knee. She was only five-four. On a guided tour through the French Quarter her freshman year, a historian had explained that people used to be much smaller. She was average, but the old architecture washed over her with a feeling from the past that piqued her curiosity. The old French Quarter, combined with the sultry blues the band was playing inside, made her long for a time she hadn't lived, and she wondered how it might have been a hundred years before. If it wasn't for her tag-along sister, she could have enjoyed a Coke inside the bar and listened to the music, maybe flirted with the handsome guitar player who was checking them out.

The song came to an end and the players reached for a variety of drinks, most of them amber-colored over ice in short glasses. "Why don't you come on in, pretty young thang." The black man with a beard holding the saxophone called to them.

Regan smiled but lingered at the entrance, remembering the old woman's words. "I can't. I've got my little sister with me." She motioned to Rain and shrugged her shoulders.

The man chuckled with a knowing smile. "Aw, I had one of those. My little brother followed me everywhere until I was twenty-five. Don't worry, she'll outgrow ya and get her own life. She's a pretty little thang too, but too young for the likes of me, ya."

Regan sensed the need to move on. She may not care for Rain tagging along all the time, but she didn't need older men scoping her out, either. As she turned with her hand on Rain's shoulder to nudge her away from the unwanted attention of the sax player, she heard one of the band members whistle at them.

Looking back, she heard, "You got a sweet voice. It's a little raspy. Can you sing?"

It was the one thing he could have said that made her stop. She turned, squinting through the strong rays of the summer sun pouring over them as they stood on the cobbled street. "Yeah, I sing. I play a little too."

The band let out a mix of hoots and jests. The guitar player pulled the strap over his head and held out his instrument to her. "Come on then, don't be a tease. Show us whatcha got."

Regan pulled Rain in and looked her in the eye. "Don't move! You hear me?"

Rain protested, "I don't think this is a good idea, Regan. Mom will tan your hide if she finds out."

Her face was mere inches from Rain as she blew out a warning in a sharp hiss. "I said, stay outside the bar!"

Regan sauntered the short distance through the mostly empty establishment. A few drunk patrons sat at the bar, but no one paid attention to the amateur show going on behind them. She took the guitar from the good-looking guy with dirty-blond hair and hitched herself up on the stool where he'd been sitting. She strummed the strings, checking if it was in tune. She knew it was since he'd been playing, but she gave a show of warming up. Regan plucked through the few chords leading into the chorus without a word, just feeling the music. The song started with remnants of classical excerpts from famous composers, diced up then smashed together with modern flare. Her voice hummed over the strings as she felt the tempo climb. As the chords led into the first chorus, she started in. Her voice was barely audible.

"Louder honey. We can't hear you." Regan's head jerked up. Her gaze locked with the woman behind the bar. She missed a note, but quickly recovered as she belted out the lyrics.

"You stole my head. You stole my heart. You swore we'd never part. You walk on water, baby. You know you're driving me crazy...."

Her eyes were closed but she could feel the intense interest of the room as everything around her came to a halt. She worked over the strings, ranging her rhythm from ballad to high-tempo rock. She wooed the band members into tentatively joining in, feeling their way into the unfamiliar chords. On the third swing through the chorus, Regan let it rip, watching Rain return her stare with an emotion that could only be defined as awe. Her little sister deified her—worshiped her talent, quick wit, and ability to shuffle through the bad things in life. Regan Landry was already famous in her small back-woods town, carrying a badass reputation around school, but her grades were okay. She held a B average, which wouldn't get her into any of the big colleges, but her family didn't have big college money anyway. Regan didn't care. She knew she wouldn't need it. Her music would make her world famous one day.

The song came to a halt and the few patrons in the bar actually put down their drinks to clap. Some even blew out raucous whistles. Regan thought the smile she was trying to tame would break her cheeks. She had trained her emotions over the last few years to hide the need she felt biting at her insides. Indifference had gotten her where she was today, not that it was super-stardom, but she knew she had what it takes. She was on her way.

"Go on li'l girl, you got some lungs on you, cher." The man holding the sax reached out a hand and waited for her to shake it.

Regan reached out and slapped it in a low five, giving him a sassy grin that he returned, flashing a gold tooth. "Awe now cher, I like me a feisty woman, but you be a bit too young for me, too. Tell me, where did you learn to sing like that?"

Regan shrugged her shoulders, "I sing in a band." Why give away free information? She did her usual, if they don't ask, don't tell, routine. She handed the guitar back to the handsome guitar player. His unwashed sandy-colored hair and after-five shadow made him look a little grubby, but his full bottom lip and hazel-colored eyes were something from the collage of Teen Beat posters on Rain's bedroom wall. He was heart-throb material and not too much older than herself, at least, not in her eyes. She guessed he was in his mid-twenties. A hell of a lot more mature than Mark, the boy she'd been on and off with. They would both graduate this year. Regan had been crazy about Mark at first, but he was gone most of last summer, and it was then that she saw the writing on the wall.

Staring into the warm hazel eyes of the guitar player, she played it casual, reminding herself that he couldn't see the erratic beating of her heart. In her short seventeen years, she knew one thing about the battle of the sexes— men wanted most what they couldn't have. If they thought you wanted them, they might be interested, but it was only for one thing. She'd learned that lesson the hard way. Danny Rogers taught her that hard lesson. He was a senior and captain of the football team She'd been a freshman and a straight A student. She wasn't cool because she played in the high school marching band. She hadn't cared about popularity then, but what happened that night after homecoming had made her instantly known throughout the school. After a week of sulking in her room and trying to avoid classes, she knew she had few choices. She could remain the un-cool marching band girl who was easy, or she could quit the band, join a real band, and own the title of Bad Girl Landry. It didn't matter that she didn't date again until two years after the homecoming gossip. People believed what they wanted to believe. She held a cigarette while she waited for the bus every morning and played in Mark Juban's garage on the weekends. They'd made out a few times and she'd even let him go as far as second base last week because she'd grown bored with their usual routine. She was glad he'd spent the summer in the

Hamptons with his grandparents. It had given her the time she needed to get over her schoolgirl crush. She stayed with him because it was their last year of school. Being with Mark for two years had mended her tattered reputation. She was even cooler now because Mark's family was wealthy, and his father was into politics.

The guitar player nodded. "I'm Chase, this is Guidrey, Ronnie and that's Dax." He motioned to the sax player, keyboard, and then drummer." He waited until everyone said hello and then asked, "What's the name of your band?"

"Bon Temps."

Chase chuckled, "Good times, not bad. I'm sure there are a hundred bands in Louisiana called that, but it's good enough."

Regan gave him her best bored look. "Yeah, what do you call yourselves?"

Chase laughed again, as the band members made a few jests, oohing and ahhing. He looked back at them. "Sassy, ain't she." The humor hadn't left his eyes as he returned her stare. "Cat's Quarter."

Regan actually liked the name, but she retorted, "That doesn't sound so original to me." There was another round of hoots and Guidrey threw in, "Dawg, she punched you good with dat one."

Chase chuffed. "Me? I think that was a universal diss, ya'll."

Regan turned back to see Rain waving at her to leave the bar. It was late and she knew she was grounded already for leaving the house without permission. No skin off her back, there was nothing to do on Mondays anyway. "Look, I gotta go. Thanks for letting me sing." She turned on her heel and made her way to the door without submitting to the desire to look back. It was a mystery to her why she wanted him to call her to stay or why she worried she would never see him again. He was just a guy. Someone her mother would count as too old for her and probably no good since he played in a band at a bar.

Regan felt his hand snag hers and his hot breath pour over her in a fresh wave. He was sucking on a mint. "Don't be in such a hurry. I didn't get your number." His hold was loose, but she didn't pull away.

"Mom's waiting for us, Regan. We gotta go." Rain's untimely reminder made her want to melt into the cobbled street where she stood. Chase's knowing smile made her want to slap her sister, hard. She would, as soon as they were alone. Her Achilles heel was music, and this guy knew how to play. They might have more than this one moment in common, and Regan would have liked to explore it, but her little sister ruined her chance.

She never once looked at Rain. Instead she smirked and tossed one shoulder back, freeing her hand. Without apologizing she repeated, "I gotta go."

"Will I see you again? We're playing here Friday after next. Come back and we'll let you sing again. You're old enough, right?"

Holding one hand in the air as she retreated to the other side of Canal, where they had parked the car, she waved. Once she was driving, she allowed herself a look in the rearview mirror. He was staring after them. He'd walked out into the street as if they'd known each other a lifetime and he couldn't believe she was leaving. When he was no longer in sight, she turned on Rain, "If you ever whine at me again like that in public, I will make sure that everyone in school knows you still sleep with your dolls."

Rain's mouth shot open. "I do not!"

Regan continued, "And, if you continue to follow me around like a lost puppy, I'm going to leave you out in the swamp."

"I hate you, Regan! And I'm telling Mom."

"How old are you anyway? You big baby. Go ahead and tell Mom. I'll be eighteen soon and she can't do a damn thing about where I go or what I do. And when she finds out you were with me today, you'll be grounded from ballet."

"She won't ground me from ballet. I have a scholarship, remember?" Rain crossed her arms and looked out the window. She was ignoring her now, and that was fine by Regan. Turning the radio dial, she scrolled through the stations. Janis Joplin crooned, "Me and Bobby McGee." They drove in silence the forty-something miles out of the Crescent City and through the back roads that snaked along the swamp.

When they got home, Rain jumped out, slammed the car door, then kicked it for good measure. Regan came around the front, tackling her as she tried to clear the car's bumper. Rain made a beeline for the door, crying out for Regan to stop, simultaneously screaming for their mother. Regan sat on top of her sister without the true urge to really hurt her. They had fought like this most of their lives. Rain was small and Regan never hit hard, but things had gotten out of hand. The Ford was a 1978, but it was all Regan had. Other kids had new Hondas and Camaros. She had a bright neon orange Mustang that somehow fit her rebel persona.

Their mother, Rona, screamed from the porch. "Regan, off!"

Regan pinched Rain hard on the arm before standing up and turning toward their mother. A swift kick in the rump sent Regan lurching forward.

Like lightning, Regan turned to claw at Rain, but she was halfway to the backyard and Regan was tired of the argument. Rain was too fast, anyway.

"Regan Landry, where have you been? You know you are grounded for a month." It was a rhetorical question. Her mother didn't really want answers. She wanted Regan to be quiet and do what she was told. She had, until a few weeks ago. Her mother taking their father back, to be used and thrown away again, made her sick. She hated her father for his white trash ways, and she loathed her mother even more for falling for the conniving bastard. Rona was weak and the last thing Regan wanted was to be like her.

Did you enjoy this sneak peek? To buy your copy of, Chase the Moon, visit https://www.amazon.com/s?k=minette+lauren&ref=nb_sb_noss_1

To find out more about the author, visit www.minettelauren.com

ABOUT THE AUTHOR

As soon as Minette Lauren was old enough to write, she composed a play in one act about the love of Seth and Beth, inspired by the movie, *Gone with the Wind*. Not deterred by the play's questionable success, she has been in love with writing ever since. Growing up in a small town outside of New Orleans, Louisiana, has fueled a lot of her creative endeavors. She travels often and takes advantage of anyplace with a view that inspires her to write. Lauren now resides in Texas, where she loves to write outdoors by her pool, with her five furry writing muses. Besides her menagerie of tail-wagging pooches, she also has a loving husband, three turtles, and four sassy parrots to keep her company. Together, they make all of her dreams come true.